"Torpedo wake to port"

The torpedo struck the *Byrne* on the port side just forward of the torpedo tubes. Too late Lieutenant Tom DeWitt thought of the Navy admonition to "hit the deck," for a man can suffer broken legs from the tremendous jolt from below. The ship's list was to port and increasing so fast she was capsizing. Dozens of lines went over the side and sailors raced along the deck, cutting loose life rafts as the men slid into the sea beside the mortally stricken ship.

Down came the lines with sailors sliding on them, and Tom felt a stab of pain in his left ankle. "Hell, I've sure cracked something," he muttered. Now to get a good start into the sea and swim like hell or be sucked under.

DeWitt was a strong swimmer and he struck out for the open sea, but the oil was closing in on him, clinging to his arms, getting thicker and thicker as he swung one arm, then the other, and tried to kick his legs. His arms felt like lead and he felt something pulling down on his legs, rolling him over on his back. He realized in horror he was being pulled down and under, and that he was losing his sight in the ever-thickening black nightmare. . . .

Pacific Hellfire

Jonathan Scofield

A DELL/BRYANS BOOK

Published by
Dell Publishing Co., Inc.
1 Dag Hammarskjold Plaza
New York, New York 10017

Dell ® TM 681510, Dell Publishing Co., Inc.

ISBN: 0-440-06760-X

Printed in the United States of America

First printing—March 1982

Pacific Hellfire

Tom DeWitt stood at the open window of the bedroom, in his ears the muted thunder of the surf, on his cheeks the tranquil breeze from the east. He was quite unaware, however, of the spell of the sea, of the soft magic of the wind. He saw only the fair skin of the sylphlike figure in the transparent gown, the deft movements of slender arms as the tall girl worked the brush through her golden hair.

His bride of two weeks—yet not his wife. Irene Carlson DeWitt.

His perplexed gaze met her blue eyes in the mirror, but there was no response from her, not a flicker of expression in the delicately molded features.

In a few moments she would turn to him, kiss him

lightly on the cheek, say good night, and get into one of the twin beds.

From that moment on she wouldn't be conscious of his presence. He would be left inert, for as long as he could stand the humiliation. Then he'd turn out the light and stretch out miserably on the other bed, knowing he could not break the barrier. He had tried but had been left bewildered, stunned at the realization that his slightest touch was as shocking to her as if he were running naked through a convent or raping a nun. . . .

The next morning he woke early, put on his swim shorts, went down to the coffee shop and drank some coffee while watching the eternal white breakers rolling in. Then he went down to the beach and slowly began to run. He picked up his pace, stretching out his legs in that ground-eating stride that had brought him two gold, one silver and three bronze medals and two tall silver cups in college. He poured it on until he had reached the one-mile mark that was used by vacationing athletes during the summer.

He slowed to a jog, then a walk, while the sweat poured from his body. He had exhausted his resentment in physical exercise; now his mind would take over to find the answer to last night and the nights before.

He let his mind drift back through his high school years. He was only twenty-three now. Dates, dances, outdoor activities . . . he had stood out in both high school and college as an exceptional student and athlete, but he had never had any notable success with girls. Pamela Waldren had been the sole exception, but then she had moved away. Pamela had been special and he had moped about for months after she moved, but eventually even their sporadic letters had stopped and they'd lost contact. With most of the other girls he'd liked, before and after Pamela, it had been one date and then a cool rebuff. When he was really lucky he'd gotten as far as a platonic relationship. The only explanation he'd ever been able to come up with was that he was perhaps too shy, too unsure of himself. Girls liked a male who seemed aggressive, who came on like gangbusters—at least in comparison with Tom's style. Tom simply came on as himself, which was an entity he had somehow never been as sure of as he might have been, given his academic and athletic successes.

Tom DeWitt was an orphan, the son of Franklin and Allison DeWitt. More precisely, as he had learned in his early teens, the bastard son of Franklin DeWitt, a young writer who had died in World War One before Tom was born, and of Allison Hunter, a socialite who had died in a train crash when Tom was still an infant. His guardians were two elderly sisters who were distantly related to his mother's family. Very distantly, he hoped, despite their proud claims to the contrary. He had no memory of his mother, no photographs of either parent, and no particular resentment toward them. Not now, anyway. He had little feeling about them at all, other than occasional curiosity and a mild regret that he hadn't known them, hadn't had a "normal" family. But he'd often thought that perhaps one of the traits he'd inherited from them was his pragmatism, for he had not spent much of his childhood fanta-

9

sizing about a family that did not, could not, exist.

He had learned the few details he knew about his parents at a bad age, though, when the two women who had raised him deemed it "proper" that he should know his background. He was thirteen, full of insecurities, and Louella's and Bertha's ill-timed and characteristically ill-considered revelation had come as a shock and only added to his uncertainties about himself. The two women had further added to his shyness and sense of awkwardness with their fantastical notion of the proper young man—and "proper" was a key word in that household—as being a cross between Gabriel and Sir Galahad. He had come to realize that no such man could ever exist, but his "aunts'" ideal of behavior had been difficult to exorcise from his expectations of himself.

So one question had been resolved. But if he had become somewhat self-conscious in the presence of girls, how then had he snared the beautiful daughter of a multimillionaire? He had inherited none of his own parents' wealth, nor any of the smooth self-assurance that went with it. He had been smitten with Irene, and had gratefully assumed that she simply loved him for himself. If she was not at first as affectionate as he might have hoped, well, perhaps she was saving herself for her marriage and was a bit reticent about the whole business. He had begun tenderly as far as the sex was concerned, hoping she would respond. She hadn't. By the second night of their honeymoon he remembered that he had never seen her mother, Martha Carlson, display any affection for Henry Carlson. Now he could only conclude that

Irene was entirely a product of her mother. She had none of her father's warmth and geniality, except, it seemed, as a purely social front. Did she love him in spite of it? And did he love her? He couldn't begin to guess, so different was their honeymoon than all he had expected.

He began to jog back to the hotel. He wouldn't try to solve this riddle at the moment. But he couldn't help feeling that Irene regarded him as no more than a figurehead husband, a nice-looking young man who made an attractive escort for all of her socials. He grimaced at the thought that for once his aunts may have been right in their prediction of disaster—which was what they had consistently predicted whenever he had done something that didn't quite fit in with their scheme of things. Marriage definitely had not fit in with their scheme, he thought, remembering the confrontation.

It was a blazing broadside he had fired at the breakfast table, his announcement of his intended marriage to the queenly Irene. At first, before his anger set in, he'd had to restrain himself from laughing at these aunts, for their reactions were as ludicrous as their physical appearances.

Bertha Mayfield was round, with round body, round face, round hands. Even her lips seemed perpetually drawn into a full round pout. He had always thought that if she ever managed to gather momentum in her slow, rocking gait, she would start rolling like a big rubber ball. Just as he understood why no man had ever wanted to marry her, it was equally clear why the husband of the other aunt, Louella Finerty, had drunk himself to death. Louella was of medium height, skinny as a crane, with a sculptured, angular face and a straight-backed, jolting walk that reminded him of the rigid, jarring motion of a pogo stick in action. Many was the time he had thought that one of the creators of animated cartoon characters could have become independently wealthy using his aunts as models.

Physically dissimilar as they were, their expressions were identical, except for their eyes. Bertha stared; big round staring eyes. But Louella's eyes were never still. He could never remember her gaze meeting his for more than a moment. It seemed to him that she avoided exchange, as if she felt he knew something about her. He knew only how far she was from the truth. Actually, he knew nothing. Her husband's drinking, perhaps?

"Thomas DeWitt, what is so funny?" Bertha had demanded after he had broken the news. Her fat face was beginning to perspire.

"They don't make the camera that could reproduce your expressions." He continued his casual attack on scrambled eggs and toast. "News of my marriage. It's like someone just told you of the sinking of the *Titanic*."

"But, Tommy dear, you're so young," Louella protested.

"Most people who marry *are* young," he replied, giving Bertha a wry smile.

There was a hostile silence. Then Louella said, "Well, dear, remember, you can always get a divorce if things don't work out."

He chewed in silence. This was what he might have expected.

"Tommy, have some marmalade," Bertha offered.

"Thank you, no. The wedding's in September."

"So soon? The marmalade's good on the toast."

"No marmalade, please." He gulped down his coffee, glanced up at the ancient wall clock.

"Oh, Tommy, your coffee must be cold!" Louella exclaimed. "I'll make you some more."

"Coffee's okay, thanks. Don't have time for you to make more. You know the Carlson Company. Henry Carlson's a regular guy, but he does expect his employees to be punctual." He tried to close the conversation on a good note. "You know, I always thought businessmen like Carlson were only interested in their specific enterprise. Henry Carlson is different. He has a den—you might call it a study—with something like fifteen hundred books in it. And his ability to relate history to current events is like some sort of psychic capacity."

Louella stirred, like a big crane beginning to move. "Tommy, I'm going to make you some more coffee—"

"No, please, no. Carlson has the whole trilogy on the civilization of western peoples—"

"Some marmalade, Tommy?" Bertha pushed the jar toward him with final determination.

This was the end. He stood up, slammed the flat of his hand on the table. Dishes and cups jingled, a spoon bounced to the floor. "Good God, no! How many times do I have to say no? I do not want any marmalade, I do not want any coffee! I've been trying to tell you about my marriage, and so far the only response I've

13

heard is that I can get a divorce if it doesn't work! No word of congratulation, no discussion, no single word of a girl who has become important to me. You're already assuming the marriage will fail, without knowing anything about it. I honestly believe you want it to fail!"

As his anger swelled, the sound of his voice began to boom in the small breakfast room, giving further impulse to that anger, releasing more of his pent-up resentment. "I almost believe you *want* me to remain single so that you'll have a pet around the house, someone to advise how to dress, how to eat, what to eat, what to say, even how to feel."

He gathered his breath for a final blast. "Has it ever occurred to you how inconsistent you are? You insist that I remain a pampered child, yet that I achieve absolute perfection in everything I undertake. It's like expecting a man to be the responsible head of an industry and yet remain a baby with no concept of life's realities, a baby fed on the dream-drivel you've shoveled at me for as long as I can remember. I sometimes think you actually believe in the sugar-covered make-believe you dreamed up for my benefit."

He paused, looking away from their shocked faces and out the window at the brilliant green of the lawn. He had delivered his broadside, and like Isaac Hull's gunners on *Old Ironsides* was sponging his guns, taking more shot from the racks, readying his powder, ladles and matches for the next broadside. If one was necessary.

But the return fire was weak, confused, sporadic. Bertha found her voice first. "Well! You speak of girls

—I'd prefer *our* kind to such as that—disgraceful little creature, Pamela Waldren—"

"Bertha!" Louella cried.

"So, you know! How gratifying!" His victory was complete. "You knew all along, since I was sixteen! The only thing that puzzles me is how you managed to keep quiet about it all these years!"

Bertha's face puffed out with indignance, growing even rounder. "He might as well know, Louella." She turned to her nephew, her expression saying oh-how-I-wanted-to-shield-you! "Yes, we knew how much time you spent with that girl. It's just a lucky thing for you that she moved, before she could lead you any further down the garden path."

He grabbed his hat and hurried toward the front door. "Spare yourselves the effort of explaining all your kind consideration. Pamela Waldren was no china doll. But she was a true lady—and a human being, which is something I doubt either one of you can really understand."

He rushed from the house, feeling like Dewey at Manila Bay, like Wellington at Waterloo, like the marines at Belleau Wood. He heard gasps behind him as he went out. No doubt they were attempting to put on the dual fainting act at the horribly shocking speech he had delivered. No worry about that. Let them fall on the floor. They'd get up when he didn't return. They were both strong as mules.

As so many men before him, Tom DeWitt had endured the furious pre-wedding whirlwind which every girl seemed determined to have, despite the fact that she reached her wedding day in a state bordering on hysteria. It seemed like a constant round of madness, with endless discussions of the wedding arrangements, debates over the selection of silver pattern, new drapes for the bedroom and new clothes, the showers to attend, the excitement and anxiety about the wedding gown, the choice of bridesmaids and ushers and so on. In the relative quiet of the day before the wedding, everyone concerned seemed to be drifting in the calm of a gentle exhaustion.

The wedding ceremony moved swiftly, smoothly, a sort of anticlimax to all of the breathless preparation of the preceding weeks. No blunders marred the ritual: everyone was in the right place at the right time, everyone said and did the proper things without flaw. Tom thought Irene's classic beauty never showed to lovelier advantage. Her face, framed in the gold-brown hair, was almost ethereal in its white perfection. Like her mother, she was completely composed, serene. Martha Carlson's pale blue eyes glistened in a way that struck Tom as more smug satisfaction than genuine happiness. Her husband, Henry Carlson, wore a look of quiet resignation. It had been obvious right from the beginning that Irene and her father were not close. That had puzzled Tom, for he himself found Henry Carlson to be a demanding but fair employer, and as Carlson's future son-in-law their relationship had become one of easy camaraderie. But Tom had stifled whatever slight doubts he may have felt before the wedding, before the disastrous honeymoon.

The honeymoon had started out well enough. Tom had anticipated Irene's fatigue after the wedding, had resolved to show every consideration and forbearance. After the whirlwind of preparations, any woman might be a long way from lovemaking and prefer a night of rest, and indeed, be grateful to her groom if he wasn't too aggressive.

In a hotel across the city that night, he held her, kissed her, and said, "Irene, I know you must be tired. Come to me when you want to."

Irene had seemed touched. And she had returned his kiss with fervor. "Darling, thank you. I am tired, terribly tired. I do so want to be a good wife. But— would you mind so awfully much, dear?"

He had said he didn't mind at all. He did, of course. Desire boiled within him. But we have time, he reasoned; the rest of our lives. We'll build the foundation of this marriage firmly on mutual consideration. I'll fool Bertha and Louella. The unbidden thought came that perhaps he would even fool Henry Carlson.

They drove along the east coast of Florida. September was a good month here, despite the occasional threat of a hurricane from the Bahamas. The hot sting of summer had gone, and the white breakers rolled in from the Atlantic in thundering gaiety. The days were warm and bright, the nights cool. They sunned themselves on the beach, walked miles on the hard-packed sand, watching the ungainly yet oddly graceful pelicans sailing in single file overhead, the tiny sandpipers racing and squeaking in the shallow ebbing water. Snowy white egrets, taller than the midget sandpipers, stalked in their stiff-legged walk, their long questing bills looking thin as bayonets. This was a world of sunlight, salt water, and the pungent smell of

17

seaweed. It was an environment that made an adult feel like a child, exclaiming over the beauty of the white and iridescent sea shells, racing after the gaudily painted concession vehicles that dispensed hamburgers, franks and ice cream.

Irene was fresh and cool in a white swimsuit, and Tom filled with pride on seeing the second glances given her by tourists of both sexes. Her skin was too fair to take much of the sun, so her exposures were brief. Not so with him. He tanned readily and deeply.

They dined at drive-ins, at swank hotels, in cozy little French restaurants. They placed small bets at the dog track, prowled around in aquariums, marine museums and several forts and block houses of Spanish, perhaps Huguenot origin. An ardent student of history, he once remarked to Irene, "Isn't it strange, how a man is a villain or a hero, according to viewpoint? Old Henry the Eighth, for instance, might well be called the father of the Royal Navy. He foresaw that the rocky little island called England would some day become too populous to sustain itself. Importing the products from agricultural countries would be her only salvation, so a strong navy was essential. Men such as Hawkins, Drake and Frobisher later flourished because of his foresight, and any foreign power that attempted to cut the British supply line was dealt with dramatically. To the British, he was a national hero; to the Americans, also, in a certain sense. But to the Spanish, he was a buccaneer, taking the gold-laden galleons that sustained them, for they had no sturdy middle class."

"I suppose," Irene had said listlessly.

Something had hardened within him. She knew well enough that Britain's lifeline was being cut at that very moment by Germany, and that as a member of the U.S. Naval Reserve, he would soon be on active duty. But not once had she shown any interest in the dire war news. And her reaction to his impending duty had been one of bland acceptance. No concern. No pride. Nothing.

And there was something else he had begun to notice. A cool barrier was beginning to build itself.

Irene was seemingly a lively, interesting companion, a good listener, agreeable to any of his suggestions. But he felt he was getting to know the real Irene. Already he recognized her strongest character trait: a serene, placid poise, maintained at all times, under all conditions. She wore it like bright, impenetrable armor. It was most evident when she met people who displeased her or were distasteful to her; a polite smile, and the turning away of her head, not precisely a rude gesture, but nonetheless final. This realization should have been another warning of the barrier that was growing, but he had not lived with it long enough for it to dispel the glow that his new marriage brought him.

Time was moving by. In the bedroom, the second night had been unsatisfactory, which was not in itself unusual. But the wall she was creating was beginning to grow stronger as time went on. He began to feel a vague sense of helplessness when evening approached. Irene did not cooperate; she endured. Several times when the warmth in him sought to stimulate a like response in her, she had actually stiffened, recoiled from him. And when her barely audible "Oh, Tommy!" held such shocked revulsion, he grew panicky with apprehension and uncertainty. He always desisted at once, his ardor dashed. And she always turned away from him, pulling the sheet over her, once again a gesture of finality. He would stand over her bed, wanting to apologize, but not knowing what he had done wrong. For what must he apologize? He could find no answer.

To be sure, the third morning had brought renewed hope. Irene was pleasant and conversational at breakfast. She seemed actually to exhibit a degree of warmth toward him. He took heart. Time, that was it; just more time. He launched into a discussion of their day's sightseeing. She joined in and his spirits soared. This was going to be a good day.

The day was. The night was not. Even as they went to their bedroom, he could sense that the invisible barrrier had become a stone fortress with a moat around it. She was inert, silent, as he took her in his arms. As his mind wondered why . . . why . . . why . . . the desire quickly ebbed from him. Her lips were cool and unresponsive. He looked at her exquisite face and saw no expression, no feeling and, suddenly, no beauty. He started to make a joke, then realized he would appear ridiculous. The best he could expect was that she would let him get it over with so she could go to sleep. He released her, got up and went to his bed.

She looked at him, as if in surprise. Then she turned over and pulled the sheet over her.

That night and the nights to follow, he lay in his bed, silent, shaken, angry.

2

THE FLORIDA HONEYMOON had lasted two weeks. By the time it was over Tom DeWitt had realized that one of the most astonishing and outrageous humiliations had become his lot. During this time he had tried to invent defenses on her behalf: Irene is otherwise normal, but not feeling well; she is more sensitive than other girls; she has perhaps been too sheltered. He must be patient, leave her alone for a while. Mutual trust and affection will gradually bring normalcy to our sex life. All of these things he told himself as they came home. In the final analysis, he believed none of it.

The worst session was ahead of him. He had always felt that living with the wife's family would inevitably bring loss of identity for the husband. And he did not like the Carlson house anyway. But Irene's mother, fully backed by Irene, had argued in her persuasive way. "After all, Tommy, no one expects you to start off with a house of your own. And it would be wasteful, don't you think, not utilizing some of the extra rooms we have here. You can live in one part of the house, decorate it as you wish, and we'll all be like close neighbors. It isn't as if we were living in crowded conditions, with not enough closet space and everyone waiting to use the same bath." And she had argued buying or renting a house would burden the newlyweds with debts.

He would not have given in except for Henry Carlson. The older man had put an arm around his shoulder, then faced him with that friendly wink and half-smile and said, "You'll have to admit, Tommy, that they have made some sensible points, don't you think?"

So he had capitulated. Had it not been for his respect for Henry Carlson, he would have refused. But now there was a bitterness in him because he would have to face Carlson with the most vile truth of his life—and he could not give this man anything but the truth. To a man of Carlson's discernment, the truth would be quite obvious anyway.

The house, located on a wooded hill above Philadelphia, was imposing. Tom conceded that. But he could not concur with the exclamations of many who saw it for the first time. "Oh, how perfectly lovely—it's like a palace." To him it looked more like a fortress, a reflection of Irene and her mother.

On their return Irene busied herself at once with selecting and ordering new appointments for their rooms, exchanging or disposing of such of their wedding gifts as were superfluous or impractical. Tom left Irene to her own devices and made no suggestions; he knew all things would be arranged according to her tastes anyway. It was her money, wasn't it? His own relative poverty humiliated him when he thought of it now. Oddly enough, he had accepted their financial disparity—until he had been repulsed when he attempted to make love to her, for in this respect they should have been equal. He did not voice objections to her desire to transform an extra room into a den for him. He couldn't pay for it. And he felt, rationally or otherwise, that it indicated the first step toward a permanent imprisonment there. So when she insisted on furnishing the den, he couldn't bring himself to tell her what he wanted in it. Which didn't seem to bother Irene. She smiled and went ahead, furnishing it with things that suited her fancy.

Tom knew of one room where he could be comfortable; it was the den of Henry Carlson. That room was a refuge from all but the distasteful conversation he now faced with Henry Carlson. The oak door was closed. He knocked on it and went in to find Carlson, as usual, seated in his favorite chair, a book open in his lap.

In an effort to begin on a light note, he grinned and said, "Per-o."

"Eh?" Carlson looked up from the depths of Tolstoy. "I said 'Per-o'".

"Ah, yes, the Great House, the origin of Pharaoh. Please sit down."

Tom sank into a red leather chair, feeling tired in every fibre. There was comfort here. The room was crowded with books, ivory elephants, German regimental beer steins, red leather furniture and good English oak. It was the only room in the house that revealed something of the man who lived there. The other rooms were stiffly elegant, artificial.

Henry Carlson put aside his Tolstoy. "I'm with you now, Tom. If you are referring to this as the Great House, you're mistaken, you know. But I am master in this one room."

"The only reason you're not master of this entire fort is because you don't want to be. You could be master wherever you lived or worked."

Carlson smiled at Tom's use of the word *fort*. "Oh, the Carlson Company is prosperous, liquid as gold. And I enjoy working there, because I'm building and creating and furnishing the materials for other men to build." His face became suddenly serious. "How was it in Florida? You came here to tell me something."

So Carlson knew, had perhaps expected it all along . . . Tom poured himself a drink. This was going to be more knotty to get into than he had feared. He took a long swallow of his drink, then slowly put the glass down. And all the while he could see Henry Carlson's eyes boring into his face. "I—I think, sir, you've known all the while what was going to happen. After all, she *is* your daughter."

Carlson stared at him and slowly shook his head.

"My God! As soon as that?" he murmured. "You've been married only two weeks."

"Yes, sir. Two weeks. It seems much longer." Tom was beginning to feel a little sick.

Carlson studied the young man's face. His own features had softened, and when he spoke his voice was gentle. "Tom—has it been very bad?"

Tom colored and looked away. "Worse than I could have imagined," he finally admitted. "Before we married, I thought I could detect a little reserve about her. But I attached little significance to it, just assumed that she was a proper young lady and all that. Besides, she kept giving me dates, and we were going places. But after we were married, when I . . . tried to make love and was rebuffed—well, you can't imagine anything worse. I tried to be understanding, but—" Tom broke off, overwhelmed with embarrassment and shame, and rose to leave. "I'm sorry, sir, for all I've said. You're the only man I'd have told. If you'll excuse me, I'll go to bed."

As Tom reached the doorway, Carlson spoke unhurriedly, softly, his low voice giving his words greater impact. "You're wrong on one thing, son. I understand completely. And Tom—try a little longer. Don't quit now."

Tom studied the face of the older man, and saw sympathy as well as fatigue. He realized how much he had come to like him. "Why?"

"I thought you would be the man to make a woman of her. You seemed tough, not easily beaten."

"Good Lord, I'm not tough!"

"You're tougher than you think."

"Possibly. But I'm not so confident. Look, sir—I'm—I guess I'm just plain scared."

"I know." In the glow of the old-fashioned lamp near Carlson's chair, his face had suddenly aged. "Remember, Tom, I told you how self-sufficient Irene is? I'm no psychologist, but for what it's worth I believe Irene is afraid of being dominated."

"Irene? You mean her lack of affection for me is a defense against me?"

"Against any man. But especially against you. Because you are closer to her, you are the man who will get to know her and find her weaknesses. But even for Irene it would be difficult to keep you at a distance forever. Her eternal poise and self-containment might be destroyed if you gave it a chance. Eventually she would have no defense against you."

Tom's mouth was agape. "That's a distorted way of looking at it. Why must she have a defense against my love? You make it sound as if this is a battle, man against his wife."

"It isn't, generally, but I believe it is from Irene's point of view. Tom, you know that the male is always the aggressor—no, that's too strong a word—I should say, takes the initiative in life, in lovemaking, in all things. We may not like some aspects of this maleness of ours, because in our present society, we are frequently up to our necks in complications and difficulties because of it. But we have been so created."

"Dominated was the word Irene used," said Tom softly. "But when a woman gives herself to a man, she isn't being dominated any more than he is. Each is giving to the other."

"Yes, in the relationship between a normal woman and her lover. Some women are not aware of this, Tom. I'm afraid Irene is one of them."

"I wish I could contest that point with you, but I can't. Why, after all you've said, do you think I should continue?"

"I thought you had a better chance than any other man. I still have that hope—the hope that your love will break through that damnable, self-contained self-centered reserve and achieve the thing that will make a woman of her." Carlson picked up his book, opened it, looked unseeing at its pages for a moment before raising his eyes to his son-in-law. "I've said too much, Tom. But there's one other thing—if you were thinking of this house as a Great House with a Pharaoh, you were right. But I did not create this house, only the means to build it. Only the means to build it. I know you do not like it. Except for my den, neither do I."

"I understand, sir." And Tom did. Carlson's explanation was in the nature of an apology. He said good night, and left the room.

Waiting came hard to Tom. Despite his sense of impending failure, he made the effort; a week, ten days, two weeks. Irene, accepting his abstinence quite casually, plunged into a series of parties, telling him excitedly, "I want to attend some of the social functions with you. And I know you, too, will like them."

"Like who?"

"The people you're going to meet. I've so many plans, Tommy. We'll have so much fun!"

It was hopeless. He had denied himself normal

physical outlets, and she seemed totally unaware of it. Did she think sex was only for lower forms of animals? He had heard of women who had had a perfectly happy life without having a man, but he had never thought it would be his unhappy lot to marry one of them. He watched Irene in her preparations for a party, happy as a child playing in a new doll house. She *was* a child. Henry Carlson is a kind man, but he's foolish to believe I can make a woman out of her. I was blinded by the attentions of this lovely girl. I allowed myself to be seduced by her show of beauty and grace, but in truth she has no more real feeling than a dead fish! She married because all of her friends were getting married and she was not to be outdone. She needed a nice-looking and intelligent escort to take her places so that her social life would be full and satisfying.

Names, places and events, these were her interests. He had to admit that she was capable in this field. She moved swiftly, efficiently, when she planned a party. Invitations, planning the menu, engaging musicians— she did it all with the practiced knowledge of a professional. She made proper seating of guests for dinner, taking into account always the personalities of these guests so that persons of like tastes and interests were seated together. Her mother hovered in the background, like a mother spaniel watching over the antics of her puppy.

Tom was more puzzled by "the people he should meet" than by her own behavior. He could not understand the value she put upon her association with them. They were artists who did little painting, musicians who seemed to be unemployed most of the time, composers who did not compose, and writers who went to tiresome lengths detailing the shortcomings of successful authors, but never seemed to get around to writing anything themselves. And there were a number of middle-aged men, impeccably dressed, faultless in manner, whose sole occupation seemed to be observing others at these socials. Without exception, they struck Tom as intelligent and sensible—if somewhat reserved—dinner companions. This last group Tom liked, for somehow they reminded him of Henry Carlson.

"Oh, they're retired men," Carlson explained when Tom drew him aside at one of Irene's parties. "Did quite well. Were always too busy to study people, so they do it here. Most of them are guests in my den. I think you'd like them."

"I do already."

"And what is your opinion of the others here?"

"Easy. A delightful collection of leeches, pimps, and prostitutes. I think Irene cannot know what they are. She's stupid in that respect, or she's a child."

Carlson laughed. "*Sehr gut.* An accurate analysis."

Tom and Carlson walked to the bar to get a drink and then strolled into Carlson's den. "There's one thing I don't understand. Irene is practical. Too much so. Unless something can be put to a practical use, she has no interest in it. I noticed that when we were in Florida. She was willing enough to go places and see various things, but she never looked at anything without considering whether it might be useful. I don't believe she could enjoy looking at the ocean. She can't use it for anything."

Carlson smiled. "I know. She looked at a part of my stamp collection once and said, quite sincerely, 'What on earth is it good for?' She might almost understand that it's a pastime, a way of enjoying myself, or that the stamps are valuable in and of themselves, but I doubt she'd understand my interest in their history or in any of the finer points of stamp collecting." Carlson paused and frowned, as if displeased with himself. "It's true, Tom, that her approach to many things is somewhat . . . uh, utilitarian, but—"

Carlson broke off at the sound of footsteps at the door. Irene came into the study, striding in that queenly and self-confident manner that had first attracted Tom. "Your guests are outside, Tommy."

"You mean your guests," Tom replied. His tone was casual, but pointed.

"I invited them," she said easily, "but as long as they're here, you owe it to them—"

"I owe them nothing," he said, matching her tranquil hardness. He had been through many of these parties now, finding that he was never acknowledged by Irene's friends as more than a figurehead host and husband, like a new accessory. He was as weary of her friends as of the hypocrisy of her expectations of him and the hypocrisy of his continued silence. "Say, that guy out there, Boldini, or whatever his name is— does he ever wash his neck? Or clean his fingernails?"

Henry Carlson suppressed a snort of laughter.

Irene's neck visibly reddened. "Boldini is a poet."

"He's a bum," Tom retorted. "Look, a man doesn't have to go around unbathed and unshaven to be a poet. I knew a young fellow in college who was a poet, a damned good one. He was six feet two, weighed two fifteen, was All-Southeastern for Tennessee twice, All-American once. Could have made the pros, but preferred to go into business with his father. He's forgotten more good English than the rest of us will ever know—and probably wrote more good poetry before he quit than Boldini will in his whole life."

Irene was not impressed. "Please, Tommy. Let's not keep everybody waiting."

She turned away as he would have protested, shaking her head in that manner of finality that he was beginning to detest. He had promised Henry Carlson he would continue his effort at this farce of marriage, but already he knew what his eventual decision would be. She had closed her mind to further discussion; she had terminated any exchange of views on any subject— so like her mother. He looked into Henry Carlson's face and smiled. It was like looking at himself in a mirror.

As he rejoined the party, he thought, in a few minutes she won't know whether I'm here or not, and neither will her friends. But this he found to be a great advantage. It gave him an anonymity he would not have otherwise enjoyed; it gave him freedom, because no one paid any attention to him.

Today he was to find that there were two exceptions. Tom found another young man who was bored.

And he discovered here a kindred being who, like himself, held a reserve commission in the navy. The young man introduced himself as Vic Hadley, and immediately they were off into talk of the war in Europe, the possibilities of their being called to active duty, the accelerated pace of shipbuilding in the navy yards and in private yards like the New York Shipbuilding Company. The general public appeared completely indifferent to the reports in the daily papers and on the radio. There were reporters and reporters; those whose main purpose appeared to be to create mass hysteria, and those who were making every effort to awaken America. The latter were the men who would very shortly be transformed into war correspondents, making every effort to bring the tragedies, while being as exposed to danger as any soldier, to their country.

Vic Hadley talked of the President's touchy problem in trying to aid Britain while keeping the nation out of the war. "The sort of job that really ages a man," he said. And so it went, while both of them imbibed more than their usual quota, becoming more loquacious all the time.

Tom was enjoying himself, sitting at the edge of the patio, discussing all of these international issues. And then he saw the second person who attracted him at this noisy affair. The girl was standing near a table, and her dark eyes were staring boldly at him. Over the rim of his highball glass, he made a detailed inspection of her; medium height, slim, dark-haired, her breasts small and high. He watched the dress swirl as she turned and walked over to speak to some people at a nearby table. The legs were good. Very good. She talked and laughed and then she turned again and threw the full impact of her gaze at him. An inquisitive, bold look. Below the ragged bob of curly black hair were heavy, arched brows, a full, sensuous mouth and eyes set wide apart. He felt the gooseflesh rising on his arms and felt the hard thudding in his stomach.

It seemed minutes that her eyes clung to his, though he knew it was a matter of seconds. This was it. His frustrated body suddenly leaped to the animal yearning evoked by this tempting girl.

"Who is she?" he asked Vic, knowing her name really didn't matter. She represented release from a long bondage.

"Frankie Britt. Smart kid. Honor roll student in school. Senior. Been kicked out of two schools for—ah—extracurricular activities of which the faculty didn't approve. She'll make it this time, though. I think she wants to travel." His new friend Vic Hadley laughed. "Better find out if you like her. There's no point in my briefing you. Go and find out for yourself. Mister, I think you'll be glad she's the opposite sex."

"You're right." Tom stood up and grinned at Vic. "I must get to know my guests."

Hadley glanced over at Boldini and his group.

"Well, some of them, anyway. Remember the time-worn saying about opportunity knocking on your door only once? Looks like that's what's happening now, my boy. I know Frankie well enough. I wouldn't let too much time go by if I were you, not if you want this opportunity. As of now, it's you she wants."

"Are you sure?"

"Dead sure. Maybe it's only for tonight. But right now, she's sending the old mating call to you and you alone. Look at those big soapy eyes raking you over. Go on, my fine buckol"

Tom could never remember when he had been so direct before. He found himself facing her, having negotiated the crowded path between several tables with a dexterity and nimbleness of foot almost incredible, considering the number of drinks he had downed.

"Your name's Frankie Britt? How may I be of service, milady? I'm Tom DeWitt, your host."

He led her away from the table and they began to dance. She clasped his left hand with her right, resting her left hand behind his neck. She pressed her cheek against his, whispered softly, "Don't have another drink, please."

"And why not?"

"Because if you get sloppy drunk, I won't get all I need."

He felt the slight tremor of her hand. Her nearness, her directness—and his neediness—stirred a passion that surpassed anything he might have felt for Irene. Frankie danced beautifully, effortlessly responding to his lead, her body bending easily to his every motion, her breasts pressed softly, enticingly, against his chest.

She hugged his neck again, pressed her cheek to his. "And you're married to Irene Carlson. God, I feel sorry for you!"

Her words sounded genuine. She knew Irene. He didn't know whether Irene or anyone else with a proclivity to gossip was aware of the seduction taking place on the dance floor, but he couldn't care less.

The circle of his arm drew her closer, and he was both shocked and amused to hear her say, "Continue with your warm-up. I'm already loving it, and being married to Irene is going to make it all the better for you."

He held her slightly further away and looked unbelievingly into her smiling face. Finally he laughed and shook his head, accepting that this was indeed no fantasy. "Come on, let's get out of here."

"We'll go to my house," she said.

In the shadows of the driveway, she paused and reached up to kiss him. The feel of her full lips was good; a gentle pressure, then the lips opening and the soft moistness of her tongue. It was a lingering kiss that sent his blood pounding faster. Then she pulled away from him and put her head on his shoulder. "Coming up for a bit of air . . . I suppose you think I'm a tramp."

He had to pull her body close to his and his hands went down and clasped her firm buttocks, began to rub. "I'll tell you a secret, Frankie. All of my life people have looked at me and said, 'Oh, he's such a nice boy.' Hell, I didn't want to be a bum, and I don't think I was. But labels like that are too easy. They dismiss too much, like all of the complexities, and don't leave any margin for error." He gave a rueful laugh. "But I guess I'm learning I'm guilty of the same thing—letting myself be fooled by first impressions."

Frankie squeezed his hand, knowing he was thinking of Irene. "Come on, time's a-wasting," she said, leading him to her car.

She had a convertible, blue and gray. She slid behind the wheel, motioned him to sit beside her. He liked the way she drove. She had quick, strong hands. Her left hand held the wheel rock steady, while her right hand maneuvered the shift lever, surely, quickly, never once grinding the gears. She poured the gas into the car, rushed through the quiet night, braked smoothly, letting the wheel spin back without hesitation. He had seen no equal. It seemed strange that a girl manifesting such sureness, such confidence, could be as unstable as she was in her college studies, in her relationships.

He studied her legs as she activated brake and clutch pedals; in their sheer hose they looked perfectly groomed. A tiny gold chain sparkled around her right ankle.

"I hope you like them," she said.

"What?"

"You know what—my legs."

"They're nice, better than nice. They give me ideas."

"Oh, now, Mr. DeWitt." She suddenly whirled to the right, and the car shot up into a driveway half-hidden by a tall hedge, and rocked gently to a stop. "You have touched the essential point of lovemaking. Do exactly what occurs to you at the moment. Delay, restrain yourself, and you begin to lose that fine edge that makes for a really good time."

"Restrain myself? Are you nuts?" For just an instant he thought of Irene, standing before the mirror, letting him see through her filmy gown. That was sex to her. Let the husband look, then to bed—and immediately to sleep.

Frankie leaned back in the car, stretched out her

right leg. "Have you guzzled so much you won't be able to get what you want?"

"It'll never happen. I'm so horny, I'll probably lose it by the time I get on you."

"Tommy! You talk so terrible!"

He put his hand on her knee. She waited, saying nothing. He leaned toward her and rested his hand on her silk-clad thigh. Her hose were rolled tightly a few inches above her knee. His hand slid along smooth bare flesh until it reached the stopping point. She caught his head in both hands, kissed him hard and then began to slide down on the leather seat. Her kisses set his blood racing again but when his hand became gentle but insistent she pushed him from her and opened the door.

"Not here, Tommy. Come into the house."

Tom found that Frankie Britt did not subscribe to the theory that the male must always be the aggressor. Obviously she believed that feminine aggressiveness—at the proper time—would stimulate the male to more heated action. Clever, thought Tom. After all, that was the whole point, wasn't it? Get him dizzy with desire, then grab him and let him soar to the heights on his sweet explosion.

Tom was unaware of covering the distance between the front door and the bedroom. He did not consider whether she lived here with her family or perhaps with another girl. They were alone and they wanted each other; that was enough. Frankie's direct approach astonished him. There was no dabbling with perfume, no fussing with hair or makeup. With her dark eyes on him, she quite simply and forthrightly stripped. At this point, he decided that Irene had done something for him after all. She had driven him to this, and he could now appreciate the night ahead all the more.

The glistening black shoes came off, then the rest. Frankie had worn the minimum. Three pieces. Dress. Lacey panties. Dainty bra. She was so lean that she needed no girdle and could roll her stockings. She did not remove these. Except for the hose, she was naked. She let him look at her for a moment, then withdrew to the bed, where she lay in partial darkness, with only the small bed lamp on.

Words were unnecessary now. His clothes were quickly scattered from the door of the bedroom to the bed. When at last he lay with her, her pliant body arched and strained up against him, and her hands pulled his face down to her lips for a long kiss.

"I'm drunk, of course," she murmured as his hands moved over her. "My pathetic excuse—and a girl must have an excuse, no matter how weak. Can't be frank and honest, like a man, and simply say—'I want it.'"

His laugh was low, throaty. His body was stimulated to a rosy, aching glow as her fingers slid down his thigh and closed hard on his flesh. "Easy, now, Frankie. You don't want to finish me before I get what I want."

"Never fear, you beast. You'll never get away after only once."

She kissed him again, this time the kiss of fulfillment. The feel and smell of her, new and strange, was almost unbearably sweet after his months of abstention, of misery, with Irene. Her gentle movements swept him into the passion he had been denied all this time. Their breathing quickened as he mounted her, grinding into her churning hips. Perfect coupling, like a hand in a glove. A velvet glove.

His hands and senses savored her surging body, its exquisite flesh and silken clasp. He groaned and went rigid as he suddenly thrust deeper within her. His hands held her tousled head while her tongue explored his mouth, and her pelvis lunged up in response to his every move until his final thrust brought them both to a fury of release.

He lay back, his eyes closed, his pulse calming in the quiet afterglow. When he moved away from her, he caught the essence of the woman smell, sharp, feral, wild. As she lay breathing heavily, he watched the thumping in her stomach. She made a slight grunt, sat up and reached to the night table for a cigarette.

"Sorry," she said, giving him a rueful smile. "I usually take a shower right before, but this head-on animal collision tonight was rather unexpected—and I suppose I was never one to delay the inevitable."

He had to laugh. "You're very frank which I like. As it happens, I also like the way you smell."

She exhaled a cloud of smoke and gave him a skeptical look. "You do, really?"

"Of course. It's part of the whole sex thing, part of what attracts two people, gets them excited."

"I'll think about that." She swung her dark eyes to his. "I'll see if I can smell stronger the second time

around. Have a cigarette. Relax. Smoke. I want some
more of you. I'm just building up for some more fun.
So you rest. You're going to need it."

It was two o'clock before he returned to the Carlson house. Frankie had offered to dress and drive him
back, but he had declined and found a cab. She had
kissed him gently and asked him to phone her. And
of course he had promised, but he doubted that he
would ever call. He felt that he had simply been there
at the right time, that her need would tolerate no
delay and that any young man would do. Hers was
not an address to be passed from hand to hand but
neither could he regard her interest in him as anything other than a matter of convenience—for both
of them, he had to admit. Much as he liked Frankie,
he didn't love her. And he didn't understand her
attitude toward life or toward sex any better than he
understood Irene's. With some self-disgust, he believed he would search far and wide to find a young
man as ignorant as he was about women. For someone who had been raised by two women, he knew
less about women than any man he knew.

As he entered the house, a couple of servants clean-
ing up after Irene's "social" looked up quickly, then
turned their faces away at once. He could not suppress a grin. Mr. DeWitt taking off on his own, and not
showing again until 2:00 A.M.? Shocking.

The moonlight threw its white glow across the bedroom as he began to undress. The sleeping figure in
the bed suddenly stirred, and as Tom stepped into
his pajamas Irene sat up. As she came fully awake

and her eyes registered his presence, Tom gave a low laugh, surprised that she didn't simply lie down and go back to sleep.

"Tommy, what are you laughing about?" She shook her head, setting her golden-bronze hair bouncing about her shoulders.

He sat down on the bed, but his smile held no humor. "I was just thinking—wouldn't it be funny, after this farce of a marriage of ours, if you underwent some miraculous change and wanted me to make love to you."

"Oh, Tommy, what a ridiculous thing to say."

"Not at all." He stretched luxuriously on the bed. "Because if you did, I would be unable to accommodate you."

She stared at him blankly. "I—oh, you're not making sense, Tommy. It's two o'clock."

"Ten after," he corrected. He was through with being patient and understanding, but the bitterness he had felt had somehow dissolved. It was time for the truth, and let Irene react as she would. Things had to be settled, one way or another. "I took one of your guests home."

She lay back on the bed. "Was he sick?"

"It wasn't a he; it was a she."

"A girl?" She raised herself on one elbow. "I don't understand."

He stared at her directly. "You never will." He felt the numbing pleasure of sleep coming fast over him. Soon—although he wouldn't say a single word—she would find out about Frankie. He could expect anger, a hot outburst, not because Irene had any real affec-

41

tion for him, but because her happily-ever-after marriage would be exposed to the world as a mere fiction. It was strange, almost startling, how little it mattered to him now. Irene would blast him, he would remind her why he had turned to another woman, and then it would be over. The eventual confrontation was a necessary evil, but it hardly seemed an earthshaking prospect. Yes, he felt sadness and a certain amount of anger for the way he had blinded himself to Irene's true nature, but there was also relief that the marriage would soon come to an end.

With a smile on his face, he closed his eyes. His chest rose and fell in easy breathing. Sleep claimed him.

3

Tom DeWitt let the engine of his little Plymouth warm up a bit. The autumn days were getting chilly. It was going to be a beautiful day.

As he put the car into gear and began the drive to his plant, the sun came flickering through the red, brown and yellow leaves. Usually he loved this time of year, but today the autumn colors were dulled for him by the news from Europe. The German juggernaut was rolling across the fields of Poland. Adolf Hitler now had thrown aside a treaty pledging to make no more territorial demands, and it seemed that nothing could stop the Wehrmacht.

"No blackout of peace in America," the President

had said. Sincere words, but how long would he live up to them?

Now, with Irene soon to be out of his life, he thought of his ensign's commission in the naval reserve. Vic Hadley also had a commission. Tom had put in four years at Georgia Tech for his, and Vic Hadley at Northwestern. Phil Armstrong, whom he had met thru Vic and who had become a fast friend, had gotten his commission during his years at Harvard. They called Phil the "erudite one." He was broad-shouldered, with big hands and bushy black eyebrows, a thoughtful young man with a keen sense of humor. It had been inevitable that the three of them would put in for active duty. The swelling numbers of workers going into the Philadelphia Navy Yard was evidence enough that the U.S. was gearing for war, and the number of British destroyers and corvettes coming in for repairs and overhaul seemed to be almost a declaration of intent.

Now, on this lovely crisp day, he was beginning to realize how many things he had taken for granted. All of the things at this time of year—football at Franklin Field, Yale and Harvard in their traditional scrap, crowds of bright, noisy young people at the games, the smell of good coffee, the tang of hot dogs and hamburgers, walking on the leaf-covered paths at little Swarthmore, the crackling warmth of fire in the hearth at the frat house—all taken for granted, and only now fully appreciated. He was about to make a major change in his life. This evening when he went home from work, he would have his last talk with Irene. He knew she anticipated something or had learned something, for both she and her mother had been studying him at the breakfast table that morning.

It had been that way yesterday, too. There was no doubt that Irene knew. It had been only a week since that night with Frankie, and already Irene knew. He lit a cigarette as he waited for a red light to change. Of course it was inevitable that she would find out. Too many people at Irene's party had seen him dancing with Frankie, had noticed how she held him, had seen them leave together in her car. And if Irene was insensitive in some respects, she was still sharper than the average person. It surprised him that he could view the upcoming scene so dispassionately. He had lived in a turmoil of frustration, uncertainty, and disappointments for five months. Perhaps the calmness he felt was because what faced him now was anticlimactic. He had become drained of emotion. Well, after "the scene" was over, he could begin to forget Irene.

He had no leisure time at the office on this day. There were more than a few irritations to cope with, and the topper came when Tom's assistant, a young man with ample enthusiasm but little experience, turned in the square footage on a run of corrugated board. When Tom finished computing the selling price of finished boxes, his eyebrows went up at the astronomical figure. Tom would normally have chided his assistant about it, but today he chewed him out

thoroughly—which sent the young man, red faced
with embarrassment, scurrying from Tom's office and
only made Tom angry with himself.

At four-thirty, he drove home, on his way to have
the boom lowered. Let's have this damned thing over
with, he thought, fighting his way through pedestrians
and traffic. Look at that fool woman, running under
a red light, her eyes fixed on a bus. Get the bus, no
matter that you're risking your life. Must get that
bus! If you miss it, by this time tomorrow what the
hell difference will it make?

The nearer to the Carlson house he came, the more
his mood deteriorated. Have your tantrum, Irene, and
get it over with. Then I can start forgetting you. Haven't
lived for five months. If you don't know about Frankie,
I'll tell you. Maybe after dinner. Would be nice to see
that old gal, Martha, get a good case of indigestion.

The confrontation did not come until after dinner.
At the table, he watched Henry Carlson. He doubted
that Carlson knew anything, but the older man's instinct was functioning. He had plainly noted the
tense expressions of both his wife and daughter. Pale-
faced, neither had had much to say. Neither seemed
to want to meet Tom's gaze directly. To cover their
self-consciousness, they launched into a discussion of
the upcoming marriage of one of Irene's girl friends.

Tom slowly ate his dinner. No doubt about it, he
thought; Irene and her mother definitely know. And
they've been really shaken, because this is the last
thing either of them expected meek little Tommy to
do. He watched them, the one dark and harassed
looking, the other blonde and flushed as if she had a

fever, talking animatedly. He could almost feel pity for them. They expected a man to live like a monk, and he had given them the roughest shock they had ever experienced. Then he thought of the kind of life Henry Carlson had been forced to live, and he hardened again.

Their talk ran on. "Eloise says this boy's family in Charleston is closely related to the Legares," said Irene. "They have a simply palatial home in a new section there, near the Ashley River."

"I've heard there are quite a few penniless aristocrats there," said Martha thoughtfully.

"Not this family," Irene exclaimed triumphantly. "The boy's father has interests in three states. Eloise couldn't have done better. The boy has finished paying for a considerable amount of utilities stocks . . ."

And so it went on, the two women momentarily having forgotten Tom and the problem he represented. Eloise's groom-to-be had stock, a new Buick, a recent increase in an already substantial salary, and he was planning to buy a house and already had a beach cottage in Florida. Eloise had, indeed, made a good catch —and they would make such a good-looking couple.

Tom looked at Carlson a couple of times during the conversation. His father-in-law had the look of a man who has heard this sort of thing before and had little interest in it.

Tom heard himself casually ask, "Does this Eloise love the guy?"

Abruptly the flow of words stopped. The two women looked directly at him. One dark, one fair, they suddenly looked identical to him. He saw wide eyes, features almost artificial in their perfection, faces turned on him like the bloodless faces of pretty dolls. His calm good humor vanished. In a voice brittle with growing anger, he repeated his question.

"I asked if this girl loves the guy. In all this conversation, I haven't heard one word of what he's like. He's a good catch, has a lucrative job, nice car, great expectations. It's kind of sickening to think that those are the only things that count to his happy little bride—or to you."

He rose and left the dining room, conscious of the look that Henry Carlson flashed at him. There was hearty applause in the older man's quiet grey eyes.

Carlson spoke as Tom reached the door. "I once saw a game at Franklin Field. The home team, playing Penn State, was a three-touchdown underdog. They played their hearts out. Almost won. They were two points behind and on State's one yard line with thirteen seconds to go, but the whistle blew before they could make it. Things were stacked against them, you might say, but they put on a helluva good fight anyway—a memorable fight."

Tom gave him a pale-lipped grin. "That's a standing ovation, Henry. Thanks."

Tom waited in the bedroom. He stood at a window and looked at the brightly colored leaves drifting from the trees, lying scattered over the grass. It was getting dark now and color was hard to see. A man inclined to the dramatic might say Tom's hopes and plans were falling and being scattered about like those leaves. But his task now was to forget; a monumental task, since his awareness of defeat was so complete.

Such a swift collapse. Five months. He was angry at himself for letting those two words keep recurring in his mind. He wondered whether another man would have had more tenacity and won out. Apparently Henry Carlson did not think so. Carlson had asked him to hang on, had said Tom was stronger than he gave himself credit for, that he was stronger than other men.

He felt her presence in the doorway before he heard her steps. He turned to face her.

"Tell me about Frankie Britt," she said, her voice shaking ever so slightly. She had lost her usual composure, and her face was chalky white. Tom at once regained the calm he had felt when he had left Frankie's house.

"You know, I am reminded of my aunts when they called me to account for some mischief when I was a boy."

"This is hardly a boy's prank, Tommy. You're evading my question. Get to the point."

"How could I evade such a fitting comparison? Oh, my aunts were never as beautiful as you are. You know, before you married me, when you turned on the charm you were quite irresistible. I fell victim in a hurry, ignoring all the little warning signs, not allowing myself to realize that all you saw in me, all you wanted, was a presentable young man, a graduate of a college with a high academic rating, someone who would make a fitting escort at all of your social events. But you see with my aunts, I always had to account for every act, every little mistake, every minute I was late for dinner—"

"I think an accounting is due your wife!" she cried in a shaky voice. Her pulse was visible, throbbing in her white throat.

"You would be exactly right, Irene—if you *were* my wife."

He watched the flicker of incredulity cross her face, then the narrowing of the blue eyes as understanding came. "You say this to me, after lying with that little tramp!"

"A tramp? I have a great many questions for you too, Irene, questions that might make you reevaluate yourself if you could answer them truthfully. Men need women in a way that's as basic as the need for food and drink. But, it's not just sex I'm thinking about. More than that, there's the need for genuine mutual affection. What's your answer for that? I'm not supposed to share your bed or your affections, yet you're furious when I seek relief elsewhere. Your attitude defies description."

She screamed and flew at him with flailing arms. As her accusations poured out, all of the pent-up anger and resentment welled up in him until he could stand it no more. He slapped her cheek with the flat of his right hand, hit her hard enough so that she fell to the floor. She jumped up, the bright red outline of his hand showing clearly. "You animal!"

His voice suddenly became quiet. "Irene, don't ever call me that again, do you understand? Never again. Damn you, I'll change the shape of your face if you do!"

She stood up, swaying, nearly breathless, an incredulous look spreading over her face. For the first time in her life, she had no words.

"Go to your mother, if you wish," he said. "Don't waste time waiting for sympathy from your father. He's endured so much he's become immune to the existence your mother created for him—and to you and your mother. He won't explode as I did. He's a formidable man. It's too bad you didn't learn more from him." He hesitated at the door. "I've nothing more to say to you, Irene. This has been a wretched affair for me and I've been quite miserable about it. That's the truth."

Henry Carlson was alone in his study when Tom rapped on the door and went in. Tom went to the bar and poured himself a drink, a stiff one. Carlson put aside a book of Sandburg's poems and smiled up at him from his red leather chair.

"Tom, you can usually measure the size of a man's problem by the size of the drink he pours for himself."

Tom sat down and faced him. "Mr. Carlson, you're dead right. Except that in my case, the problem has ended. You might call it a case of enlightenment and release."

He took a good pull at his drink, waiting for it to dull his anger. The long walk outside in the garden had helped. Still, this was not going to be an easy interview.

"You're leaving Irene," Carlson said quietly.

"Right again. And it was because I went to bed with a girl—well, I've been hurting the way only a man

51

can hurt. Irene found out about it and we've just finished a good lusty row about the affair. She called me an animal, began beating me with both hands and I slapped her to the floor. You'll no doubt hear about it from her and her mother."

"I don't doubt that. Who was the girl?"

"Frankie Britt. Does the name mean anything to you?"

"Oh, yes, Frankie. Been here quite often. Brilliant student in school. But other areas of her life haven't exactly been up to the same standards. She's not really a bad girl, though. She's plenty smart, and from what I recall when she was in high school, full of life. The school authorities said she needed better parental disciplining. She has no parents. Maybe what she needs is someone to really care for her."

"I understand," Tom said, suddenly thinking of his aunts. It was funny; what Frankie had needed was more disciplining while he had needed less. But what they both needed now was not so very different.

Carlson's placid voice brought him out of his revery. "Who else have you spoken to about this?"

"You're the only person I'd discuss this with. She tried to make me feel—" He stopped short, the memory of the scene renewing all his anger. "It was as if I were uncouth or obscene for being a normal man!" he burst out. "I don't claim to be an expert on women, but I never expected her to react as she did. The sight of my naked body, the slightest touch seemed to revolt her. And the crowning horror of all was my so-called brutal penetration of her, a cruel masculine attack upon her dainty feminine person—Forgive me, sir, I'm being too personal . . ."

"I think factual would be a better word. Go on, Tom. Let it out."

Tom shook his head, ashamed of his outburst. "I tried to walk out some of my anger in the garden before I came in here to see you."

"You haven't told me all you meant to. And you must do it, or it will eat you up."

Tom smiled despite his low spirits. Carlson was talking to him as a friend, as a peer. He didn't wonder that men worked their backs stiff for him. What a tragedy this man had to be wasted on the bloodless, self-centered Martha.

"That's really about all there is to say. I'm not sure this would all have come to a head so soon if it hadn't been for Frankie. She made me feel good about myself again, however briefly, and after that I knew I had to do something to stop feeling as miserable as I've been . . ."

"And of course Irene found out about it and there was a scene, and you want a divorce. I mean, I think it's mutual."

"Yes, sir. Excluding you, I never want to see anyone in this house again."

"I have a good friend who's an excellent attorney. He can arrange things quietly, discreetly. Name's Trevor. Between the two of us, we'll make it as painless as possible. I think I guessed it tonight at dinner. Knowing Irene, I was surprised that she was able to restrain herself as long as she did."

"She made up for it tonight. It was one helluva scene. As for myself, I was surprised that I didn't really care that she had found out about Frankie. Isn't that one helluva note? To be married only five months, and not care if your wife knows you've laid another girl?"

"There's one thing, Tom."

"What's that?"

Carlson paused, as if unsure of himself. "She *did* care enough to blow up about it."

"You're right, as usual. She was enraged, but not because there was any affection involved. It was because I was upsetting her little dream world."

Henry Carlson suddenly looked very tired. "I think I've heard enough, Tom. But just so we can both be sure she hasn't finally been shocked into turning over a new leaf—what were her last words?"

"Something like this—'I've been willing to put aside my self-respect, ignore your flirting with other girls, so that we can go on as before. It positively sickens me to say it, but if I must go into unpleasant details, I cannot bear the thought of having you put that thing in me after it's been in that trashy girl. I would feel unclean every time. But I will make the sacrifice. You'll continue to be my escort wherever we go in all our activities, or at parties here. And when you're swollen with that animal lust, you can go find some tramp who will relieve it.' "

Carlson let out a long sigh. "Not exactly a bargain for you."

"I told her I'd see her in hell before I'd accept such an arrangement."

Carlson studied him carefully. "Have you anything more to say, Tom?"

"No. Only that I hope you and your attorney friend can break this thing off as quickly as possible."

"Can do." Carlson stood up, put a hand on Tom's shoulder. "I'm truly sorry I encouraged this marriage, son. My only excuse is that I believed you could, in time, transform Irene. When she was very young, I believed a strong man could make a woman of her as she grew older. It's only a grain of consolation, Tom, but you made the best effort. But I can see now no man can make a woman of Irene. You sleep in the guest room tonight. I'll get busy in the morning."

"I'm making another change, too. As you know, I'm in the naval reserve. I met two friends at one of Irene's parties here, and what with the Germans running all over Europe we've decided to request active duty. The navy's beefing up everything. It's obvious in this yard, and I've had letters from friends in other naval districts who write of the same increased activity. The Charleston Navy Yard in the Sixth Naval District is building destroyers like mad. They had about four thousand employees in 1940. I'm speaking of trained, skilled workers of every type. They have nearly eleven thousand now and it won't be long before it'll be fifteen thousand. It's hardly classified information that the United States is doing everything short of a declaration of war now, and German espionage agents know it as well as anyone. Roosevelt will continue his present policy as long as he can, but I truly believe he has no confidence in being able to do so much longer." He sighed. "I'm fed up with that damned box factory anyway."

Carlson smiled. "To use an old cliche—the change will do you good."

Carlson looked around his study, and as Tom watched his face he had the sudden feeling that the older man, too, had a change in mind. He started for his room. "Good night, sir."

"Good night, Tom. And when you're through with the tailor, drop around to see me. I want to see how you look in navy blue."

If Tom had guessed that Carlson had a change in mind for himself, he could not have guessed how drastic a change it was.

Martha and Irene found Henry Carlson's diary lying open on his desk the next morning, when they had been unable to locate him. The diary entry was actually an open letter to them. Their eyes round with disbelief, they read:

"With the entries of this date, so has ended my diary, as everything else has ended. My son-in-law—I wish he were my son—endured the utmost in insensitivity from a daughter in whom I had some vestige of hope. I myself have endured as much as I intend to endure. The following is all I will offer by way of explanation. My more extensive efforts to explain have fallen on deaf ears in the past. Perhaps in abbreviated form some part of it may seep through to the two women who have been such a disappointment."

They gaped at each other in genuine astonishment.

The idea of either of them fitting this description was beyond belief.

"Irene, just what you expected of marriage is, and has been, way over my head. That you would take a man's name but not be a wife to him is, I believe, a derect reflection of your mother.

"You were infuriated when he broke free from almost complete abstinence from normal relations with his wife. But have you any idea of how he felt each night when he looked at a beautiful woman and she sent him to bed with a polite good night? Have you considered how he felt without any of the companionship that is supposed to be one of the great blessings of marriage, or how it felt when his wife shared only the most superficial aspects of life, or of herself, and rejected him in as fully and demeaning a manner as possible? I regret to say that I doubt you've ever considered his feelings. I doubt you even have the least conception of who or what Tom DeWitt is.

"I tried to find excuses for you. When you were in high school, I used to sit in this room and wonder how long it would take for you to learn. I know now how futile my hopes were, both for you and for my own marriage.

"I'm sure you realize, Martha, that this means two divorces. You'll realize after a while that it's best. You can have the property here if you like, and I'm sure you'd like. A double divorce should provide some entertaining conversation for your parties for a time, but I warn you that the people here will never let it be forgotten that your son-in-law cheated on your daughter. They'll keep it alive. Somehow I feel that after a while you'll give up this house. In any event, I shall try to be fair in the settlement.

"As you read this, I am looking for a place up-country and have taken Jenkins with me.

"Enough for now. It has not been an easy letter to write. But—*su ende.*"

The two women looked at each other, pale and shocked.

"*Su ende?*" asked Irene. "What does it mean?"

"It's German. It means *the end*. He's right, you know. It is the end."

4

Tom DeWitt kept his word. He had reported to the office of the Fourth Naval District after receiving orders from the Bureau of Navigation—later known as the Department of Naval Personnel. After the tedious procedure of undergoing a physical and wading through a small mountain of paperwork, he had been given a uniform allowance—insufficient to actually cover the cost—and had made a few purchases at the Ship's Service. He was then given orders to become a member of the military department of the Yard's office, where his duties consisted of making contact with incoming vessels and assigning them to piers where the planning and production departments took over. He was also to engage local pilots, who were familiar with the Delaware and other waters in the area, to get these ships underway once they were ready for sea. These functions were done in the capacity of yard duty officer, rotating with other officers. Phil Armstrong and Vic Hadley had also run the same gauntlet and had the same assignments. All three of them believed these duties to be temporary. Sea duty was not far away, a sharp silhouette like a ship on the horizon.

Tom found himself at home with his new life more quickly than he would have thought after the disastrous marriage. He enjoyed the feeling of accomplishment at getting a ship into the yard, seeing that the production department finished the necessary work, and watching that ship get underway to resume its duties. Each incoming ship presented a different problem. He met its executive officer, took him to the production department, and discussed the work to be done under the supervision of the officers assigned there for EDO—engineering duty only.

Tom liked his work. There could be rough days, however, some of them quite serious. One of the more serious incidents occurred on a cool September evening when his watch was routine to the point of being dull. As he sat in his office, Chief Boatswain's Mate Charles Bowen, known as "Spring Line" Bowen, rushed in. His face, usually a florid red, was pale with anxiety.

"Bell, sir—in the dispensary with what the chief pharmacist's mate thinks is a bad appendix."

"The coxswain at the boat house? One of my boys?" DeWitt stood up. "Have you called the medical officer with the duty?"

"Can't locate him, Mr. DeWitt. I've two men running all over the Yard."

"Then send out some more!" Tommy grabbed the phone, got the girl on the switchboard. "Mildred—where is the doctor?"

"Don't know, Tommy. I tried his office, and we know he's not at the dispensary. Sometimes he goes to the main gate when an A.W.O.L. returns, and after the duty officer has him logged in he has the man checked for—ah—V.D. I don't know where else to try."

"Okay, Mildred. I've had no A.W.O.L. this evening. I'll try elsewhere."

He put the phone down and stared at Bowen. "Spring Line, if I can't locate the medical officer at the places he should be, then I—"

"Yes, sir. Try the places he shouldn't be."

Tommy jumped up, reached for some keys on the wall. "The station wagon, chief?"

"Yes, sir. It's right outside."

"I'm off to the officers' club. Which is the last place in the world I want to find him."

A grim-faced "Spring Line" Bowen watched DeWitt race from the office toward the station wagon. Then the phone jangled and he picked it up. Bell was worse. The chief pharmacist's mate was scrubbing up to try the surgery himself. Then the phone rang again—this time with better news. An excited blue-jacket garbled at him that he had found a doctor at the hospital, that the doctor was on his way to the dispensary.

Bowen thanked him, then hung up. He glared at his list of phone numbers, then began to dial the officers' club. Knowing DeWitt as I do, he thought, I hope I'll

be in time to get him before he does something drastic
—if he finds that doctor.

He was not in time. Tom DeWitt had located the
medical officer—at the officers' club bar, sloppy
drunk. He turned bleary red eyes on DeWitt.

Enraged, Tom wasted no time. "I have something
for you, you stupid bastard!"

He did—a straight left and a crunching right hook
that sent the inebriated officer flopping on his plump
backside and brought exclamations from the twenty-
odd officers present. Tom stood over him, both fists
clenched, his arms shaking.

"Get up, you damned sot! Get up, so I can beat
the damned hell out of you!"

The medical officer, Lieutenant-Commander Ralph
Starke, put a hand to his smashed nose. It came away
bloody, and he saw blood running down his shirt
front. "I'll have you court-martialed," he screamed,
"for striking a superior officer!" He pulled himself up
and gestured to the group of sober-faced onlookers.
"Get security—put this man under arrest!"

"You do that, Mr. Starke," Tom replied. His arms
weren't shaking now. They were rock-steady, with
clenched fists at his sides. "I can't call you *Dr.* Starke—
you're not worthy of the caduceus on your sleeve.
Call security. I'm putting you on report for being
drunk on duty and for negligence. Hell, don't you
know you should be available when you're on duty?
There's a man with acute appendicitis in the dispensary. My men have been running all over the Yard, trying to find you! I've never seen a doctor who didn't
care for the men in his command, much less a doctor

who'd get so pie-eyed drunk he couldn't help anyone if he had to."

He paused. Three men had entered the club: Chief Boatswain's Mate Bowen, a straight-backed young ensign, Barry Terence, wearing sidearms, and a medical officer Tom did not know. All three presented tired, sober expressions. The doctor spoke first.

"Mr. DeWitt? I'm Doctor Rimmer. I'm afraid that Coxswain Bell didn't make it. His appendix had ruptured, and there was peritonitis. I did all I could. His next of kin will be notified at once. I'm very sorry . . ."

Tom nodded dumbly. He glanced at Starke, still leaning in the corner, his expression now more foolish than angry. Tom looked back at the three men who had just entered. Why couldn't he scream? All he could do was stand like a graven image, his limbs frozen, his lips compressed. Suddenly he was aware of the meaning behind the presence of Ensign Barry Terence, who looked embarrassed and apologetic.

"There's someone from the administrative command in my office, isn't there? I'm going to be relieved, isn't that it?"

"Tommy—" Terence coughed and shifted his feet about nervously. "The chief phoned the officers' club and they reported what was going on. I'm—"

"Okay, okay. Let's get to my office." He paused and turned back to face Starke. "One of my boys died, and he died because you were here drunk. He was eighteen years old. Are you sober enough to understand that?"

Starke glanced away from him to the group of officers looking at him. He found no sympathy there.

In Tom's office, he found a commander wearing an

arm band and sidearms waiting for him. "Mr. DeWitt? I'm Commander Leslie Callahan. You are restricted to your quarters until further notice. Give me your side-arms, please. Mr. Terence has the duty as of now."

"Yes, sir." Tom unhooked his belt with its regulation .38 and handed it to his superior. "The gun is loaded, hammer's closed on an empty chamber. The C.P.O. of the watch has the log up to the minute."

"Very well, Mr. DeWitt. Chief, take custody of this weapon. You may go to your room." He started for the door, then hesitated. "Mr. DeWitt, I take no pleasure in this."

He was gone, and Tom had scarcely heard his words. He was thinking of a boy named Bell. And the letter he had to write his parents. The navy would notify them, to be sure. But it was customary—manda-tory, in a sense—for a man's superior to write the parents in such a case, a personal letter. There was a coldness in his stomach that refused to relent. This was tougher than that unhappy fracas at the officers' club.

The next morning he was paid a visit at his room in B.O.Q. by Vic Hadley and Phil Armstrong. They sat quietly, saddened by Bell's senseless death and by Tom's predicament, and waited for him to speak. He told of his act at the officers' club, watching their faces as he spoke. Robust Vic, with a square-jawed face a bit too rugged to be handsome, and Phil, definitely handsome, with his jet-black hair, black brows and blue eyes—both faces wore expressions of understand-ing. These were two quiet gentle men, capable of all hell's fury when the situation demanded.

"Well," Vic finally said, "if that bird was yelling about you striking a superior officer, he's definitely nuts. A medical officer is a staff officer, and no staff officer is ever superior to a line officer. So he can't use that particular charge."

"He shouldn't even be called a medical officer," Phil grumbled, clasping and unclasping his big hands.

"We're all wholly in accord with that," said Tom. "What bothers me most right now is that I have a very hard letter to write."

"Yeah. We know." Phil stood up. Both young men left the room, leaving Tom to grumble and stare at a blank piece of paper.

"Dear Mr. and Mrs. Bell: Your son died here because the officer who could have saved him was drunk at the officers' club." That was what he would write if he were to tell the truth of it.

Tom was getting a headache. This whole affair was so senseless. Bell was dead because of a drunken medical officer. And Tom, who had found so much unexpected pleasure in his new life, was perhaps facing the end of his brief naval career. He suddenly thought of his father, Franklin DeWitt, a war hero of World War One. According to Bertha and Louella, the DeWitt family had a long history of distinguished military service, as had his mother's family, the Hunters. Tom had never bothered to check into it, never bothered to find any of his relatives. For now, though, without even knowing any of them, he felt vaguely unworthy. Here he was, only in his twenties, and he already had one broken marriage behind him, and the possibility of a court-martial ahead of him. And, he reminded himself, Bell, poor Bell, was dead. As he sat alone in his cell, he felt that somehow he had failed in all the most important aspects of his adult life. . . .

Tom was released from these unhappy thoughts a few days later by events that gave him a new zest. He was not only completely exonerated and restored to duty, but Starke was relieved of his command.

Best of all, Tom received a kind and understanding letter from Bell's father That, more than anything else, helped to restore his peace of mind.

5

Tom WAS ENJOYING the relaxed atmosphere of the Hunt Room in the Bellevue-Stratford Hotel. This evening the place swarmed with uniformed men and their friends, wives and girl friends. The warmth of the atmosphere was relaxing after a hard day's work.

Informality, friendliness, the pleasure of making new friends. A new friend. The thought gave Tom some hope, for the girl he had followed in here and who now sat alone at a small table had definitely brought that gleam into his eye. He took his gaze away from her and listened to the chatter of his friends, Phil and Vic, who had joined him at their usual table. In a moment he would look at her again, and if she didn't freeze him with a hard glare, he'd amble over to her table and try to get acquainted.

In the flood of people moving along the street, this girl's legs had caught his eye. First he had noticed her quick moving feet ahead of him. The heels clicked along and the neat shoes twitched a bit from side to side, as any woman's when walking rapidly. He saw next the clean, hard, chiselled ankles, above the shoes. Then his eyes moved up and were captured. She had trim but beautifully rounded calves, and each step she took sent a pleasing ripple along the flesh under the sheer hose.

Her body generally gave the impression of solidity, but with slim waist, neck and arms. He wondered if she might be a ballerina; her proportions and grace certainly were those of a dancer. He caught a glimpse of her face as she turned her head. Round face, large mouth, up-tilted nose. Just a kid! Then he heard her speak and was further confused.

"Oh, hi, Charlotte!"

No kid, Tom. That voice, throaty, mellow. And eastern. Eastern? No, not quite. There was a bit of Virginia in it, or Maryland, maybe. Baltimore. That's a good guess. Could be a Bryn Mawr student. But whatever, she's either a dancer or an athlete.

He smiled at himself. Damned if he wasn't doing a lot of analyzing because of a pair of handsome legs. Remember, good looks and sparkling personality do not necessarily go together. But this girl isn't beautiful. Cute, wholesome, but not beautiful. Her hair looks gold-brown from here, complexion is good, carriage is magnificent. The voice is an enigma: resonant, rich, it seems a bit at variance with the little-girl look of her face. Cute is the right description. As her nice underpinnings swung her into the Bellevue-Stratford, he had altered his course and followed.

He noticed that Vic and Phil had not missed his minute study of the girl. He knew that she was aware of his attention, too, though she was making an elaborate pretense of being unaware of him.

"Go on. If you don't go on over there and introduce yourself, you're chicken." Vic nudged his shoulder.

Tom was formulating his maneuvers. He'd apologize for his being obvious. He would go on from there according to her reactions.

"I don't know," Vic teased, "whether she's worth all of your planning or not. Besides, she may have half a dozen suitors."

"I think her nose is too short," Phil joked. "She stalks in here and orders a martini, but she looks like a schoolgirl."

"Stop picking my girl to pieces, will you?" Tom grumbled.

"*Your* girl? Get over there and we'll see whether she's yours or not."

He took a deep breath and walked over to the girl's table, hearing a snicker or two behind him. His heart was drumming under his stiff white collar.

"Hello," he said. Hell, he thought, a frog's croak sounded better.

"Hi." Friendly, rich voice. Mildly curious, the wide brown eyes. Her hair *was* gold-brown, and she smelled of tweed. He looked at her mouth, then at the hands that held the cigarette and glass. Her left hand quivered slightly, and it occurred to him that she might be a bit nervous, too. When he saw the increased rate of her breathing, he suddenly knew beyond doubt that this girl was no pick-up. She wasn't like Frankie and thank God she had none of that icy calm of Irene.

He stuck with his plan. "I'm being rather obvious. But since my two friends over there don't know you, there's no one to introduce us. I'm Tom DeWitt. The sandy-haired, muscular character over there is Vic Hadley, and the tall one with the black hair and thick eyebrows is Phil Armstrong."

"They look nice. My name's Gail Westbrook, and I'm waiting for the girl who shares an apartment with me."

"Look, here's something better. Come over to where Vic and Phil are. There are four chairs and we'll find another for your friend. We're really a lot nicer than we may look. Want to give it a try?"

She smiled up at him as she pushed back her chair, and they walked side by side toward Vic and Phil.

"You're just recently on active duty," Gail said. At his surprised look, she went on to explain. "You know, the bright gold stripe and star/ When the braid on the sleeve and visor begins to turn slightly green, you'll look like a deep-water sailor."

Tom laughed. "You're very observant, Gail. Go to the head of the class."

Gail looked curiously at Vic and Phil as they were introduced. "I think they'll do, Tom. But we're one girl short. Oh! Here comes my friend. Isobel! Over here!"

Tom looked as Gail's roommate came walking toward their table. Physically, she was a direct opposite of Gail. She was tall, with regular features, clear skin and clear blue eyes beneath square-cut black bangs. Everything about her was neat; shoes, hose, dark blue dress with broad belt, patent leather purse. The nails of her hands were well kept, her perfume was sweet but not heavy.

"Gail, I thought I was meeting you here tonight, not the navy. No objections, mind you."

"These are, left to right, Tom DeWitt, Vic Hadley and Phil Armstrong. They're going to win the war if we have one."

"That reassures me." Isobel sat down, pulled out a cigarette, and there was a clicking of lighters from the three men at the table.

Drinks were ordered all around, and the conversation was soon rolling, with their table contributing its share to the laughter and good humor of the surrounding crowd. It was perhaps an hour later when Isobel leaned over to Gail and whispered, "Did you have any plans in mind when you asked me to meet you here tonight?"

Gail's eyes cut sharply to Tom. "They may have been changed."

Tom, who had overheard said, "I have an idea. When we finish these cocktails, I'll take Gail to dinner at— let's say, Bookbinder's. No better spot for atmosphere and food; that is, for the middle-class pocketbook."

"I accept," Gail declared, flashing him a pleased smile.

"Great," said Vic. "Tom has Gail, Phil has Isobel, but I'm left alone."

"Wait a minute, I'll fix that," said Gail, looking

around the room. "Ah, you're in luck, Vic. I'll be right back."

She went over to a group of half a dozen girls, and after a few minutes' chatter came back with a date for Vic. "I feel like a matchmaker," she said. "This is Terry Beardall. Terry, this is Vic Bradley."

Terry was a nice-looking brunette with a bright smile. The men were quick to notice her proportions passed inspection in every respect. They dispersed, each couple going to a different restaurant and promising that a reasonable and just history of their evening would be given when next they met.

Things went well at Bookbinder's. The restaurant had a Revolutionary War motif, with large open hearths and pyramids of cannon balls set in cement. There was nothing plush about the place, but then the taverns of 1775 weren't plush.

Gail had enthusiastically demolished her lobster, frequently wiping her fingers on the red cloth around her neck, and now they sat over coffee and dessert. "You know, Tommy, you're really quite a good-looking young man. You wear your uniform well, and I like the way you talk."

"At last, an honest woman!" he said, laughing to cover his embarrassment. He fell silent as the waiter approached their table. The evening was coming to an end all too soon. It had gone well. He was liking Gail more and more, and she was definitely good for his ego.

"What happens now?" he asked. "The waiter put that check down with a positive slap."

"We'll go to my apartment and exchange notions about things for a while. Then I'll run you home."

"Not necessary to give me a lift. I have my little huffing, puffing Plymouth to get me back to B.O.Q."

"Bachelor officers quarters, right? I come from Wilmington and I've been working here for a while, but some navy expressions still elude me." Her tone became grave as they got into his car. "Things aren't looking well in Europe, are they?"

"From the German point of view, looking great. They're slicing through everything that tries to oppose them. The French have an army of six million men, trying to stop them with French 75 field guns and other equipment from the last war."

"Lightning war," she said. "What's the German word for it?"

"*Blitzkrieg.* You know, after the first big war, a French general named de Gaulle wrote a book on the rapid advance of tanks and armored cars. They don't try to run over the strong points; they run around them. Right now the French are finding German armor past them and masses of German infantry facing them. Their only choices are to encircle them, retreat, or stand and be slaughtered. All because the French High Command thought little of de Gaulle's book. The Germans, too, read the book. It made sense to them. Can you imagine Polish cavalry stopping panzer divisions?"

As he started the car she suggested, "Let's change the subject. It's depressing—and it's been such a delightful evening."

When they reached her apartment she invited him

in, and he felt a warmth running up through his stomach. Seated comfortably in an easy chair, while she reclined on a sofa, he grinned and said, "This is in the nature of an apology. I don't recall if I made any comment on your good legs, but it was the sight of them that led me right into the Hunt Room. I didn't see your face for a while."

She laughed. "No apology is necessary, Tommy. I'm flattered. If you like my legs, I certainly don't mind having you look at them."

Frankie Britt had said much the same thing, he recalled, but she ran second to Gail Westbrook in almost every way.

"Would you like a nightcap?" she asked.

"Love one." Anything to prolong this evening. He watched as she crossed the room to fix their drinks. Yes, she did move like a dancer. He was getting warm and removed his coat. The sight of her muscular calf against the sheer silk excited him. She was muscular, smooth, forceful, yet she possessed a pure femininity.

When she brought the drinks and set them down, she became aware of his scrutiny. She laughed again, spun a couple of times before him. His eyes followed the silken legs as she sat down again on the sofa.

"You know, Gail, you've just brought something back to me—a book I read. A man from time to time viewed a famous sapphire, and always had the odd desire to put it in his mouth, to roll his tongue around it, as if tasting its cool, blue color. That was the effect the soft lustre of the gem had on him. I think I understand him now."

As soon as the words were spoken he realized he

might have embarrassed her, let alone himself, by coming on too strong. But a glance at her face revealed that she took his remarks seriously. There was equanimity and the trace of a thoughtful smile.

She kicked off a shoe, rolled off the stocking, put her foot upon the sofa. When his eyes met hers again, he saw that there was invitation in them; crossing the distance between them, he bent and kissed her smooth knee. He looked up at her.

"I seem to taste things, as some people get virtually dizzy, smelling things. I've even heard people say they taste soft, flowing music." He grinned, feeling self-conscious. "Do you suppose it's unnatural, this tasting of things?"

"Nonsense. It's that person's reaction . . . like wanting a kiss." She leaned back on the sofa. "Kiss me, Tommy."

Her mouth was warm and moist, her tongue moved slowly. She pulled away. "You see? Just another reaction."

"Sure, but not like the others. You know, to get back to what I started to say before, when I first saw you, I thought you were a ballet dancer."

She was amused. "No, no ballet. I've always been active. I played a lot of basketball and softball, and did pretty well on a girl's track team. I swim, and once in my senior year, I did some fencing. But you made a good guess. Most ballerinas are slim in the waist and arms and muscular from the hips down. I've watched the football team in practice, and some of the players are built sort of the same as the girls who take ballet—although they're much larger of course. Go out to Franklin Field some afternoon and watch."

"Nothing doing. With the call to sea duty hanging over me these days, I'm spending my time with gals, not guys." He looked at her intently.

She put her mouth to his. Her kiss was both tender and insistent. With her increasing ardor, her soft arms went around his neck. As she began to slide down deeper into the sofa, he caught a glimpse of gossamer white panties, the dark triangle showing through, and carnal desire began to thunder in him. It was accelerated, too, by the fact that she had been aroused. While her hands worked in his thick curly hair and teased his ears, he took off her blouse and his left hand sneaked its way past the dainty barrier of white silk panties and began a gentle but persistent caressing. He had been excited by the sight of the white skin between her panties and the top of her stockings—such a short expanse of flesh and yet it had been so arousing to see. Why? A man would see more of a girl in a swim suit on a beach.

He watched the handsome, beautifully muscled legs draw in close together, then stretch out and go rigid. His fingers began a deeper investigation but then she sat up, pulling herself free of him. "No, Tommy. I'm practically snorting, and when I reach that stage, it's time for you to go."

"I didn't hear any snort. So that's your stopping point?" he said, disappointed, but trying to inject a bit of levity in his words.

"You bet. Your hands were getting out of bounds— way out of bounds."

"You've got me steamed up like a heavy cruiser getting ready to get underway. And then comes the order 'All engines stop. Secure the sea details. Secure the bridge.'"

She stood up, went to her mirror and began to rearrange her hair. "I'm sorry. You know, I was steamed up, too. I said so. You caught me with my guard down . . . Did you intend to make me tonight?"

He took his time before answering. For two people who hardly knew anything about each other, they had been unusually frank in their conversations tonight. It was best to keep it that way. "I didn't *plan* it, no."

"But you were prepared." She nodded at the little package on the floor. "It slipped out and betrayed you. You know, in all of our conversation—and contact—so far, you wouldn't know I had a face. You never mentioned it."

He went to her, grabbed her round face in his hands and kissed her hard. "Well, I *do* like your face. It's cute."

He retrieved the little package, red to his collar. Then they both laughed and she hugged him. "Tonight, Tommy, we haven't seen the last of each other. Good night, sweet guy."

"You surprise me—you've surprised me all the way."

"Good! I'll try to keep it up. If you're interested in dinner some time, I know just the place. And Dutch treat. I work, and a young man with one stripe is not loaded. Okay?"

"Aye, aye, young miss. Good night."

* * *

Tom felt good about his evening with this oddly captivating girl. He knew he was too restless to go back to his quarters and turn in just yet, though, so he stopped in at a hotel along the way, intending to sit in the bar for a while and wind down with a drink.

As he walked into the lobby he had to pause by the revolving door to let a group of people pass him on their way out. In that moment he looked idly about the high-ceilinged room and was caught by the sight of a familiar face. Coming off the elevator was none other than Isobel. But she was not with Phil Armstrong, as he might have expected. She was with another man. And she now wore a soft yellow skirt and blouse with tan pumps rather than the blue dress and black patent leather shoes he had seen her in earlier.

He watched as she and the man walked over to the check-out counter, where the man—who was fairly ordinary looking and a good twenty years Isobel's senior—apparently was settling his bill. Isobel gave her companion a smile and a light peck on the cheek, and it seemed to Tom that the man positively leered at her before turning and walking away from her.

Not wanting to be discovered, Tom hastily walked into the bar, taking a more circuitous route than the man's direct path to the revolving door.

He sat down in the dimly lit room, confused by the scene he had just witnessed, and ordered a drink. What had happened to Phil? And above all, what was Isobel doing here, in different clothes, with a man old enough to be her father?

The questions were no sooner posed than he saw Isobel, her dark hair glistening as she stood in the doorway of the bar. She scanned the room briefly, then walked in and seated herself on a barstool next to a lone man. Tom noticed uncomfortably that she sat facing his table. She took out a cigarette and turned to the man next to her and asked him for a light. Then there was some small talk, Isobel looking serene . . . and seductive, Tom thought.

She looked up when the bartender brought her drink, and in that upward glance she spotted Tom. She looked startled, then smiled uncertainly. Tom was hard-pressed to know which of them was more embarrassed to have been discovered there.

As he smiled back, she picked up her drink and came over to his table, seemingly completely self-possessed once again.

"I guess we're both going it alone tonight," she said, laughing. "Mind if I join you?"

"Not at all."

She sat down next to him, and he felt as if she were studying his face to see how much he had guessed. Evidently she was satisfied that he took her presence here as mere coincidence, for she visibly relaxed and sat back.

"You don't look too happy. Didn't things go well with Gail?"

He smiled. "No. Things went well—too well, maybe."

"Ah! I get it. She headed you off at the proverbial pass, right?"

Tom nodded uncomfortably, wondering where this was heading.

"Look, Tom, let me put your mind at ease. I've

known Gail for a while. Gail doesn't chase around—"
Tom thought he detected a slight hesitation, a slight
blush, before she went on. "I was surprised as anything when I walked into the Hunt Room tonight and
saw that she was sitting with you guys. That's not at
all the Gail Westbrook style. I've never seen anyone
get that far with her that quickly. And then going out
to dinner with a guy she hardly knows? You must
stand pretty high with her, believe me. Believe me
also when I tell you that she really keeps a lid on
things. But as I say, it looks to me as if she's letting
down her guard a lot with you. Hang in there."

Tom looked at her in surprise. It's curious, he
thought. His suspicions about Isobel might or might
not be correct, but in either event she was just as
nice as he had originally thought. And he found
that her words and manner encouraged him to confide in her. "I want that girl the worst way. There are
so many things about her; that big friendly mouth,
the wide-eyed way she looks at you, the way she talks,
soft, rapid, earnest—I love her voice."

Isobel giggled softly. "And the best legs I've ever
seen in my life!"

Tom laughed, admitting the thought had occurred
to him too. "But the thing that gets me about her is
something you rarely find. She appears so ready to do
things for people, as if she really *cares* what happens
to people. She's *genuine*, that's it."

"It fits, Tommy, it sure does. I've heard envious
women try to find fault with her, the way she looks,
the way she acts. But they can't match her in any way."

"Any advice, teach? I don't want her to get away."

"Sure. You may not take it. But here it is. Marry her. Things move fast during a war. It's a time when we realize we have to get everything we can out of life while we can. People do things they wouldn't do under ordinary circumstances." Isobel smiled. "If I were you, I'd lock her in the bedroom for two weeks."

He had to laugh, but he was puzzled. "You may be right, but why this frontal assault you're recommending?"

"Because she needs it. She's drawn a bit too fine, she's holding too tight a rein on herself. I don't mean just sex; she needs companionship, too. She needs to *belong*. Maybe because she has a wide-eyed round face and looks like sweet sixteen, men in their twenties steer clear of her—jail bait, you know. But did you ever watch her hands while she's sipping a martini or smoking? Nice hands, strong, sure movements. She holds anything she touches firmly. A kid? Did she feel like a kid when you held her?"

He slowly shook his head. "No. Isobel, it seems important to you that somebody cares for her."

"Right. I'm very fond of her. She's absolutely straight. It isn't in her to do anything that would hurt anybody, although I think she's been hurt herself. She's first-class merchandise, Tom, and if you let her get away from you, you've really lost something. Hang on to her, boy. Keep her, even if you have to give her a baby to do it."

6

Tom's next date with Gail was a drive to Atlantic City. There were things to be seen there: the famous boardwalk, of course, the imposing line of hotels that faced the sea, the well-known Steel Pier, with its multitude of concessions and entertainment. They talked of anything and everything. She was planning more sights for their agenda when he broke out the anchor detail.

"Gail, you've walked me half to death. I had the duty last night, and a hundred stupid phone calls didn't give me much sleep. People wanted to know how President Roosevelt and Secretary Hull were going to handle the strained relations with Japan. I imagine most of them had been listening to all the scare stories they were spitting out on the radio, and wanted information from the navy. Just how they figured the duty officer at the navy yard had any inkling of our government's plans is beyond my comprehension. And they had advice, too—oh, how they were loaded with advice!"

"You said you figure our involvement in Europe inevitable," said Gail. "But if we have to fight Japan, we'll be at war on two sides."

"That's right." His lips compressed into a worried line.

"Do we have a navy big enough to fight in both oceans?"

"Gail—I couldn't tell you that even if I knew." He could guess easily enough, though, and it made him uncomfortable. "Look, I need some sustenance, and I bet you do too by now. You can make out a list of other sights to see while we eat. Okay?"

"Good! I know a place not far from here. Do you like lobster?"

"Love it."

"Then it's Hackney's. They say it will accommodate two thousand people. It's near the waterfront." She laughed. "It's sort of amusing, with the waitresses spruced up like lobsters in red uniforms, and long red shells over their heads to resemble lobster claws. But the food is excellent."

Tom devoured the lobster, now and then looking at Gail, thinking about all the things he and Isobel had discussed about her. As the food began to restore him, the hot desire came alive again, and he knew he was going to make a pass at Gail when they got back to Philadelphia. He felt inexplicably afraid.

She held the paper toward him over the table. "And there's more. Fairmount Park is loaded with museums and such."

He looked at the list—Independence Hall, Liberty Bell, Valley Forge, and much more.

"I didn't put nearly all of them in there. There's another famous sea food place." She scribbled another name. "That's it for the time being. I guess we'd better be getting back."

"Okay. We'll start on the check-off list pretty soon."

It was getting dark as they started back, and Gail looked a bit worried. She put the key in the ignition and mumbled, "I wish we hadn't tried to see so much the first time."

"Trouble? Are you sick?"

"Oh, no. I just don't particularly like driving in the dark."

"Want me to drive?"

"No. I'll be all right. Guess I indulged in too much lobster."

But she wasn't all right. She handled the car with her customary ease and good reflexes, and made good time. They were almost within city limits when it happened. She was passing another car when a glaring pair of headlights and the blast of a horn from an irritated driver signalled an oncoming car. Tom saw Gail's face turn white, but she said nothing, not even an exclamation, as she accelerated with a hard stamp on the pedal and shot through, barely escaping a head-on collison. The driver she passed was too stunned to show any reaction, but Tom heard a loud curse from the car they had almost hit.

Gail drove on about a quarter of a mile, then pulled over to the emergency lane. "Tommy, drive me home. I've got a slight headache."

"Sure, sure." He got out and ran around to the driver's side. He didn't believe she had any headache. He couldn't swear to it, but it seemed to him she hadn't seen the oncoming car until it was too close. Luck, just plain luck that there hadn't been an accident. No, not completely luck. She was a good driver.

Back in her living room, they sat on the sofa, and Gail put her head on his shoulder. Her eyes were closed. She declined a smoke. She had been shaking when they entered the apartment, but she was breathing more easily now. He put his arm around her waist.

"Gail—it was your eyes, wasn't it? You didn't see that car coming until it was almost too late."

She unbuttoned her blouse, put his hand inside. "Hold me, Tommy. I need it. I love the touch of you. No other man, just you."

His hand moved gently. "You haven't answered my question."

"Yes, my eyes. It's the second time in a month. I've been intending to see an ophthalmologist, but I've been stupid and keep putting it off."

"You'll make an appointment tomorrow?"

"Tomorrow's Sunday. Right now, I want something else."

He leaned over, kissed her. Her mouth seemed to overwhelm his own in her response. He put a hand to the back of her neck and began to massage it gently. Her whole body seemed to relax. His other hand became more aggressive. It went past her knee, past the panties. Her body was limp in surrender. Then she stood up, walked toward the bedroom, throwing off her clothes. "Not on the sofa. Somehow that seems vulgar and cheap. Come to me now and give me what I need." She turned and smiled at him, a wide frank smile, friendly, with a sort of mischievous light in her eyes—almost like a small girl who is about to sneak away to the movies against her parents' orders.

Her expression and manner seemed a reflection of his own delight. Surely he could not be the same person who had been so miserable a few short months earlier.

Her smile faded as she put one knee on the bed. "Tommy, I've . . . I've had experience before. Only once. I was a kid, in my teens, and anxious to dance on the Broadway stage. This man was attractive, and he had contacts. I found he told the truth about that. And I can't be certain he misled me entirely. By the time he told me he could find nobody who needed dancers, he'd already had me. I just thought you ought to know."

"So?"

"So . . . I just thought you should know that I'm not exactly pure of mind and body. Especially not of mind," she added, grinning.

He drew her to him and kissed her. This girl was beginning to get a hold on him. He liked her frankness, her honesty.

In the bed, their lovemaking moved swiftly toward

consummation. During the evening he had detected her mood, her resolve to go ahead with this. The near-collision had upset her but she was past that now. She had become passionate in her kisses and caresses and only the greatly anticipated act itself remained. She sat back on her heels on the bed, watching, running her hands over his body as he removed his clothes.

He was between her legs and now he reached for the night table where he had laid one of the little rubber contraceptives. But her hand seized him firmly, there were a few searching probes and he went deep into the feminine flesh. "We'll use those next time," she said. "But just for once, I'll take a chance." So he was held in the unbelievable warm silken clasp. He moved a little and the responsive action of her legs thrilled him. They came up, hooked around him, squeezed him tightly, and his delight soared as her body began to move. Her murmured words were the last force that snapped what remained of his restraint. He wanted to prolong this. But it just couldn't be done; he went into a fury of action.

His senses, acute, enlivened, sent their messages to a brain intoxicated with pleasure: the odor from his own loins, pungent, sweaty, and then the sudden feral smell of her, feminine, razor-sharp, stronger than his own. It came up from the moist union of their bodies and tingled in his nostrils. He wanted to drown himself in it, to steep himself in her delicious femininity. With each plunge of his rigid flesh, the joy of her raced through his groin and coursed through every fiber of his being. He wanted this to last forever.

But man is not so constituted. His ecstasy brought him up quickly, his whole body rocked by electrifying spasms. As the last movement quivered away, his body went lax in a warm pleasant shudder. She had not finished, but continued to enjoy him. Her fingers caught his hair in a tight grip, pulling his head down so she could drench his mouth with her kisses. With her body heaving faster, her legs holding him in a crushing grip, he could not reconcile this potent woman with the wide-eyed, innocent face of the "school girl" Gail he had first met. It seemed she fought him in her joy. A few gasps and hugs, and her climax was complete.

He looked straight into her face, and she had an embarrassed expression, her head lowered, for all the world like a child caught stealing apples. Her hair was in wild disarray. When she lifted her eyes they were soft and reproachful, but there was a smile tugging at the corners of her mouth.

"Please, sir—would you dismount?"

His laughter pealed out. He could readily understand Isobel's affection for her. He rolled to one side, reached over and kissed her throbbing throat. He cupped a breast in one hand, felt the firm flesh.

"Gail, I know this sounds corny, but you don't know how much good you've done me. It really is the first time I've ever wanted something so terribly and got it. I saw you swinging into the Bellevue-Stratford and I thought—my God, I want that girl. Not for years have I felt so good."

She pursed her lips and looked at him knowingly. "That's right. I've got a great set of gams."

"It started that way. I'm not so sure now."

She looked at him gravely. "You've sweet, Tommy." She gripped his shoulders with her small square hands, kissed him hard. "Thank you, darling. I enjoyed that so much."

He sat on the edge of the bed and tried to think. *Darling.* When had anyone, even in jest, called him that? Gail wasn't kidding. It had come too spontaneously.

She left the bed and walked toward the bathroom, then turned for a moment. "You helped me, too, Tommy. I needed that, for a million different reasons."

She closed the bathroom door. He stretched his legs, flexed his biceps. This had been the best day of his life. "The male chases," he said aloud. "And when he catches the girl it turns out that he's the one who's been conquered."

The door opened presently and Gail stood there, wearing only a pair of scuffs. "I heard what you said, Tommy. About the male being conquered." She held a brush and began to work on her hair, brushing with one hand, arranging with the other, glancing first at the mirror, then at him. "I hadn't thought of it in that way before." Her full mouth broke in a smile. "You didn't mind the defeat?"

"You're fishing for compliments. But, yes, the defeat was delightful." For the first time he was seeing all of her; deliberate on her part, for she stood in the full light. He liked the way her back curved in a deep arch above the firm buttocks; the way she stood with her feet planted squarely, her legs slightly apart; the way her small breasts quivered with the motion of her arms, and the large reddish-brown areolas surrounding nipples that became erect with her consciousness of his scrutiny. His eyes lingered on her pubic hair. It was several shades darker than the hair on her head, a thick mahogany V at her crotch, tapering down and dropping off to a long tuft. It was still wet at the edges. Her belly was ivory smooth, except for a crisp tendril of brown hair that ran up from the triangle to terminate at the navel. The single effect was stimulating; a tawny-haired, naked girl whose body was at once both athletic and all woman. She gave him a direct stare.

"Are you gaping at my pubic hair?"

"Yeah. I never saw so much."

She smiled. "I like your gaping at me. You've gone over every inch of me. And I'd be worried if you didn't."

He suddenly began to feel jealous of the man who had possessed her. He wanted to know about him yet he didn't. Maybe Vic was right. She was getting to him, and it was more than carnal desire. At the moment she looked heartbreakingly sweet and little-girlish, despite that lethal man-sapping power lurking in her beautifully conditioned body.

She came out of the bathroom and gave him a chance to wash up. She was sitting on the bed smoking a cigarette when he returned. Her eyes went over him casually and she gave him a warm, frank smile that seemed to say: "We are partners in this marvelous lovemaking, and it seems a friendly and harmless thing." He somehow felt that if he were to find himself standing naked in front of city hall, somehow Gail would appear and make him feel at ease.

"A bright-eyed, moon-faced kid with curvy legs who can leave a man as limp as a string," he said.

She grinned. "Is *that* the way you see me? We may just have to check that out." She came toward him and began to caress his chest, to fondle and stimulate him. He wondered if he could weather the intense, enduring strength of this girl in her lovemaking, but he began to respond to her toying and teasing and they brought each other to a renewed erotic pitch.

"Golly, Tommy, I must be a bad girl!"

"No. You're a good girl who has been very careful to keep a lid on things," he said, remembering his conversation with Isobel.

"You'll have to go home after this, Tommy, but not now—"

He was surprised to find his body throbbing in its impatience. He took her in his arms, saying, "I like the way you smell."

"Haven't you said that before?"

"Maybe. But this is different. You smell like a little perfume, fresh bath soap and like girl; the combination runs me wild."

The second time was more violent than the first. He didn't understand it, but then there were so many changes that had taken place in him in such a short period of time that it seemed impossible to understand anything beyond the fact that life was most assuredly getting better for him.

Gail's large brown eyes remained open, looking into

his during the whole of their lovemaking, and for him it made the whole experience that much more intimate. He had a brief image of Irene, her eyes shut tightly, her body rigid as if warding off an assault. And there had never been any talking or any humor with Irene, as there was with Gail.

The bed creaked, and their moving bodies were perilously close to the edge. Gail giggled and said, "Wouldn't you like to see a movie of this lovemaking?"

"I absolutely would not," he declared. "How can adults look so ridiculous?"

"When I was a child, I once looked out into a meadow and saw a stallion lunge into a brood mare. Scared me half to death."

"I never saw anything like that. Just dogs, and I thought they were funny."

They expended themselves in a frenzy of ecstasy. Shortly thereafter she moved away from him, propped her head on the pillow and regarded him gravely. "A cigarette, please."

She blew out thin wisps of smoke, watching him as he leisurely dressed. He smiled at her. "You've brought me something new and good in my life, Gail. Tell me—the first time I made a pass at you, would you have given in if I'd persisted?"

She shook her head. "No, indeed. I wanted it as much as you did. But that would have made me a pushover. Besides, I saw those condoms you dropped."

"But the intent was not there. Just about every single young man carries a package, just in case—and many of the married ones do too."

"I guess I'll accept that."

"Gail, I want to be good friends, not just—"

She looked surprised, then reached for his hand and nodded up at him. Her expression was hopeful, sad and happy, all at the same time.

He pushed her stubby nose with a thumb. "You know, I think we're going to have a good relationship."

"Not if you keep disfiguring my features. I'll make you give me some more loving. Want to try?"

"Ah—no."

She laughed and walked to him to help him straighten his tie. "You're sweating. I'll get a towel so you can wipe your neck and chin."

"Am I? I wonder why. Look in the mirror. Your hair's tousled, your nose is shiny, your lipstick's smeared all over your face. You're a mess."

"I'm a happy mess. I feel so warm inside . . . Better get along now. Work tomorrow, you know."

She put on a negligee and saw him to the door. He looked down at her. Without her high heels, she seemed small, and it was hard to realize that all of the womanhood he had just experienced was inside that negligee. He caught her face in his hands, kissed her hard.

"Squeeze me, Tommy . . ."

He drew her to him and her body folded into his, warm and supple. How could anyone feel so soft? He rumpled her hair, kissed the willing mouth again.

"I'll phone you." He opened the door and then turned back to her. "Gail, sometime I'll try to explain why tonight meant so much. It's important to me that you understand. What I mean is—don't think that you're not important to me. You are."

Her eyes filled. "Thanks, Tommy. The most important thing to me is what you've just said."

He went out into the night, and it was pleasantly cool. He stretched his arms. Every muscle in him was relaxed and pliable, his satiated body was at peace. The stars from their infinite distance looked like friendly, winking comrades.

He still glowed in his exultation over the evening. Every intoxicating detail of her person swam around in his head: her moist open mouth; her eyes dark and hot, widening in her pleasure; the sweet full curves of her strong legs; her throaty laughter at her own antics; the strong thudding in the small breasts; the stimulating girl smell of her body; the feel of her deft sure hands on his; the indescribable joy of her flesh. But most important, her acceptance of him for what he was, as he was; her treatment of him as a whole man. When had he felt so good? He could not remember.

He realized all at once, as he walked in the quiet night, that he was thanking God for Gail Westbrook.

7

FOR DAYS AFTERWARD, Tom DeWitt moved in a haze of visions of Gail. When he stood the duty in the captain of the yard's office, his preoccupation affected the functioning of this most vital part of the Yard.

When a heavy cruiser, approaching for overhaul, requested a berth, the orders Tom issued to the chief warrant boatswain in charge of the waterfront office almost made the latter swallow his cigar.

"Sir!" the man protested, "you can't put that cruiser in that slip! You've already got two destroyers, a cargo ship and a PT boat in there."

Tom, looking up at the colored pins on the board indicating the berthing facilities, saw that it was so.

"Okay, Wilkins. Send them a message to berth at pier 314. Send it by blinker and get their acknowledgment."

Vic Hadley walked into the duty officer's office with some papers from the production department. "She's really got you going, hasn't she, Tom?"

"You couldn't get to first base with her, muscle man," Tom grumbled, edgy as he waited for the cruiser's reply.

"Maybe not. It's just that it's not easy to see how some couples match up. But they do, and many times make a go of it. This war's upset a lot of guys, because they're thinking they'd better get a chick while they have the opportunity. "

"Vic, all you think of is sex." Not that I don't think of it some too, Tom reminded himself, grinning at the thought. But besides being easy to fall in love with, Gail was easy to *like*. She was wholesome and hearty, frank in her opinions, clean as the dew on a mountain flower. She took your hand in a firm grasp, gave a straight yes or no when that was all that was required. When she kissed you, it was a warm, wholehearted, lusty kiss. She did nothing in half measures.

How could he explain this to Vic? And especially the intimate parts, which he had no intention of discussing anyway. Once aroused, Gail would walk toward the bedroom, smiling at him, beginning to strip. She displayed a rare quality at such times; exuberant, roughhouse lovemaking without the loss of her dignity as a woman. She could joke about various phases of it without being vulgar, be aggressive herself but not cheap and tawdry. And always her sense of humor evoked his honest laughter.

Somehow he got through the rest of the day without any more errors on the job, although he had to consciously pull himself away from thoughts of Gail to do it.

That night, as he lay in bed next to Gail enjoying a deliciously slow buildup to lovemaking, she licked the edges of his ears, causing him to laugh.

She sat up, leaned back on her haunches, regarded him studiously. Then she launched into a mock tirade. "Listen, how can I get erotic when you laugh? I go all out on things I like. It's that way with swimming, basketball, dancing. And now with your lovemaking. I want to savor every portion of it like I do a dry martini or a good steak. I do everything deep; it's my way."

She came back to him, laid her cheek against his chest and inhaled deeply. "I like to feel the hair on your chest and enjoy the man-smell of you." Her hand slid down his stomach, his abdomen, then to his groin. "All this masculinity, this giver of life, this power, and I think of how each time I have you, I get some of that fine, clean strength, and it makes me feel wonderful."

"You're unbelievable, Gail."

"You've said that before. In what way?"

"Well . . . it's like a book I once read. The hero was a soldier in the last war, and he was in love with an army nurse. She was like you, if I analyze you correctly. She said, 'I wish we could do something really wicked. Everything we do seems so innocent.' "

He began to stroke the back of her neck. "What I'm trying to say is, you can say and do things that some people would say were obscene. But with you they seem honest and clean and decent."

"Like the girl in the book?"

"Like the girl in the book."

She straightened and looked him squarely in the eyes. "There can't be anything obscene about us. What we do seems right and proper."

He let his hand rove through the mass of mahogany hair below her ivory-smooth belly. To him this was one of her natural adornments, as pretty as her expressive deep eyes, shapely hands or exciting legs. How much of his caressing was mere lust? It was pleasure, certainly, the most delightful sensation a man could experience. Was it anything more? Some day, perhaps soon, orders for sea duty would come through for him. He had to know before that happened.

"Gail, I've something on my mind—Say! What's that odor down there?"

She giggled and put her head against his shoulder. "I put cologne on it."

"You nut!"

She grew sober. "Tommy, I know there's something on your mind—I guessed that earlier this evening. And I'm as tight as fiddlestrings, trying to figure out what it is."

"I've been looking for something to buy you—"

"Really nice?" she interrupted.

"Yes. I think I've made up what I loosely refer to as

my mind. You know, the personnel office has been very busy. Some of the fellows here are getting orders to sea. Phil Armstrong already had his to the Pacific fleet."

"The Pacific? I would have imagined he'd go to the Atlantic. Do you know why? I hate to be mystified."

"No idea. Orders to military personnel are cold impersonal things, just words on paper—'You are hereby directed,' that sort of thing. But I guess it has to be that way. The officer who issued the orders doesn't have the time to give you a rundown on your duties. You find out when you get there.

"You know how it is. You hear scuttlebutt around the place that something is going to move, but you don't believe it because it hasn't come from any official source. But the scuttlebutt continues and nearly every time you learn it's the truth. So any officer has to tell his wife or girl friend that she shouldn't be surprised if he doesn't show in a few days. One day he doesn't show. And after a while she gets a letter from him and he's at sea, either on convoy duty or somewhere with a task force that's building up."

From the look she gave him he knew she understood that he too might have to leave soon. She digested the news in silence, then sighed and squeezed his hand.

"Tommy, I know how newspapers and these radio commentators exaggerate about this war—I suspect some of them just want to make names for themselves. But the news is that the German army is running all over Europe. Is it as bad as the papers say?"

"This time they're right, Gail."

❋   ❋   ❋

Tom's decision to talk with Henry Carlson was quickened by orders that came through for Vic Hadley. Vic was assigned to an Atlantic mission, on board the heavy cruiser *Augusta*. He jubilantly waved his orders at Tom.

"See? I'm slated for damage control, Tommy! I'm to be division officer of the R Division of the construction and repair department."

"The R Division?" asked Tom curiously. "I'm not hep to all the departments, Vic."

"I'll have the artificers, you know; the carpenter's mates, the shipfitters, the painters, the sailmaker, and probably a chief shipfitter, two chief boatswain's mates—and very likely a warrant boatswain and warrant carpenter. Battle station will be one of the repair parties. Which one—well, that will be determined after I get there."

Tom grinned, slapped Hadley's big shoulder. "Happy for you, Vic. You've always been a guy who makes things, who takes everything apart to see what makes it go. You're a natural for that kind of work."

"Sure hope I can fit in." Vic's ruddy face twisted in a frown. "Don't know where the ship is."

Tom laughed. "That's the least of your worries. They'll get your butt on board the *Augusta*—and right quick!"

With Vic's orders coming through, Tom knew his own couldn't be far behind. And that meant it was all the more urgent that he pay a visit to Henry Carlson.

Tom had seen Carlson on numerous occasions since

his departure from the Carlson fortress. Carlson had been as good as his word in arranging a speedy and relatively painless divorce from Irene. Tom had been shocked at news of his father-in-law's own divorce, but not unhappily so. And he was pleased that Henry Carlson appeared to be thriving in his new independence. He had bought a home in Woodbury, New Jersey, a pretty little wooded acreage, and had taken his butler, Jenkins, with him.

On this evening, Tom had been welcomed into Carlson's new den, where Tom had found him surrounded by all the familiar books and objects that had made his previous den uniquely his own.

The room was silent now as both men considered the question Tom had posed. Henry Carlson stared at Tom over his glass. His young visitor hadn't touched his highball, but was pacing nervously about, waiting for an answer to his request.

"Sit down, Tommy, and give me a minute or two. I'm trying to think."

"The Pacific, sir. Phil Armstrong went to the Pacific —and you know a couple of admirals in Washington."

Carlson's smile was patient. "And you want me to use my influence with the heavy braid in order to get you out there? Armstrong's orders were cut by mistake, I think. You know that. Your sea duty will likely be in the Atlantic." He studied the amber liquid in his glass. "A good part of our navy's there. And eventually the Allies will launch a counterattack involving our navy. You'll get to sea soon enough, Tommy."

Tom took the first pull at his drink. "Look, I'm not anxious to have people shooting at me. But I want to be a part of turning the Japs back. The navy's greatest task in this thing that's coming will be in the Pacific. You recall what Billy Mitchell said? 'The attack will come from the Japanese.' He's right. Out there is the world's largest, best prepared navy."

"Better than our own, Tommy?"

"Better than our own."

Carlson smiled, again with interest and infinite patience. "Then how do you think we'll beat them?"

"Our production, for one thing. And they may have Yamamoto, a brilliant man, but we have half a dozen admirals who know how to get the best out of what they have. And when it gets down to the nitty-gritty, we have better men. They'll outlast the Japs." He sipped at his glass again. "How about those admirals you're chummy with?"

Carlson's eyes took on a thoughtful look. "Hm . . . Brubaker is one. Finish your drink, Tom—then I'll chase you out. I've a few phone calls to make, and perhaps a telegram. I'll need total concentration. All right?"

Tom stood up and a wide grin broke across his face. When Henry Carlson concentrated, things happened. "See you. And thanks for the drink."

He left the house in quick strides. He'd have to tell Vic about this—no, on second thought, not yet. He'd wait until his orders came—if they did. And Vic would punch him with his big, hard fist, call him a lucky apple-polishing son of a bitch, and they would go out and get drunk together. There was Phil, too. He'd find him in the Pacific. Perhaps at Pearl Harbor.

8

JAPAN . . . an exotic, fascinating world, little more than a name to western civilizations. Only the affluent could afford to travel to the beauty of this Asian culture. To the average American, it was remote, geographically and psychologically, except for an occasional name or incident that received worldwide publicity.

In 1937 the American gunboat *Panay* was shot to pieces by the Japanese, causing a temporary furor. The American press exploded into its usual exaggeration. On the editorial page of one prominent newspaper appeared a sketch of an Asian soldier standing with fixed bayonet. The caption beneath this picture read:

The Yellow Peril. In the sky behind the soldier was a red ball.

Japan apologized and memory of the incident began to fade. Americans knew of Japanese planes bombing Chinese cities, killing civilians, but most people thought of it as "a foreign scrap." The Japanese wouldn't bother the United States. There were also those Americans who burned with a sense of shame, convinced that Japan felt America was too timid to defend her property overseas. But who could prove the intent of a country so unknown, so vastly different from America? There was no substantial evidence to support either viewpoint.

There were two Japanese names that were well known to the American public: Emperor Hirohito and, to a lesser extent, Admiral Isoroku Yamamoto, the latter of whom had visited the United States and made friends there, as well as a reputation at poker.

Of the American military commanders who knew most about Japan, the one whose name was least known but whose opinion proved most reliable was General William Mitchell, USA. At a "trial" because of his early advocacy of a strong air force, he had insisted on answering the question of where he thought a massive air attack on this nation could come from. "I'll answer that question. The attack will come from the Japanese."

And so while Tom DeWitt performed his duties in the Philadelphia Yard and awaited Henry Carlson's word, on the other side of the world was a tightly built office, well guarded, in which only top secret proceedings were conducted. This was on the island of Honshu.

Political leaders of other governments did not know how the enormous sphere of Japanese influence and control had been planned. Here and there a western agent had hinted at Japan's military preparations, but was unable to supply enough evidence to cause any genuine concern. Only the top men of Japan's military machine knew of the goals set out on the map of the Pacific. They were Tojo, Shimada, Nagama, Yamamoto, Nagumo and other staff members.

The minister of war, General Hideki Tojo, was unknown to the world. But after the war had started, every American and Allied sailor, soldier, airman and marine regarded "Old Tojo" as the driving force behind every vigorous and well-trained Japanese offensive.

These men sat at a table studying the encircled portion of an Asian sphere. Broad-shouldered, solemn-faced Tojo moved his right index finger along the curve. "Malaya, Thailand, Philippines, Dutch East Indies," he murmured, more to himself than to the others.

"The Philippines will bring in the United States," said Yamamoto. "Each of you must expect that and be prepared to deal with this enemy. I have planned for it."

Tojo's black eyes flicked up at him. "Yes, that's understood."

Admiral Nagumo, a superbly skilled carrier man who had been picked to lead the attack on Pearl

Harbor, experienced a moment of uneasiness. Admiral Nagumo reported how stormy the weather was on the route they had picked; a northern route, between Midway and the Aleutians, then south to Hawaii.

"Disagreeable," Tojo agreed. "And refueling will entail some hazards, but one of our observers recently made the trip from our point of departure all the way to Hawaii and didn't see a single ship. That is of paramount importance. But our conquest must include the United States. Oh, they will recover; we can accept Admiral Yamamoto's information about America's war-making potential. But by that time, being committed to Europe as they are, a separate peace agreement with them is probable. They cannot fight a two-ocean war with a one-ocean navy." He looked at Admiral Yamamoto. "We have committed considerable forces to sweep this new territory into our empire. This must come in one great blow. What have you allocated for Pearl Harbor?"

"Six cruisers, with Admiral Nagumo's flag in *Akagi*. Also two battleships, two heavy cruisers, a screen of nine destroyers with the light cruiser *Abukuma*, and three fleet submarines, five of the two-man midgets, and eight tankers."

Tojo nodded. "Eight tankers! I'm glad you were able to get them. It will speed up our operation. You have done well, Admiral. That force, along with the element of surprise, should burn Oahu from one end to the other." He rose, his face placid. "We'll retire now. Between now and tomorrow, let me have any helpful ideas that may occur to you."

There were bows all around, General Tojo left first,

then the others followed. The room was bare, and the guards closed the door.

The officers who had consulted with Tojo took his words seriously. Some of those who had misgivings voiced them at a meeting later that day, and the general, quietly confident, ordered them to rectify any discrepancies in the details of the attack.

"We are familiar with the general strategy; now let us test some of the doubts that may be lingering in your minds."

Nagumo spoke. "A number of staff members have run a dummy test on the game board at the war college, one group representing the Japanese striking force, the other the American defenders. On the assumption that the American carriers are alerted in time to sortie from the harbor, our game gives us the victory, but we lose two carriers."

Tojo replied that the three carriers would be outnumbered two to one, whether this happened or not, but that he was still confident of total surprise. "Can you think of any defects in equipment?"

"Torpedoes," said Yamamoto.

"Our torpedoes defective? After all the practice we've devoted to them?"

"No, sir, I did not mean defective. They're good. They have one thousand-pound warheads and will run at the depth set. The American torpedo runs too deep, has a five hundred-pound warhead, sometimes detonates before it reaches the target. What I meant to say is that I have a forty-five-foot bottom at Pearl Harbor to contend with on the short, low runs which our torpedo bombers will have to make. Another point: our intelligence advises that the American battleships are berthing in pairs at Ford Island, not Lahaina waters, as previously believed."

"Torpedoes," said Tojo. "In that shallow water, they may stick in the mud. See what you can do about them. And I want our dive bombers to get in plenty of work on ground targets. Now, you are sworn to secrecy; not even our flyers or seamen are to know our rendezvous or destination until Admiral Nagumo informs them. For the submarine commanders, there is one order. If you see a lone ship of any nationality, sink it and go on. We are on the threshold of a new world. Speed and silence are the keys that will open it to us."

In his chair, Yamamoto studied the huge map of the Pacific before him. His mind was not concentrated on the points of attack marked thereon; rather, he was concerned with the contingencies, the possibilities of errors in the whole scheme, and with the facts which had given him confidence in this attack. The greatest advantage was that with the battleships at Pearl Harbor eliminated, General MacArthur could expect no reinforcements in the Philippines. MacArthur had said himself that without help, he could probably hold out only three months with what he had. Three carriers and cruisers and destroyers could afford no relief. The Japanese had ten carriers, faster destroyers with more firepower, and cruisers of which many were the old four-stackers with four-inch guns. And the Japanese torpedoes were far superior. Even if MacArthur held until reinforcements reached the Philippines, it would be an obsolete fleet facing a modern one that outnumbered U.S. ships in every category.

Britain? She could render no help. Yamamoto respected the manner in which she had fought her way back to survival, with R.A.F. Spitfires inflicting enormous losses on the Luftwaffe; but the Japanese would neutralize Singapore, so Britain's contribution in the Pacific would be negligible. All of Britain's resources were in the Atlantic, her army trying to hold Rommel in check as the British and Germans shuttled back and forth in the cities between Gibraltar and Alexandria.

Every detail ran through his mind; he set November 25 for the fleet to get underway, figuring it would take thirteen days to reach Oahu from Tankan Bay including time for refueling. The entire fleet would, of course, be limited to a speed that was no faster than that of the tankers, in his opinion, fourteen knots. Yamamoto was forced to smile, despite the many pressures to be endured. This last consideration would bear heavily upon Admiral Nagumo, who had appeared skeptical of the whole venture from the start. However, he knew Nagumo was a good carrier man; once the action began, he would become fully and unreservedly involved, like the professional he was. That was why Yamamoto had chosen him in the first place. And he had no qualms about Commander Mitsuo Fuchida, who had been picked to lead the planes. Yamamoto would take him aboard the flagship *Akagi*.

Intelligence relayed from Honolulu revealed that there were approximately a hundred ships at Pearl Harbor. But his only concern were the eight battleships and Hickam and Wheeler Air Fields; destroy them, then head with all speed northwestward for Japan. . . .

The carriers began to rendezvous at Tankan Bay; the flagship *Akagi* and *Kaga* and the largest carrier, *Zuikaku*, the light carriers *Hiryu* and *Soryu*, and the largest and newest, *Shokaku*. Nagumo watched the other ships as they arrived. They were the heavy cruisers *Tone* and *Crikuma*, and the battleships *Hiei* and *Kirishima*, the latter aging, but still a formidable punch with her good crews. The nine destroyers to screen the force were under command of Rear Admiral S. Omori in light cruiser *Abukuma*. The heavy cruisers were commanded by Vice Admiral G. Mikawa. The fleet submarines were to scout well ahead of the striking force, the I-19, I-21, I-23. With the arrival of the all-important tankers, the attacking force was complete.

Once underway, the carriers steamed in two parallel columns of three, with the tankers behind and the battleships and cruisers watching the flanks. The destroyer screen sometimes sailed in a pyramid formation, with the apex destroyer's sonarmen sounding the water ahead, and sometimes they sailed in a half-circle.

They tried their first refueling on November 28. The rough weather made the ships pitch and the hoses from the tankers waved like giant whips. This did nothing to help the temper of Admiral Nagumo. These operations took time, with the ever present danger of being discovered. But with the refueling done and the striking and supporting forces underway again, Nagumo felt better. He had the most efficient carriers in the Japanese Imperial Navy, and the cream of the crop of combat pilots. Should any of the American battleships manage to sortie, he had two battleships and two heavy cruisers that could handle them. The U.S. personnel would not be alert after a Saturday night ashore and only one-fourth of their crews aboard the ships. Everything hung on one factor—not being observed. That was the one factor. His face became grim as he looked ahead at the dark rough sea.

The refueling was easier by November 30. The general attitude of the men on all of the ships was one of curiosity and impatience. The very strength of their force told them something was in the wind, but they could get no clues from their officers, particularly those on the carriers, who were entirely unapproachable.

Nagumo spent his time on the bridge or in his room, pondering the island of Oahu. As far as he knew, the task force had not been seen. He wanted to get closer to Oahu before informing the personnel of their mission. The envoys from Japan were still in Washington negotiating for some kind of settlement. If diplomacy settled the taut relations between the two nations, his attack would be cancelled, he would set his course northwest for Honshu and no one would know what had almost happened.

Then Yamamoto radioed the task force: "Climb Mount Niita"—code words for "proceed with the attack." A second message gave the date, "December 8," which was December 7 in Oahu.

The men were mustered and told their destination. There was shouting and the cry of "*banzai*" throughout the ship. The word was passed that not the smallest object must be thrown over the side. Each seaman was jubilant. He could tell his grandchildren how he had done his part in smashing the Anglo-Americans and wiping them from the Pacific. Nagumo kept receiving radio messages from Yamamoto. Still no indication that Washington suspected anything. By now Nagumo had dedicated himself to this task, just as Yamamoto had predicted, and had decided if he had received no word to the contrary he would attack on December 7.

There were two more refuelings. December 4 and December 6 were significant days, for the tankers were sent back and Nagumo went to the attack. The float planes from the heavy cruisers had sent back the information he wanted; all eight of the American battleships were lined up at Ford Island and there were some cruisers southeast of the island. But there were no carriers or heavy cruisers at Ford. The Japanese were now about 400 miles from their targets. Freed from the crawling tankers, they were speeding along with sea foam flying from their cutwater.

Now came a series of events, seemingly trivial, but pertinent in the later inquiry into heavy U.S. naval losses when CINC-PAC Admiral Husband Kimmel was called to account. Early in the morning (0342) an American minesweeper, *Condor*, saw what appeared to be a white wave moving toward the harbor entrance. This was reported to the DD *Ward* on picket duty; the *Ward* went to general quarters and began to search for the "white wave," now identified as the periscope of a submarine.

At 0458, the gate vessel reported, "Gate open, white lights." The man making the report meant the gate of the antitorpedo net. Another minesweeper *Crossbill,* came on through, then the *Condor.* The gate remained open, since the tug *Keosanqua* was due to pass out at 0615. To the men involved, it didn't seem worth the trouble to be opening and closing the gate when entrances and departures were so frequent. The destroyer *Ward* continued the search but with no results. Her report to the *Condor* was heard by nearby radio stations, but none reported the talk-between-ships to anybody. This sort of ship-to-ship conversation was heard all the time with nothing but routine information exchanged.

Admiral Nagumo had figured on two waves of torpedo planes, dive bombers, horizontal bombers, high-level bombers and fighters. The numbers of these as they were launched would be designated by Commander Fuchida. They were holding back about forty fighters in case any American ships managed to sortie or any of their planes got off the ground. This second possibility Nagumo believed unlikely, and as things turned out most of the hangars and planes were blasted before they could even be manned.

Nagumo had worried a great deal for naught. He could see that now in the alert way his pilots were checking their craft, the squadron leaders stalking about, stopping here and there to peer in a cockpit or bend to look down at landing gear.

The striking force was, indeed, ready. They had been seen now, so the element of surprise was lost. A Navy PBY saw the streaking planes with the red ball on them, as well as several ships. The DD *Ward* was first, probably because she had noticed the "white wave" and identified it as the periscope of a submarine. One ship noticed a thin line of planes coming in from the northwest; another saw more planes coming in from the south. But the ships appeared indifferent to these sights. Morning colors were observed as usual and men were going to their stations. About 0755 the thunderstorm struck. Due to some misunderstanding the signals between the Japanese fighters and the first wave of bombers, all planes were attacking together.

Disbelief was the general reaction, even though the S.O.P.A. (Senior Officer Present Afloat) had sounded general quarters and hoisted the signal, "All ships in harbor sortie," even as bluejackets raced to their battle stations, forward and up and port and down, according to navy traffic rules. Stunned men, many still sleep-drugged, had not thought war was ever a possibility as long as negotiations were going on in Washington. The antiaircraft fire was the first to begin cracking, the 5 inch, the little 3 inch, and the 1.1 Swedish type. The big turrets of the battleships were in poor position at the moment to counter the torpedo planes coming straight in, releasing their torpedoes.

The *West Virginia* staggered under the impact of six torpedoes, the *Oklahoma* took five, the *Arizona* two. The *Tennessee*, inboard of the *West Virginia*, was relatively safe at the moment. Ensign Phil Armstrong, running along the deck of the *West Virginia*—or the *Wee Vee*, as her crew called her—saw a curious thing. A Japanese plane struck some part of the *West Virginia*'s basket mast, the plane exploded and the pilot was thrown forward into the foremast, caught there, hanging like a puppet. Phil stopped, looked on the deck where a dead bluejacket lay. A .45 automatic lay within reach of his motionless hand. His head ringing with the cracking of guns, explosions of bombs, Phil picked up the weapon and, holding it in both hands, levelled it at the Japanese.

"Welcome to Pearl Harbor, you Jap bastard!" And he emptied the gun at the pilot.

A flying sliver of steel hit Armstrong then, cutting like a saw, disembowelling him. Phil went down heavily on his back, his arms outspread, his gun bouncing against the barbette of a turret. He was looking skyward. Half the Japanese pilot's head was gone. Armstrong's smile of victory turned to a grimace, and froth ran out of his mouth.

"I got one, Tommy! Hear me? I got one!" he whispered.

Two bluejackets came up, managed to get him into a stokes stretcher. A coxswain, maneuvering a sixty-foot motor launch, came alongside. He looked up, shook his head.

"Just leave him there till this mess is over. I got to the wounded as quick as I could and picked up as many as I could. Those guys have got to get to the medics quick."

The men with the stretcher looked down at Phil Armstrong. The blue eyes looking up through the heavy smoke were sightless.

There could be no doubt of it now. What had at first been dismissed as American planes flying off course or carelessly dropping a bomb was the real thing. Head-quarters on Ford Island broadcast the report that shook the United States and the world:

AIR RAID, PEARL HARBOR—THIS IS NO DRILL.

Gone was the shock and panic that had first gripped the men of the Pacific fleet. Going to battle stations, on the alert, with one's task force in formation and flexing its muscles, is quite different from the way these men had been awakened, with but a fourth of the personnel on watch in "Condition Three." Anger and fury gripped each man now, and waters around the stricken ships were filled with men swimming with all they had to get to their ships and fight with whatever was left in the way of armament. They fought with 50 calibre machine guns and 3-inch antiaircraft guns, but more than half had to busy themselves fighting fires.

The Japanese planes kept gliding down Southeast Loch with horrible efficiency, and more ships were hit. *Oklahoma* was hit with too many torpedoes on one side to counterflood, and began to capsize. The order was given to abandon ship, and the men began to slide down the starboard side as the ship was rolling over. Coxswains in twenty-six-foot whaleboats and sixty-foot launches moved through the oil-covered waters, picking swimmers who were struggling against the heavy oil that was coating their arms and legs. Even the best were in danger of drowning from the weight of the oil on their bodies, and the suction of the capsizing ship was also an imminent danger to them.

One bluejacket watching the unbelievable accuracy of the Japanese bombs and of the torpedoes streaking through Southeast Loch, making more hits on the *Tennessee* and the *Arizona*, screamed in frustration, "You scientific bastards!" It was far from his intent, but he was paying tribute to the efficiency of the Japanese Air Corps, and in one sentence summing up the difference between the two opposing fleets.

Now a long line of bombers headed for Hickam Field and found what they wanted; the pilots were running for the planes in a neat line. It was too easy. The hangars were blasted and the men were strafed. The barracks went up in flashes and smoke, some thirty-five to forty men being killed instantly. Wheeler Field was next. Ten dive bombers came in from the northwest, blasing the army fighters to bits and strafing the barracks. Men running to their battle stations saw nothing but planes with orange-red balls on them in any direction they looked.

Haleiva had the army's P-40 fighters being gassed up and their pilots pulling on their flying suits, expecting to take off shortly, when they were hit. All of Ford Island was blazing with red and yellow fires and rolling clouds of smoke as more bombs fell and Battleship Row took more torpedoes.

More antiaircraft guns, 30 calibre, 50 calibre and a few five-inch .38s were in action now, and here and there a Japanese plane went flaming into the sea or to the ground on Ford Island. But it was too little, too late. The attack had begun at 0755 and a mere ten minutes had elapsed, but that was enough for Admiral Nagumo to have achieved most of his objectives—the destruction of the U.S. battle line and of Hickam and Wheeler Fields. There were of course scattered sections of resistance that gave a good account of themselves. For some reason a great deal of publicity was given the two-man midget submarines that had first attempted entrance into Pearl Harbor—and understandably, because it was a new tactic. But all over the United States people talked of the midget subs as though they had been instrumental in the Pearl Harbor disaster. Actually, the *Monaghan, Curtiss* and *Ward* did an excellent job none of the five midget subs survived.

The *Oklahoma* was definitely gone; she had rolled over until her masts were sticking in the bottom. And now the *Arizona* took the worst of it all. Three more bombs hit forward, one went down the stack and she sank so fast that more than a thousand men were trapped below.

California took her first torpedo at 0805, then two more in quick succession. Her voids had been left open for inspection and the water rushed through rapidly. The *Tennessee*, inboard of the *West Virginia* which was now a mass of flames, began to take her turn at punishment; one 16-inch shell burst forward near the number two turret, then an armor-piercing bomb burst through number three turret aft. Captain Mervyn Bennion of the *Wee-Vee*, was struck through the stomach as he stood on the bridge, but refused to leave his post. Ensign Delano remained with him during the attack, keeping the captain posted on how the ship and men were doing. Delano could find no morphine for the captain and told him a few white lies about the whole disaster. The fact that at least fifty percent of the ship's crew were firing while the rest were fighting fires would not exactly have lessened the pain Bennion was enduring.

Admiral Kimmel hurried to CINC–PAC headquarters, and he felt the surge of nausea that only a man in his position could feel when he stared at Ford Island. The *Arizona* and *Oklahoma* were complete losses. *California* was going down and *West Virginia* had sunk. *Maryland* and *Tennessee* were unable to sortie because of the outboard ships pinning them in. *Pennsylvania* was in drydock. The old target ship had sunk, and destroyers *Cassin* and *Downes* and cruisers *Helena Honolulu* and *Raleigh* were badly damaged.

"When did they start their bombing and torpedo runs?" he asked his aides.

"We're not certain, sir," one of them replied. "So many people saw planes at different times and believed they were our own on practice runs. When the first bomb fell, it was believed to be a mistake. Then all hell broke loose. It must have about 0730."

Kimmel looked at his watch. "All this done in such a short time! My God, it must have been a big striking force. Our three carriers and most of our heavy cruisers are at sea." He looked around at the drawn faces. "That, gentlemen, is the Pacific fleet. What about the airfields and hangars?"

A young lieutenant who had just arrived saluted and said, "Admiral, the hangars at Hickam and Wheeler are blown to bits, and we must have lost two hundred planes, army and navy—though that's just a guess, sir. Some of them might be repaired."

"Make a careful check," said Admiral Kimmel, "then report to me just how many planes we do have in operative condition, and how many can be repaired."

"That leaves us virtually no air defense if the Japanese return for a second attack," Commander Murphy commented. "There are plenty of military objectives for bombing. But I think this was a hit-and-run raid by a sizeable carrier force with its main target being our battle line, and of course the two main air fields. Right now there's a lull; doesn't seem to be many Jap planes in the air. I don't believe they'll be back."

Kimmel's smile was wan. "I didn't think they'd come the first time. But I've heard from our intelligence— and the information seems to be accurate—that the Japanese are creating an Asian sphere of their own with highly disciplined forces."

"With your permission, sir," inquired an aide, "is it likely they'll return with transports to land troops?"

"No, I think Commander Murphy is right. They had no intention to actually invade." Kimmel remained relatively optimistic, despite the roasting he knew that he and General Short would soon be facing. "They've achieved their purpose. However, you're wise to consider that possibility. When you've eliminated what will *probably* happen, then consider what will *possibly* happen. But I don't think their ground troops could take Oahu. Even now General Short has his troops moving up to higher ground to man hidden coast defense guns, concrete pill boxes and other strategic spots. We have sixty thousand men, well-equipped, and they're seasoned career troops. The Japanese would absorb enormous losses trying to ascend that high ground. And if they did succeed, consider what a long supply line they'd need to maintain possession of this place."

Admiral Kimmel witnessed one determined and courageous act—there were hundreds—that was particularly outstanding. That was the sortie of the U.S.S. *Nevada*. She had the northeasternmost berth of Battleship Row and was not moored to any other ship. It takes time for a battleship to get up steam, but she had two boilers already hot and was underway in about forty-five minutes. Yard workmen and sailors cheered to see her moving out with her colors waving, a sight that many of them would not see again. The officer taking command was Lieutenant-Commander Francis Thomas USNR, with Ensign Taussig directing the work in the fireroom. Others working the *Nevada* free were Chief Quartermaster Robert Sedberry and Chief Boatswain Edwin Hill, while men manning the 5-inch .38s and 5 calibre machine guns shot down four Japanese planes. The *Nevada* took a torpedo and bombs that settled her in the mud, but she had made a gallant effort.

Japanese planes returned to inflict some damage on the *Pennsylvania* and the cruisers, but in the meantime a still nervous Admiral Nagumo was arguing with Commander Fuchida who was in the last plane returning to the *Akagi*. Fuchida said there were plenty of targets left and the populace was hysterical. This, of course, was not true. There were isolated cases of panic, but in the main, Pearl Harbor was a beehive of men already at work on the sunken and damaged ships and setting up what weapons they could find if a second attack came.

Nagumo felt that he had accomplished what he had been sent to do, and ordered the fleet northwest to Tankan Bay. He radioed Yamamoto about his action. Yamamoto was pleased but not surprised about the efficient job Nagumo had done; it was exactly what he had expected. In the short time from about 0755 until 1000, the biggest threat had been eliminated.

Admiral Husband Kimmel had been right this time. There would be no further attack on Pearl Harbor. The Japanese forces cut the seas on their northwesterly course toward home, leaving a profoundly shocked world and a charred and sunken battle line at Oahu. They had wiped out the battleships and airfields, damaged several cruisers and sunk two destroyers. But they left the power plant, repair shops, heavy cranes and fuel tanks untouched. It is not known whether Fuchida was directed to these targets by Nagumo, who then changed his mind, or whether he was instructed by Yamamoto to bomb and torpedo only the battleships and the two major airfields.

In any catastrophic event such as this, many acts of heroism are reported, some true, some false, and some even humorous. It was told, for example, by millions of Americans, that at Hickam Field an army chaplain made for a nearby machine gun, put it atop the altar and began firing, that he kept yelling as he fired at the attacking planes, "Praise the Lord and pass the ammunition, and we'll all be free!"

No one can be certain this actually happened, but it was the sort of thing that catches on with the public.

Melody and lyrics were written about this chaplain's spunky effort, and most people preferred to believe that the story was true. In the navy yards and private shipbuilding yards throughout the U.S., the song was roared out by men who clapped their hands and stamped their feet.

Of course there continued to be isolated reports exaggerated to the point of absurdity. At the Charleston Navy Yard, the communications watch officer walked next door and said to the yard duty officer, "Here's a dilly for you. I've just received a phone call from a person who wouldn't identify himself, and he told me he had just seen a blimp full of Japs over Stono River."

The duty officer snorted and shook his head. He had heard everything that day, but this was the topper. The Stono was a small river in the Charleston area, and even a conservative estimate would put it some ten thousand miles from Pearl Harbor.

"I have a couple for you," he countered. "Admiral King should be fired, General Marshall should be fired, and Admiral Kimmel should be sent to Portsmouth Naval Prison. And, oh, I forgot General Short—Leavenworth for him."

Paradoxically, the Japanese attack, destructive as it was, also had an enormously constructive effect; it unified America as no other event could possibly have done. Forgotten was any tendency to underestimate a potential foe, gone were the minor political differences. America had been stunned, frightened, panic-stricken. But now came hot anger, and the unbending urge to fight.

9

TOM, GAIL AND HENRY CARLSON followed the news of Pearl Harbor as assiduously and in as much outrage as anyone else. The report of Phil Armstrong's death shook Tom to the marrow, putting him in a white-hot rage of grief for his friend and making him all the more determined to get to the Pacific. Gail could only look on in quiet consternation, knowing the day would soon come when Tom would indeed be in active duty, thousands of miles away.

As it happened, Tom's earlier prediction to Gail turned out to be all too true. One day he simply didn't show up.

She came home from work one night, in a rush to get ready for a dinner date with Tom. He had a key to her apartment, and as she let herself in she sensed immediately that he had been there and gone. With a sinking heart, she glanced about the living room and saw a small square package wrapped in white tissue on the coffee table. She picked it up, unwrapped it and gazed at a dark blue velvet box before slowly opening it.

The brilliant reflection of an engagement ring flashed in the light. Her eyes started filling, and she had to wipe them clear to read the card beside the box.

"Gail—looks like salt water under my feet now. I hope you like the ring. Put it on. I'll give you the other one when I get back."

Barry Terence was back from duty in the Atlantic. His destroyers and others, accompanied by two oilers that had been converted into small carriers with forty planes each, had been assigned to search for submarines while escorting a convoy of small ships bound for Britain. He dropped into the communications office at the Yard. Tommy DeWitt wasn't there, he discovered. He hadn't really expected to see him anyway. But where was he, in the Pacific?

Crossing the Yard, he could see the change. The pace had grown faster as the war news rolled in—all of it bad. He wondered whether the war correspondents were doing an honest job, or just trying to sell newspapers and establish names for themselves.

He swore to himself he had never seen so many people in offices who knew nothing, had nothing but misinformation, and did half their assignments wrong.

He went down to the building ways at the waterfront, where he found a bedlam of hammers, shrieking whistles, dust, hurrying, harried men who now and then swore at each other. Mad clear through, these men were fighting a war right here at home.

He sought refuge at Point Affirm. Naval officers and marines filled the place. He ordered a bourbon on the rocks, then spotted Vic Hadley, also back from a mission, and joined him at his table. Barry had forgotten how pretty the girls were. He took a deep, greedy gulp on his drink. That was better. It warmed his stomach, went down his legs to his feet. It was good to hear a young ensign, heated by several drinks, expressing himself in impassioned terms.

"Look, they're everywhere! They've landed in the Philippines, they're attacking in the Dutch East Indies, they've bombed the *Repulse* and *Prince of Wales* to the bottom—"

The speaker looked around a circle of interested faces. "They're in Hong Kong, in Siam and islands in the central Pacific. The red rays of that rising sun are everywhere. How do they have so much of everything?"

A ruddy-faced lieutenant, a mustang wearing a World War I victory ribbon and the Navy Cross spoke up. "It didn't take so much to overrun Malaya, Siam and some of those other places. But as far as comparing them with our fleet, they have a few more ships than we have, but not enough to whip us to a frazzle. The big difference is that while Japan and the U.S. both have ten carriers, we have only three in the Pacific. I'm not saying anything but what's known everywhere. The important thing is that what they have is *ready*."

The others studied his weathered face solemnly.

"Yep, that's right. I know what you're thinking," he continued. "Economy. The richest nation on earth had to use dummy torpedoes in practice, while the Japs used live fish and corrected their errors. Now we're paying for it. Don't you see? They were ready. A force in being is superior to a greater force in potential. A man can have an arsenal in his basement, but if he's surprised at the front door by a thief with a .38 revolver, of what use are all those weapons beyond his reach?"

The honest red face now had a shadowed look about the eyes. It was the look of a man who saw beyond the men he faced and didn't like what he saw. "I recall when our battleships had long-range battle practice in the Pacific, always in fair sunny weather. There were always Japanese fishing ships in the area—except they weren't fishermen. They were reserve officers in the Imperial Navy. And they didn't like what they saw. The American long-range gunnery was too good to suit them. So they developed a technique of fast, hit-and-run night attacks, with the use of searchlights, and our ships were taking salvos before they had a chance to man their battle stations. We can expect this and have to learn how to beat them at their own game."

"You were at Pearl?" Barry asked.

The man nodded. He didn't have to tell them which ship it was. The big man wiped the sweat from his face. He looked at the backs of his battered and scarred hands, the result of too many fisticuffs in Singapore, Panama and Norfolk. "I'll have another drink, then shove off. This old man's tired. We've paid the price for being stingy. But we have the Academy men, mustangs and good reservists, too."

He's looking at us, thought Barry. He means us.

"In every war we've had a handful of professionals and reservists who've been trained to hold off the enemy while the nation gets ready and finally throws its Sunday punch. Yep, that's what you've been trained for, and that's what you'll do. Well, I've a few things to do at the waterfront office. Be seein' ya."

As the old mustang reached the door, Barry said, "Sir, you know I think I'm a little scared—Vic here, too."

"How scared?"

"You said we had to hold 'em. You know how thin our fleet is spread in the Pacific. You said so yourself."

The pale blue eyes held theirs for a moment. Then the leather visage broke in a smile. "I'll bet my next month's pay you can do it. You're worried about whether you can do the job—but you're concerned about your country. And you'll have some help, a real tough admiral to lead you; he'll fight like a killer shark, and he'll end up with five stars before this thing's finished."

Vic looked surprised. "Who is this admiral, this Jack Dempsey of the navy?"

The mustang spoke in a voice almost gentle. "Bill Halsey."

* * *

Barry Terence, taking over Tom DeWitt's stint in the military department, found the chaos over Pearl Harbor giving way to cool efficiency. The girls at the switchboards cut off all nonsense calls, of which there were many, and the attitude among all the workers at the Yard seemed to be one of feverish dedication. Everyone was in a rush, he thought, looking up as the aide to the commandant ran into the office.

"Look, Terence, the old boy wants the location of all the cans at the piers. Also find a place for the two new tankers. Don't phone me. Just jot it down and bring it to my office, and I'll take it from there."

Barry rubbed his chin, looking at the berthing arrangements. He grinned at one spot in the slip; the monster new *South Dakota* was getting the finishing touches, was already in commission and had had her first gunnery practice in Chesapeake Bay. She sure looks ready, he thought.

Barry looked at the chart of the waterfront, changed a few colored pins. He didn't have to ask what the aide meant by *the cans.* He wanted to know where they could put the British destroyers and corvettes that were coming in for repair and overhaul from the gruelling Battle of the Atlantic. The men of the Yard were getting to understand the limeys better. Reserved at first, they became cordial enough with a bit of knowing. A man who works thirteen hours a day because his fleet's ships are spread so thin does well to get the scotch to his lips and enjoy the camaraderie of his foreign allies.

The succeeding months were hard ones. The American press, for once, was trying to bolster morale. They expanded every fragment of good news, but were hard pressed to find anything but bad news. But Barry could sense a change. The nation had recovered from its initial alarm and near-panic. The sleeping giant was awake and beginning to flex his muscles. The scattered forces of career men and reservists were everywhere, fighting delaying actions. "Hold 'em, hold 'em! That's what you've been trained for— that's what you'll do!"

Far away in the Pacific, that's what the defenders did. MacArthur fought hard with no naval or air support from December 8 until March 11, 1942, when he was ordered out by the president, leaving "Skinny" Wainwright in command. Many unthinking people, bitter over another defeat, had acid criticism for Mac-Arthur, who had held the Philippines with valor and could hardly have ignored Roosevelt's order. Beneath MacArthur's somewhat flamboyant uniform was the most experienced officer the United States had in the Pacific, a man who had spent most of his military career there, and certainly was the most logical choice to lead American troops back into the Philippines. His speech, when he said vehemently, "I shall return," was also the object of derision. It was an unfortunate choice of words, one that increased his lack of popularity. His low standing with the public was no doubt responsible, in part, for the story that he left the Philippines with several boats filled with his and his family's personal belongings, including rather valuable objects of art, when those boats could have been filled with

U.S. Army nurses, who were later captured by the Japanese. There is no shred of evidence that this was true.

Back on the home front, the common complaint of naval personnel and workers in the yards was that once again the United States had gone to war unprepared, with obsolete equipment, despite what seemed adequate appropriations for defense. The captain of a destroyer just in from sea told Vic Hadley, Barry Terence and the other officers in Philadelphia's communications office:

"We have no shortage of torpedoes in this can. But we don't know what will happen when we fire them. They may hit the target and fail to detonate. They may detonate before they reach the target. Most often they run too deep and go under the target. Time and again we have them in our sights and return to base with maybe one hit on the whole cruise."

An officer who had been at Pearl Harbor said ruefully, "The antiaircraft guns on the battleships and cruisers were outmoded and there weren't enough of them. The 1.1s are inferior to the new 40 millimeters, and the new 20 millimeter single barrel is an excellent little antiaircraft gun. But the ships at Pearl had practically none of those, and every Jap in Honolulu knew this."

"Don't forget the Zero—that thing flies circles around our Grumman Wildcat fighter." The speaker was a junior grade lieutenant with wings, a gold ribbon and battle star on his coat. "Faster than Britain's Spitfire. We *do* have an advantage in the Grumman—two, as a matter of fact. More firepower, and about three hundred pounds of protective metal around the pilot. You can't dogfight with a Zero, but if you can make one running pass and get one blast out, your target is through."

"That's good news," said Barry, "and we need all of *that* that we can get. Speaking of which—there's talk about the battleships *North Carolina* and *Washington* coming through the canal. There's also a new carrier about ready. No secret. Any yeoman or ship-fitter here can tell you that. I wonder why it is that the damned officers are the last to know about up-coming events?" There was general laughter at this.

"Well," said Barry, "it's time for me to brief the night duty officer coming on. He's had experience before, but he's new to this yard. In the meantime, let's pray that our guys can hang on out there until we can get more of everything out to them—"

One young ensign broke in. "Right! We'll flood the Pacific with carriers, battlewagons, cruisers, blacken the skies with planes, and send destroyers as thick as mosquitoes, and marines with their funny little tanks —Say, something wrong, Vic?"

Vic Hadley had been a silent sit-in on all the gabble of conversation. Now the other junior officers turned, suddenly quiet, to look at him. His face had gone pale.

"I'll be okay. I lost a good friend at Pearl. I guess when Barry said to pray it made me thing of him. His name was Phil Armstrong."

"What ship?" asked one man.

"The *West Virginia.*"

He left a room of silent men.

Vic walked along slowly, trying to soften that hard

knot in his stomach. How vividly he recalled his last conversation with Phil. The big guy was talking about his orders to the Pacific—and about his own self-analysis. "I remember, Vic," he had said, "I had a steady girl in high school who felt I should be some kind of knight in shining armor. She was a sharp, good-looking kid, and our friends thought we made a nice couple. But we didn't think alike. Once some smart aleck tried to start dating her, really coming on strong and hanging around her all the time. She could have been rid of him simply by telling him to get lost. But she really wanted me to fight him. I wouldn't, and she told other kids I was yellow.

"I stopped dating her. Then the same guy made a pass at my kid sister and I flattened him. I wasn't proud of this fight, Vic, because it wasn't any fight. He was tough—but I hit him just twice, and it was all over. Yeah, you've got my message. I fight when it's important to *me*. That's the way I see this war. I don't even know any Japs or Germans, so how can I hate them? But the way things are going now, it seems to me that we don't have any choice. People say we have a big ocean on each side of us, that they present a barrier to potential enemies. You know they don't. They're actually two highways leading right to our shores, and a nation with a big navy that can conduct amphibious operations could do it."

All of which had sounded eminently sensible to Vic. Now Phil was gone. The man who had fought only when it was important to him had died before he had a chance to fight.

He suddenly felt very alone. Should he call Isobel?

Isobel had known Phil, if only briefly, and it had been good to be around her after the news of Phil's death. And since Phil had made it clear that he had no special interest in her, Vic felt no compunctions about dating her. They'd seen each other several times, and Vic found that he was liking Isobel more and more.

He found a phone booth and dialed Isobel's number. "Isobel, are you alone?"

"Vic? Yes, I am."

"I'm coming over—I have to talk to you. Why don't we go out to dinner? You think of a place before I get there."

When the door opened, she was there, smiling, the lovely panacea to the horrible aching in him. She immediately sensed his mood and crushed herself into him, with her arms around his neck. "You've been thinking of Phil . . . oh, God, I'm sorry!"

He stroked her head. Pressed into him, she felt strong, yet delicate and tender. He was fast learning something. Isobel could pour strength into him when he needed it. They walked together to the sofa, and he collapsed on his back with his legs spread out. "He was one helluva of a guy."

"I know, from the things Tommy and others said about him." She sat on the edge of the sofa, smiling down at him. "You know, Vic, I'm going to introduce you to a good place for dinner tonight."

"Let's have it."

"Wannamaker's Tea Room—in the department store."

"A tea room? Hell, you can't get enough to eat on those fancy little plates they serve, Isobel. Besides, it's a place where a mob of overdressed females exchange gossip about their neighbors or people they don't like, expanding every bit of it."

"Vic—have you been there?"

"No, but a tea room is a tea room."

"It's not what you think!" Isobel laughed. "It's a big place, glistening with bright lights, full of laughing, happy people. And you can make a perfect hog of yourself, if you like."

"Happy people? Good, that does it! And I'll tell you what we'll do after that. We'll park Tommy's car and take a walk near the Schuylkill River. There's going to be a big moon tonight. You'll like it."

It was a perfect evening. Vic ate ravenously. He would never have believed that even he could come up with such an appetite. Full and content, he drove Isobel out to Fairmont Park and parked by the Schuylkill River.

They looked at the moon-bathed statues, the glistening river and the silver limbs of the winter-stripped trees.

"It's nice, here by the river," Isobel said softly. "It reminds me of something Gail once said. 'Night brings different things to different people, I suppose. To me it brings a sort of magic. For example, a painted picket fence may be ugly in the daylight, but it becomes a palisade of tall black and silver bars in the moonlight. A dead tree becomes some weirdly beautiful creature from another world.'"

Vic nodded. "Well put. But it's camouflage. A world of delusion. Like snow. Broken broomsticks and rusty tins in your backyard may be covered with snow, but their ugliness is still a fact even if it's hidden."

"Sure. But the magic comes every night, not only in winter under a coverlet of white. Moonlight or pouring rain, it's magic. The rain rushes down and drowns all other noises—"

He laughed. "Like the Philadelphia motorists sounding their horns?"

"Right. And if it thunders and lightning flashes, it's the night shouting its strength and fury, you see."

"And the magic is gone when the daylight comes. Well, that's the way she sees it. And you, Isobel?"

She seemed suddenly tired. "Let's not talk about that, Vic. Take me back to my apartment. I need you, Vic."

He gripped her hand tightly. "Come get in Tommy's aging percolator."

In her apartment, Vic laughed softly. It was the kind of laugh that is triggered by nervousness, even embarrassment. Recently he had been feeling that way when he was intimate with Isobel. He felt her nakedness and heard her say, "I'm going to tear you up for thirty seconds and then the bit of heaven will be gone, just like the magic."

As usual, she was in a hurry. He had scarcely shed his clothes when she slid under him, locked him in her relentless embrace and had her fill.

Back in his room, a pleasantly tired, sated Vic Hadley dwelled on what he had heard this evening. He liked what Gail had said about the magic of the night. He knew of Tom's broken marriage and that unfathomable Irene. For Irene, the night had meant party after party, glittering dresses and tinkling glasses. For Gail, it brought a beautiful transformation of all that was ugly. And for Isobel? It meant going on the prowl.

Tom had told him that he and Gail had discussed Isobel's late hours after he'd run into her that first night in the hotel bar, and that both of them had only been able to conclude that she was "uh . . . supplementing her income," Tom had said. Vic had been shocked at first, but Tom had also said that Isobel was damn smart, and probably one of the best friends anyone could ever find. Fine . . . that was the word Gail had used to describe her.

Vic had discovered for himself that this was true. He also suspected that he was falling in love with her. With a beautiful raven-haired girl who was normal in every respect—except that she was a prostitute. Vic hadn't discussed it with her, but he knew that it wasn't because she needed money. And so far as he could judge it wasn't a psychological thing. She seemed to have an overwhelming and purely physical craving for sex. He couldn't understand it. He couldn't figure out quite where he wanted to fit in that particular picture. And he really didn't want to think about this puzzling situation, not just yet.

For now and for the foreseeable future, night to him would mean the plunging and pitching of his destroyer in the wintery seas, watching the lumbering of the cargo ships in the middle of the formation with their precious equipment that Britain so desperately needed, falling wearily into his bunk, his last wakeful moments conscious of the chung-chung-chung of the depth charges from the destroyers on the other side of the convoy. When he reached Britain, he would enjoy a warming drink in a blacked-out restaurant with his allies, England's navy, their drawn, weary faces somehow managing a laugh, likeable limeys who wanted to know the difference between New England and California. They were always astonished at how many of the American cities and towns on the east coast bore the same names as those of England. A pleasant, all-too-brief interlude; then back to sea. A man just didn't think beyond that. Somehow, some day, it would end.

10

EVERY MAN on Oahu worked unceasingly, with one thought in mind—*time* was the factor. Some of the battleships here could be floated and repaired so that they could make the yard at Bremerton under their own power. This was the yard that could virtually convert a battered ship into one that looked like new. True, the Pacific fleet was not completely wiped out. There were three carriers at sea, with a lot of heavy cruisers and light cruisers with the 6-inch .47s so fast the Japanese were later to call them six-inch pom-poms. What was needed was a victory, a pounding of some of the Japanese-held islands to pick up the spirit of the American public.

During lunch period at Pearl, one shipfitter shoved

a newspaper at a friend. Munching methodically on a ham and cheese sandwich, his friend read aloud, "Japanese inhabitants being rounded up by local authorities . . . all of Oahu's in a state of panic—" He threw aside the paper. "Hell, we're too busy to panic. Besides, we've got a good many ships at sea. By the way, where in hell are they, anyway? Haven't heard a word about them, except we're damned lucky they weren't in the harbor when those bastards attacked."

That was a good question. Where were these carriers that were later to play such a crucial role in the battle for the north central Pacific? The U.S.S. *Enterprise*, commanded by Vice Admiral William Halsey, had delivered twelve Grumman Wildcat fighters to Wake Island and was steaming back to Pearl Harbor. The *Lexington*, commanded by Admiral Wilson Brown, and the *Saratoga*, were steaming southwest to support Wake Island, then under attack. Frank Jack Fletcher, destined to give the Japanese some very bad times, was old *Sara's* task force admiral. During these days of feverish work at Pearl Harbor, when every man was throwing himself into the massive efforts to repair and fortify the Pacific fleet, shock after shock was emerging from what had been mere rumor, and the Americans learned the true extent of what they were up against. The Japanese torpedoes had a better guidance system and 1,000-pound warheads; all of their battleships were faster, and we had no heavy cruiser with the speed of *Tone*, which had 152,000 horsepower. The *Sara* and *Lady Lex* were conversions, ships that had originally been laid down as battle cruisers.

They did have speed, but although our navy air corps was the world's best (and proved it) they fought critical engagements with obsolete machines. The U.S.S. *Ranger*, in the Atlantic, was the first carrier laid down as such.

And what of the navy's combat planes? The Grumman Wildcat fighter did well compared with the Zero, but the Douglas Devastator torpedo plane was obsolete and the best the navy had at this time was the dive bomber, the Douglas SBD.

Aside from the disposition and condition of our Pacific fleet, Admiral Kimmel and General Short were, of course, the principal subjects across the nation. How could they have permitted such a catastrophe to happen? As professional military men, how could they be guilty of such laxity that a big carrier task force of six carriers with battleship and cruiser support could appear, as if from nowhere, and launch such a devastating attack?

Wake Island . . . This tiny island, some one thousand miles from Midway, an American possession since 1899, was of little importance until the Japanese attack on Pearl Harbor, when it became an integral part of that operation. The Japanese did not ignore it. It was a strategic position, because of its proximity to the Japanese-held Marshall and Gilbert Islands. Fortified, it would be a threat to the Japanese, constituting a base from which the fast American task forces could attack those islands. Tom DeWitt, assigned to the heavy cruiser *San Francisco*, was among those involved in the conflict over Wake. It was an experience that heightened his fighting spirit, as it did for so many others—and that once again brought him close to a court-martial.

As far back as June, 1941, Admiral Kimmel had begun to put military personnel there and a few guns. He did not believe the Japanese would pay much attention to it, since it was his opinion, as well as General Short's, that any attack would come from the south.

So the first defenses were light; in August, 1941, a marine detachment landed, with six officers and 173 enlisted men. Subject to Kimmel's orders was Major James Devereux, barely able to make the marine minimum height of five feet five inches, slender, courageous, and tough as a pine knot. He was a good leader imbued with that exceptional marine esprit de corps that enabled him to face the hard issues and do his best—which proved to be a very good best—with whatever weapons he had at hand. On October 15 he had begun fortifying Wake for what he felt was certainly coming. His defenses consisted of six 5-inch .51 calibre guns taken from old battleships (these would be his principal coast defense guns), twelve 3-inch guns, eighteen .50 calibre machine guns, and thirty .30-calibre machine guns.

Wake was a mere spot in a tremendous ocean, but it did have trees and the cagey Devereux used them to best advantage. In November a transport arrived with nine officers and 200 men. This gave the Wake garrison a total of 383 men. It also confirmed what Devereux had felt lay in the offing—a major Japanese offensive move to the east. Amphibious landings on the islands which they intended to include in their own sphere, as outlined by the Minister of War, General Tojo, would involve numbers of carriers, surface vessels and planes considerably in excess of what Admiral Kimmel and General Short believed they had. A major attack on Pearl Harbor? Major Devereux believed in facts. And thus far he had no information Japan had such capabilities.

Wake actually consisted of three low islands: Wilkes, Wake and Peale, shaped like a thumb and forefinger, with the open end pointing northwestward. Batteries of two 5-inch guns were placed at Toki, Kuku and Peacock points, so cleverly camouflaged that they could not be seen from 100 yards offshore.

These 5-inch guns constituted Devereux's main defense, and he placed his 3-inch guns in batteries of four near the larger guns, and the .50-calibre and .30-calibre machine guns were placed at strategic spots along the beach. Devereux had done an excellent job of setting up a defense. But the insurmountable headache for this capable little commander was a shortage of manpower. He could have used twice the number of men he had, for some of the 3-inch guns were difficult to move around as needed.

On December 11, the first bombing attack (thirty-six bombers from Kwajalein) struck eight Wildcats being serviced and completely destroyed them, killing twenty-three officers and men. The Pan American station was strafed. The clipper in the lagoon was riddled, but managed to escape, loaded with civilian passengers.

This bombing attack was followed by the invasion force, commanded by Rear Admiral Kajioka in the light cruiser *Yubari*; he was followed by 450 naval landing troops in two converted destroyers and garrison troops in transports, escorted by six destroyers. There were also two old light cruisers *Tenryu* and *Tatsuta* as support force.

From their battle stations, the marines, wearing khakis and World War I helmets, clutched their Springfield bolt-action rifles and waited.

Devereux, standing by one of the 5-inch guns, heard one or two nervous coughs. "Hold your fire," he said easily. "Let's not waste any ammo, boys." He looked around at the other positions. The men were statues, watching him. What wouldn't he give for five hundred more men like these?

He let the flagship come within 4500 yards and watched as three of the destroyers made a turn. He lifted his arm high in the air. "Battery A!" he called, using an old British command. "Mark your targets . . . fire!"

A marine, watching Devereux like a pointer, turned to his gun. The 5-inch flashed, with that sharp, biting crack that only a 5-inch can emit. The *Yubari* was hit, then hit twice more. She swung in sharp, and with smoke streaking from her she made flank speed (all she was capable of) to get out of range.

"Battery L!" They let the destroyer *Hayate* have three two-gun salvos. She blew up and went down instantly.

Under the accurate 5-inch gunfire, the destroyer *Kisaragi* blew up and sank.

With the .50- and .30-calibre machine guns chattering away, the first Japanese attempt faded, the ships withdrawing, Admiral Kajioka stunned at his losses—500 Japanese dead, two destroyers sunk, one light cruiser damaged. The marines were yelling with joy at their victory. An amphibious landing had been beaten off—which rarely happened—and the leathernecks were throwing up their arms and jumping in the sand. A veteran sergeant remonstrated with them in typical marine language and got them back to their posts.

Devereux, staring at the sea, knew it had appeared too easy. It wasn't going to be easy. The attack on Pearl Harbor was over; but which way were the Japanese going home? North of Wake or South? They might divert a part of their fleet to attack Wake—and Wake had no sufficient defenses—unless the U.S. carriers came to them and brought marines or army troops. He did not know it, but Admiral Nagumo's task force had not found the U.S. carriers on either side of Ford Island or anywhere near Oahu; and as Kimmel did not know where the Japanese force was, it was something of a Mexican stand-off. He heard a voice behind him.

"Sir, will they be back?"

"They'll be back. They intend to occupy this island, and they have more troops than they've thrown at us so far. Japanese never make the first move until they believe they have the enemy heavily outnumbered. No, Sarge, we wait. Just wait until they make their second attack, or some of our forces bring us reinforcements."

The sergeant spat into the ground. "We'll give 'em hell if the yellow bastards do come back."

Devereux returned his salute. Of the men he had here—and they were all of them good soldiers—he knew he could count on this man to the last bullet.

Two things were on Devereux's mind as he gazed at the sea. If Kimmel sent reinforcements to Wake, he might not make his landfall in time. And secondly, they would be outnumbered anyway, with only three carriers in the Pacific.

Kimmel had not forgotten Wake, though he himself was in the midst of chaos. He had hoped to offset the numerical superiority of the Japanese by sending two carriers on diversions: Task Force 11, the *Lexington*, commanded by Admiral Wilson Brown was on a raid against Jaluit; Task Force 8, the *Enterprise*, commanded by Vice Admiral Halsey, was to operate to the west of Johnstown Island and cover Oahu, a rather passive role for a personality like Halsey's. For Wake's relief, he formed Task Force 14, with the carrier *Saratoga*, the three heavy cruisers *Astoria*, *Minneapolis* and *San Francisco*, nine destroyers, the fleet oiler *Neches* and the *Tangier*, and a seaplane tender converted to a troop transport. But they had only two hundred marines, which was all they could spare.

Major Devereux was right on both counts. The relief expedition was late, due to the fact that the *Saratoga* group was late leaving Pearl Harbor, and the others were delayed by refueling in rough weather, with the fuel lines parting. Secondly, Admiral Nagumo's Pearl Harbor striking force sent carriers *Soryu* and *Hiryu*, with heavy cruisers *Tone* and *Chikuma*. With them came the original invasion force which had taken such a severe beating. Rear Admiral Kajioka was back, in the patched-up light cruiser which the marines thought they had sunk, the *Yubari*. More landing troops were included in this second effort, and the count stood at about 2000 Japanese against 500 marines.

The marines were being worn out by constant bombings, long hours and too little sleep. The invincible Major Devereux was everywhere at once, "laying the guns," operating machine guns, and giving first aid to those men who were hit. Inside his wiry frame was rage against the Japs and a growing despair for the fate of his men. But his men knew they had a leader; weary, their bodies getting weaker every day, their saturnine faces gave no evidence of their duress. Reports of their stubborn resistance reached Pearl Harbor, the west coast, the entire country. Praise ran high for them, and because people must have some one to blame, Admiral Kimmel and General Short were doubly cursed for being incompetent, lacking in foresight, indifferent to the threatening clouds hanging over the nation, and too trusting of a foreign power determined to wipe out the Pacific fleet.

The days passed, and the number of marines on Wake dwindled. At one point a small group of marines fought 500 Japanese until all but one of the marines were killed or wounded, and the lone survivor fainted from exhaustion.

It was too late now. The relief force would not be in time. Something had happened to that task force. Devereux saw 2000 Japanese on the beach and more coming up. Behind him he heard his men clip their last cartridges into their rifles, and the clink of bayonets being fixed. It was not in his authority to surrender, and he knew marines surrender hard. He saw Commander Cunningham walking to him. Here was the man who had the rotten job, the decision as to whether or not to surrender. Back in November, 1941, Commander Winfield Scott Cunningham and a few navy petty officers and bluejackets had come ashore to take charge as a naval station.

Now was the sickening moment. Devereux couldn't surrender, and his men wouldn't. He heard Cunningham's hoarse voice say, "We can't have them slaughtered. We've no choice, Jim."

Devereux's throat was tight. "All right. Take a few steps forward, take off your sidearms and pitch 'em on the ground in front of your adversary there." He indicated the Japanese captain who had walked toward them and stopped, half a dozen enlisted men with rifles at the ready.

Cunningham complied with a grumble. One of his bluejackets had tied a white handkerchief on a stick and stood at his commanding officer's side. Major Devereux casually unhooked his canvas belt with its clip and Colt .45 and tossed it on the ground near Cunningham's weapon. The bluejacket walked with Major Devereux toward the Japanese and stopped. The Japanese captain brought up his hand in a smart salute. From behind Devereux came the hoarse shout of the marine sergeant.

"Major! We'll fight for you until we're all dead— but if you return that yellow bastard's salute, I'll knock your teeth down your throat!"

Despite his defeat, Devereux's white teeth showed

beneath the thin black moustache. He took the white handkerchief from the sailor's hand, walked forward and stuck it in the sand in front of the Japanese officer. He said nothing to the Japanese captain, but turned and spoke to his sergeant. "Come forward and stack arms."

The men wearily complied with his order. They looked at their Japanese captors with stoic unyielding faces.

"It's over," sighed Commander Cunningham.

Devereux ached in every muscle. What had become of the carrier rescue mission? He had already instructed his radioman to send the message which was becoming a battle cry of a sort.

ENEMY APPARENTLY LANDING.
THE ENEMY IS ON THE ISLAND. THE ISSUE IS IN DOUBT.

"Heads up there!" he called to his sagging men. "You're marines, damn it—march down there like it!"

The Japanese captain stared as the stiff-legged marines marched past him to be taken in custody. What kind of creatures were these, anyway? He wondered what the admirals of the two carriers offshore were thinking.

A total of 470 officers and men of the armed forces and 1,146 civilians were taken prisoner. Devereux was not to know for sometime that Kimmel had been relieved, and that Admiral Pye, acting at Pearl Harbor until Admiral Chester Nimitz could get there, had recalled the *Saratoga* task force because he was unable to locate the Japanese striking force and because the *Saratoga*'s men would have been outmatched before they could evacuate the marines. Naval personnel were as bitter as the marines on the *Saratoga*, yet no one man felt as bad as Admiral Pye himself in giving the order.

Wake Island was not bought cheaply by the Japanese. Eight hundred twenty men were killed, 1,133 wounded, one cruiser was badly damaged, and four destroyers, one submarine, one gunboat and nine planes were sunk. It would be difficult to find anyone who disagreed with Commander Masatake Okumiya, Imperial Japanese Navy, when he said it was his opinion that his navy had suffered a defeat.

Tom DeWitt, in the communications department of the heavy cruiser, *San Francisco*, would not have gone along with the Japanese's officer's view. Shaking, with a nauseous feeling in the pit of his stomach, he had watched the *Sara* turning—and then the rest of her Task Force 14 following—and he had stormed up to the bridge, yelling in a strident voice he hardly recognized as his own.

"That stupid bastard! Why did he give such an order?"

He addressed his comment to Lieutenant-Commander Evan McCoy, USN, acting executive officer. The cruiser's exec was confined to his room with a bout of the flu.

McCoy's head snapped around and he replied stiffly, "Mr. DeWitt, what is your assignment aboard this ship?"

"The communications department, sir," came Tom's choked answer. The hot blood had rushed to his face and his heart pounded in his chest. He wanted to strike out at something, to hit something, smash anything, in the rage that had possessed him at the sight of the dispatch ordering the *Saratoga* and her supporting ships back to Pearl Harbor. He stood shaking, a rigid, immovable figure.

McCoy seized him firmly by one arm and escorted him back to the signal bridge. "You're out of order, DeWitt! In the first place, Admiral Pye, who sent that message, is acting commander-in-chief of the whole damn Pacific fleet. Secondly, we don't know if the Japanese carrier force that struck Pearl diverted carriers to help take Wake Island—or how many or where they are! And another thing—we have only two hundred marines to land there, certainly not enough to be of any substantial aid to Major Devereux. And last, Mr. DeWitt, it is not your function to advise your superiors on their course of action."

"*Somebody* should do some advising! We're leaving those men—and civilians—to be captured without a single effort to help." Tom was fairly yelling now, and two signalmen nearby busied themselves with the flag locker to avoid watching this unusual verbal clash between a junior officer and the acting executive officer. They did not see Tom DeWitt lift his hands, as if to grasp the lapels of McCoy's coat, poise his trembling hands a moment, then lower them.

McCoy's face whitened. "Get below to your duties, Mr. DeWitt. Is that understood?"

"Understood—sir!" DeWitt left the signal bridge, going down the ladder on legs that fairly shook.

Lieutenant-Commander McCoy returned to the bridge. He didn't even hear the quiet order from the officer-of-the-deck to the bluejacket standing by the engine room control.

"All engines ahead full."

"All ahead full, sir."

McCoy removed his hat and passed a hand over his sweating forehead. Damn, what a blasted headache! The profane, vitriolic language from men on the bridge was merely a murmur in his ears. That upstart junior grade lieutenant! How was it possible to make a man like that understand?

Tom DeWitt understood. But his rage at turning his back on comrades who needed help blotted out all rational thinking, especially with Phil Armstrong's death still fresh in his mind. McCoy realized this when a white-faced radioman faced him, handing the acting executive officer a scrawled message that was easily recognizable as DeWitt's handwriting.

"He wanted me to send this. He was—adamant, sir. I can't send it."

McCoy shook his head. "No, of course not. Mr. De-Witt is upset—perhaps rightly so. Go back to your job. I'll handle this." He left and went below.

He knocked and then entered Tom DeWitt's room, and was a little surprised to see Tom seated at his small metal desk, his head leaning upon his folded arms. He looked up at his superior with a countenance devoid of all wrath, imprinted now with resignation. He watched as McCoy waved the paper at him.

"This—this is ridiculous, DeWitt. 'To the c.o. of marines at Wake Island—Task Force 14 did not desert you. The gold braid at Pearl did.' Surely—surely, DeWitt, you couldn't expect to send this on your own!"

Tom DeWitt stood up, weary but still hard with anger. "No, sir, I did not. It was spontaneous—the way I felt. I was wrong in trying to send it. But I'm not wrong in feeling that we've let those men down."

McCoy crumpled the paper in his hand. He had regained some of his composure and now became the disciplinarian once more. "Mr. DeWitt, although your conduct borders on insubordination, at this crucial time we cannot go through the procedure prescribed by regulations. You will be confined to your room until we reach Pearl Harbor." His hard stare was a challenge, but Tom stood at attention and said nothing.

As McCoy turned away, he said over his shoulder, "DeWitt, every man in this task force feels just as you do—also Admiral Pye, who had to send the order recalling us."

"I know that, sir."

Then McCoy was gone, and Tom was left with a quiet frustration. Yes, McCoy was right, and Admiral Pye was right, but if Tom DeWitt had been the task force admiral, that task force would have gambled, would have made a quick run into Wake and picked up those marines, chancing on what they might meet.

"There will come a day," he said softly, "Yeah, you butt-headed, bragging gy-renes, there'll come a day." He stopped muttering and wiped his cheeks. Why in hell was he crying?

His orders came before Task Force 14 reached Pearl. He accepted the paper in silence, reading the coldly formal message:

24 December, 1941

From: Cinc Pac
To: Lieutenant (j.g.) Thomas DeWitt,
    D(V)G USNR
Subject: Change of Duty
1. You are hereby detached from your present
duties and will report to the commandant, Fourth
Naval District, Philadelphia Navy Yard, for such
duties as the military department at that station
may require.

He sighed. The message went on, but in essence it
meant—back to the captain of the yard's office, and
then to duty on the Atlantic. Ah, well, he was getting
off easy and he knew it. Beyond this one incident there
was the fact that McCoy and Tom had never hit it off.
McCoy always seemed as unbending and impersonal
as a military tribunal. There could be no doubt that
McCoy had had a hand in this transfer. Well, he supposed he had asked for it with that crazy outburst.
Why had he done it? It seemed the last few years had
brought out a depth of feeling he hadn't known he
possessed. The marriage with Irene, his friendship
with Vic, Phil, and with Henry Carlson, his love for
Gail, and then Phil's death—his emotions in each instance had come so strongly, as if he'd held them in
for his whole life until they'd finally burst forth of
their own accord. He hardly recognized himself anymore. But it did hurt, to go to the trouble to get into
the Pacific and then be snatched out of it.

* * *

At a pier inside the harbor, Tom went down the gangway and walked swiftly, trying to avoid looking back. But he couldn't have missed seeing the cluster of junior officers and enlisted men on the main deck forward, staring down at him as he moved along.

Their sun-tanned faces held something he could not read. Had he been able to, he would have seen regret at seeing him go, understanding, and even admiration. Every man in the task force, including McCoy, had burned over the last-minute recall from Wake, but they had all followed orders in unquestioning military fashion. Each man aboard, however, had silently applauded Tom's reaction. It was the reaction of a man outraged at leaving his comrades to the unending assault of overwhelming enemy forces—a reaction that spoke for each man aboard the *San Francisco*.

Tom's anger was echoed by the American public, weary of yet another defeat. But out of the disheartening atmosphere had emerged their first hero, a staunch marine Major Devereux who had fought overwhelming odds from the eighth of December to the twenty-third, a man who had disappeared behind the bleak curtain of imprisonment.

Though American war production was gaining only slowly, Vice Admiral William Halsey did not wait. He persuaded Admiral Nimitz to undertake a raid into the Marshalls and Gilbert Islands, a fast hit-and-run to keep the Japanese guessing as to the location of the American carriers. The *Saratoga* took a torpedo that sent her back to base but Halsey decided to follow through with the raid with what he had. So, late in

January, he divided his task force into three groups: his own, with the *Enterprise* and three destroyers, to strike Wotje, Maloelap and Kwajalein; Rear Admiral Raymond Spruance in the heavy cruiser *Northampton* and heavy cruiser *Salt Lake City* and one destroyer to bombard Wotje; and Captain Thomas M. Shock in *Cheste*r with two destroyers to bombard Maloelap. Rear Admiral Fletcher in *Yorktown* had the strongest force to work on the three southern islands; light cruiser *St. Louis,* heavy cruisers *Louisville* and four destroyers.

Due to clouds and being sighted by enemy planes, only the groups under Spruance and Halsey achieved any success, but the attack was nonetheless a psychological shock to the Japanese. For the first time they saw a real possibility of the Marshalls and Gilberts being taken over by the United States, which would pose a threat to their own ambitions in Australia. Spruance's shore bombardments created chaos on Wotje, and Halsey's attack on Kwajalein Island sank a transport, a net tender and subchaser. Another subchaser and gunboat were badly damaged, as were light cruiser *Katori,* an ammunition ship and a submarine tender. Eighteen planes were destroyed and ninety men killed, including Rear Admiral Yashiro, the area commander. ....

This strike into the Marshalls and Gilberts could not be termed a major victory, but it gave the nation another hero who had dared to take what was left of the Pacific fleet and strike deep into Japanese-held territory.

Back at Pearl Harbor, Halsey walked about, looking at everything. Good progress was being made. Follow-up, that's what they needed. Something to follow the raid just completed. But where?

His aide, walking at his side, said, "Sir, we have some ships transferred from the Atlantic. Those battle-wagons are old, but there's no better gunners than they have. And that *Yorktown* looks good. But what can we do with them?"

A stiff-lipped Halsey shook his head. "I don't know, yet, young man. I don't know."

11

TOM DEWITT was at length back in the States, having shoved from his mind the unpleasantness of the McCoy affair. No one returns from sea duty without a physical check-up, so Tom had to endure this routine procedure after arriving at the navy yard in Mare Island, California. And there was the irritating delay of paperwork before his pay accounts, health record and officer's qualification jacket were given to him. His annoyance mounted when he could not get an eastbound plane. His feelings were not helped when he obtained a lower berth on a transcontinental passenger train. The train, creeping like a caterpillar from San Francisco, was crowded with other servicemen of all branches, most of them ordered to stations or posts in the central, midwest or eastern sections, and with civilian passengers with harassed expressions, having been put through a questioning by transportation authorities whose principal demand was—"Are you certain, sir, that this trip you're making is really necessary? Space on all modes of transportation is critical."

Tommy felt pity for these people. Civilians were being hit in rapid succession by gas rationing, automobile tire shortages, and the issuing of tickets that told each family how much sugar or meat they could have. Who knew how much further curtailment might be levied? But they seemed to be enduring it. He'd have to take a lesson from them. He would endure this nuisance. It was only temporary. And soon he'd be able to see Gail, Henry Carlson, Isobel and Vic. . . .

He found Gail first. As he closed the door to her apartment, he was met by a wave of warm fury, warm arms around his neck, her body swinging so that her feet left the floor.

"Tommy—Tommy! Oh, God, it's been so long!"

He turned her around, embraced the compact body in the clinging blue knit dress. "Gail, my brown-eyed, moon-faced girl! God a'mighty, you look sweet!" He kept kissing her cheeks, tasting the salt of her tears running into the corners of his mouth.

"Tell you what," he teased, "first thing we'll do is to go to the brightest, prettiest restaurant you ever saw."

"Are you kiddin'?" she cried out. "You've lost your mind!"

It happened so quickly, the trail of clothing on the floor all the way into the bedroom, and they were two young beasts in the bed. He looked at her as she reached for him, and said, "I'm glad it's not the wrong time, the wrong—"

"Time of the month? Well, you can see it's not. Don't you have any of those pretty rubbers with those patriotic red and blue ribs?"

He kept kissing her throat and cheeks. "You're raving mad. They don't provide those where I've been. You'll have to settle for bare skin. I'm the reckless kind. Besides, didn't you get the ring I left? Tomorrow we'll go get the mate to it."

"One thing at a time! You've been working too hard —your face is thin. But you'll be relaxed very soon . . ."

He laughed. How long had it been since he had really laughed? The full, natural laugh, not the nervous laughter that came with duty at sea. His feeling for her filled him completely.

"Oh, heaven, heaven, heaven . . ." she murmured, her body clinging to his after they were both spent. "Thank you, darling. It was wonderful!"

He fairly gaped. "You're thanking me?"

"Yes, yes, yes." She brought her head up from his chest and looked into his eyes, "Now you're looking sober again."

"Maybe it's because you're unbelievable. Besides, you know I have a poker face. And my job right now doesn't exactly evoke any mirth, either."

She smiled. "I feel smug, being intimate with such an unusual guy." She sat up. "I'm going to be hungry very soon. But first, let's wash up."

"You first, fair lady." He nodded toward the bathroom. "Anyplace special you want to eat?"

"Sure is," she called from the bathroom. "Arthur's

Steak House. It's near the waterfront. Looks like an unpainted wooden shack, but the food's terrific."

Arthur's was exactly as Gail had described it. While they dined, Tom told her, "I've just a few days' leave, so I guess we'll have to cram a lot in. First thing we do tomorrow is pick up your ring. And I think I'll have Vic Hadley as best man. How will you feel, walking under those crossed sabers?"

For a moment Gail stopped chewing and her eyes were suddenly moist. "Finish your steak."

They returned to her apartment, drowsy and full of Arthur's steak. There were twin beds and both felt so listless they took separate beds. Deep in the night Tom awoke. Gail was up on one elbow, looking at him from the other bed.

"Husband-to-be, would you like some more?"

He was up at once. "What a foolish question!"

Once again, that all-embracing warmth. Her face drew into an earnest gravity as desire gripped her hard. Then the torrent of delight overwhelmed them both, the fulfillment of their love and the promise of their future sweeping them ever higher.

The next day went just as they had wished. She protested at the size of the diamonds in the wedding ring he selected. But he grinned happily. "We don't have to be frugal about something like this, Gail. The point is, do you want it?"

"Oh, Tommy, it's gorgeous! It takes my breath! Of course I want it!"

The marriage was simple. Muscular Vic Hadley stood straight and important. There were a few navy and marine officers and their wives or girls as guests. One thing was present over all—the shadow in the minds of the wedding's participants. All of them had lost friends or relatives in the war, and all of them had known Phil Armstrong. The *West Virginia*, on which Phil had died, could at least be brought back to life to fight the war. Grim-faced yard workmen were working like mad to get the *Wee Vee* underway to Bremerton, where she would emerge a new and tougher battlewagon.

There was no honeymoon. Isobel had temporarily moved in with a friend to give them complete privacy, and so Tom and Gail spent their time enjoying each other's company and planning their future. Gail seemed full of surprises. One day she grabbed at him and announced, "We're moving, Tommy! A nice little apartment, furnished, across the river in Woodbury, a good change, away from the big city. We'll even have Henry Carlson as a neighbor. It's a little Pennsylvania-Dutch town with enormous trees, farther from the Yard, but—"

"I know, restful." He laughed. "What else?"

"Vic's arranged a party for tomorrow, at the Warwick. He and Isobel will be there, and Henry Carlson, too. Good things come in chunks, Tommy! You're back, Halsey took a whack at the Japs, and Henry's going to be with us! Let's go take a quick look at our apartment, and then we'll have lunch at a nice little spot I've found."

Gail, vivacious, doing half her talking with her hands as they drove to Woodbury, was enchanted by the little town, the red brick apartment building, the red and brown leaves. It was furnished with old-fashioned appointments, but it was well-kept, spick and span.

They ate heartily at the little restaurant Gail had found, and Tom found himself swept up in Gail's enthusiasm for their new home.

"You see," he said as they left the restaurant, "we're in walking distance of home. Don't have to drive . . . Say, did you ever see a doctor about your eyes while I was gone?"

She faltered. "Well, no—but I will, I really will. It's just the headlights of cars at night that bother me. It's okay otherwise."

"Well, no more promises. Next week you'll see an opthamologist."

"Don't nag, Tommy." She was silent for a time, but then perked up. "When we get home, I'll give you a proper congratulation for your promotion," she said, giving him a suggestive look.

"Can't wait—except long enough to stop by this little house in the next block. Let's drop in on Henry and see what peace and tranquility have done for him."

Henry Carlson met them with a soft smile, embraced Gail and kissed her, then put both arms around his former son-in-law. "God, Tom, you look great!" He stepped back, thrust his hands into the pockets of his jacket. "I don't have to ask—it's rough out there, isn't it?"

"It is indeed, and the Pacific must be a mess, despite Halsey's raid. We need another follow-up, for the American people. My guess is that we'll have to install a holding action until we can get more of everything out there. And Halsey is the man to do it."

"What we have to do, we will do," said Carlson, moving over to his small bar. "Just a small nipper, to celebrate seeing my son again." He poured each of them bourbon-on-the-rocks.

With Gail holding onto his arms, a warmth crept into Tom as he watched Henry Carlson. There was a peace, a contentment in the way Henry moved, that convinced Tom that here was a happy man. When this nightmare war was over, Tom promised himself that he and Gail would do their damndest to create the same contentment for themselves.

12

Few men had the instinct for following up a successful blow, even a minor one as in the Marshalls, as did President Franklin Roosevelt. This second blow was a strike deep into Japan, to accomplish two objectives at once: to further boost the morale of the American people, and to deliver a shock to the Japanese people. His fertile mind began to formulate a plan, verifying what an enthusiastic Democrat had proclaimed in 1932: "Now we have a sailor in the White House!" His reference was to the fact that during Republican administrations no new ships had been built for the navy. Since that time, however, the shipyards had been busy laying the keels of every category of warship, and they were now busier than ever.

In January, 1942, Roosevelt sent Winston Churchill a dispatch, advising that he had a nice surprise up his sleeve, thereby giving some encouragement to the "old bulldog" who had suffered so much for Britain.

Roosevelt got down to brass tacks. He conferred with Admiral King and his operations officer, Captain Francis Low, and they obtained the consent of the commanding general of the army air force, "Hap" Arnold. They began to work out the details.

"You're going to bomb Tokyo?" Arnold rubbed his chin. "From where?"

"From carriers," said King. "My selections are *Hornet*, under Captain Marc Mitscher, and *Enterprise*, Captain George Murray. This is Task Force 16, under command of Vice Admiral William Halsey. We've picked the medium bomber, B-25, sixteen of them. We're reasonably certain they can be launched from the *Hornet*."

"You can't recover them," Arnold warned.

"True. It will be a one-way trip, hazardous, with the planes landing on Chinese airfields. Every man will be a volunteer. Admiral King advises that the *Hornet* can take only what the deck will hold, because of the B-25's wingspread. The *Hornet*'s own planes must go below. The planes of the *Enterprise* will cover the B-25s."

"Some stunt," said Arnold. "We launch the army's planes, then head for home at flank speed. But the navy's bombers don't have the range. Have you considered, sir, that the B-25s cannot drop many bombs? They'll have to carry so much gasoline to reach China."

"The amount of damage we do is secondary, General. The important factor is that the Japanese will know that Tokyo can be hit by our bombers. More important, they won't know where the planes came from."

So exuberant army flyers began to practice on Florida's Eglin Field, which was marked off in the dimensions of the *Hornet*'s flight deck.

April 1, 1942: the planes were ready. They were flown across the country to San Francisco and loaded on the deck of the *Hornet*. On the next day the *Hornet* steamed out from San Francisco for her rendezvous with *Enterprise* and their top secret mission. *Hornet*'s escort was the heavy cruiser *Vincennes* and light cruiser *Nashville*, along with four destroyers and the fleet oiler *Cimarron*.

After eleven days *Hornet* met *Enterprise*, with her escort of two heavy cruisers, *Northampton* and four destroyers, at a point between Kamchatka and Pearl Harbor.

There was satisfaction on Halsey's face as he ordered, "Flank speed."

The army pilots were making their final check-ups on their planes. The medium bombers were loaded to the limit; four 500-pound bombs each and a full load of 1100 gallons of gasoline. With this weight Halsey and the army flyers figured they would have to get within 400 miles of their objective before the B-25s could take off.

A Japanese picket boat spoiled what would have been a safer flight for the army bombers. It spotted the incoming force, and although it was quickly sunk by the light cruiser *Nashville*, Halsey had lost the advantage of surprise. Nonetheless, he chose to continue with the plan, launching the planes from about 650 miles out.

As the ships in this striking force lunged ahead, a veteran quartermaster on the *Enterprise*'s island remarked to the admiral: "If I may say, sir, we're in it now. This is the point of no return."

Halsey calmly looked the man over, from his gleaming shoes to the seamed face and spotless hat, and smiled. "You might say so—Sims, isn't it?—and you're damned right! And don't forget to say a word for those army air force men. Because after they're all launched, we're setting a southeasterly course for Pearl and getting out of here. They'll be on their own then—not an enviable position. I only wish we didn't have most of our carriers in the Atlantic."

"Aye, sir, it'll be up to them to lower the boom on those Nips."

"They'll do their job, Sims. This flight they're making is one of the most courageous deeds in all military history."

Lieutenant Colonel "Jimmy" Doolittle, who had volunteered and trained the men for what they hoped would be a surprise for the Japanese, was on the first B-25 launched. Yells of encouragement from the carriers' sailors accompanied each succeeding plane.

The targets selected were power stations, chemical plants, truck and tank factories. Unfortunately, some bombs hit the wrong buildings, for which three of the flyers captured were executed.

But Halsey's task force, ploughing back through the seas toward Pearl Harbor, had accomplished its purpose. Of eighty men involved in this risky flight, he was to learn that seventy-one had survived. He was aware that relatively little damage had been done. But every Japanese now knew his capitol could be hit by American bombers—and from where?

There were two humorous aspects to this undertaking. Halsey's order, coming from the island, had never been made before, nor would it again:

"Army pilots—man your planes!"

And President Roosevelt, when quizzed by the press about the source of the B-25 bombers, smilingly said:

"They came from Shangri-la."

Minister of War General Tojo was a literate and well-read man, and knew the American president was rubbing it in through his reference to author James Hilton's *Lost Horizon*. He found no humor in the remark, nor in contemplating the turnabout effected by the attack.

His aides had a B-25 bomber drawn to scale, as well as drawings of the U.S. carriers *Enterprise* and *Hornet*. While Shimada and Yamamoto calculated distances and fuel capacities, Tojo turned a darkened face up to them.

"These are most accurate, sir," said one of Tojo's aides. "We have checked them many times."

Admiral Nomura, who had never been overly enthusiastic about taking on the United States, muttered, "You can look at these cut-outs and see there is no way you can get those bombers on a carrier! What, then? Were they land-based? Did they fly all the way from Midway?"

Tojo scowled. "Well, they didn't come from the sea.

That much is obvious. It's clear our intelligence is faulty."

"From what I've seen and heard, the people do not seem frightened about it," offered Shimada.

"No!" Tojo's big palm struck the table. "Some of the people are alarmed, but the impact hasn't fully struck all of them." He leered at Shimada. "Suppose you lived in San Francisco and knew that Japanese planes could bomb you at will even though it seemed impossible? Oh, don't speak of Pearl Harbor. The Americans are alert now."

"What is our next step?" Yammoto asked.

"We proceed with our plan to control the Coral Sea, take Port Moresby. That strutting peacock Douglas MacArthur is building up too much air power in Australia. We cannot permit that to continue."

Inside the planning office at Philadelphia Navy Yard, Vic Hadley dialed the number of Isobel Strawn. He heard her throaty voice on the line and a few goose pimples stood up on his arms.

"Vic, why haven't you called me sooner?"

"I've been busy since our ship got into this damned yard, and that's the truth."

"No girl in every port?"

"Very funny. We've been on convoy duty, getting across all manner of stuff to the British and I've seen nothing but salt water. My eyeballs are sticking out, looking for periscopes. Those krauts are cagey, running in wolf packs to pull the destroyers away from the freighters and transports."

"Are you doing any good?"

"You know I can't tell you much. The destroyers use ash cans, and a sub will come to the surface when it's crippled, and our eight-inch guns send him below in a flash. Roughest part—Tom may have told you this—is that when we get close to Britain, those German land-based aircraft really get after us. We still need more of everything. Makes you feel bad to see a cargo ship go down with a load of brand new tanks."

"Should you be saying all these things on the phone?"

"Isobel, I haven't said a word the Germans don't already know, just as we know there's something big building up in the Pacific. The Nips have something up their sleeves. Say, are you going to be alone for a while?"

"Good grief, I was wondering when you were going to get around to it."

"If you're alone, I'll be right over. I have something special for you."

"Then get over here. I can hardly wait . . ."

She opened the door for him, he put a large box on the sofa, grabbed her, kissing her soft mouth, inhaling the smell of that jet-black hair. "God, you look sweet!"

For a moment she pulled away from him, a puzzled look in her eyes. There was something gentle in the way he held her, not like before. Oh, God, no, she thought, don't let it happen!

"Well, let's see what's in the box," she said.

He picked it up, carried it into the bedroom, lifted the lid. The contents were covered with tissue. "First, let me have a naked Isobel. I mean it. It has **every-thing** to do with it."

For a moment she stared at him. She was wearing a white blouse, beige skirt and scuffs. "Just for being so weird about this box and seeing me in the raw, you'll put a little extra on the dresser before you leave," she joked.

Vic was momentarily disconcerted by the remark, for he had never brought up the subject of her other men. Did she simply assume that he knew? He shrugged the thought away and tried to match her joking mood. "No, I won't. Now, stand by the bed. After I put each one down, look at it. And when you come to the one you like best, lie on it." Lord, that alabaster body and glistening black hair . . .

"A negligee!"

White, lacy, transparent. He looked at her. She shook her head. "Not quite."

Others followed, one on top of another; foamy pink, turquoise, and then—

"That's the one!"

It was horizon blue. She put it on. It was edged with delicate lace and was nearly transparent, so that the dark nipples and black triangle could be seen. There was one left in the box, a black beauty, but this one was her choice. She regarded herself in the full-length mirror. She put the others back in the box, then took off the blue one and lay on the bed.

"My present, Vic?"

"It is. Now let me have mine. I'm burning alive."

During the course of their lovemaking, he found a difference in her, could sense it somehow in the undulations of her body, could see it in her puzzled eyes. When they had spent themselves, she got up, put on her new negligee and studied him seriously.

"Vic, there's something I have to tell you, and you listen carefully to all of it."

Still in the bed, with sweat running down his chest, he nodded. "Go ahead. I won't say one word til you're finished."

She lit a cigarette and began what he instinctively felt was a confession. "I was very young when I realized that I had good looks and a figure to match. Many girls, before they mature, adopt an attitude of 'if you've got it, flaunt it.' I was no different. I would squirm into a swim suit plastered as tight as wallpaper against my skin, so tight in front that anybody male with eyes could see that bulging bush down there. I enjoyed watching the boys on the beach and around the swimming pools gape, and watching the older men rake me over, from head to foot. I knew damn well what was in their minds. Young girls like that are such damned stinkers, Vic. If one of the men said something in the way of an invitation, I was ready to call the police. I guess I was the worst exhibitionist of them all.

"Well, as I said, most girls grow out of that, but with me—well, I grew out of being a tease, but I also grew worse. I wanted the touch of boys. If I kissed and embraced with a boy, I enjoyed hearing him breathing hard, and I would move my thigh around so that it rubbed him between his legs. And one night, at a school party, I sneaked down the hill toward a river with a boy I had been teasing a long time. This time he couldn't restrain himself, and for the first time ever I found myself responding. He put a light raincoat on the ground, I found myself pulling at his clothes, and he tore my pants to pieces. At first, it hurt . . . and then it was greater than I had ever imagined it could be. He didn't make me; I made him. I tore him up. And from that time, I was . . . I guess I was enslaved.

"It's not a nice story, Vic, and I feel dirty telling you about it. I met a young man two years out of college and I really cared for him. I felt that I was actually in love with him. We were married, and from a sex standpoint, he must have thought he had hit the jackpot. But I wasn't a good sex companion. I was an animal. I was after him all the time and soon he realized he had married a girl who was definitely different from any other girl he had known.

"I don't think he had had much sexual experience for a man his age. The poor guy was competent at his job, worked hard, but had no rest when he came home. I was dragging him into the bedroom before he'd had a chance to eat. And if we went out to dinner, I wanted him as soon as we got home. We divorced— probably the first divorce ever for over-consummation of a marriage. I wouldn't take any alimony, you can be sure of that. As a matter of fact, I never wanted to see him again, as though it was his fault. I was ashamed, that was the truth of it. I'm not a very religious person, Vic, but many times I've prayed for him because he'd been unfortunate enough to marry a girl who had something wrong with her."

Vic knew enough about her so that he should not have been surprised by the story, and yet he felt chilled clear through now that all his suspicions had been confirmed. He silently began to get dressed and he put the things back into the box. When she tried to give him back the blue one, he smilingly refused. "You wanted it, kid, and you look good in it. . . . I don't know whether you feel worse or better, after telling me all this. One thing about it, Isobel. You've been frank with me. I'll be the same with you. You know you're sick, and I guess in a way you're asking if I can do anything about it. I don't know; it sure as hell doesn't look encouraging to me."

She stared at him, wide-eyed, frightened that this might be the end. "Vic, Gail doesn't know about this— at least, I haven't told her. But she's sharp, Vic, and I'm sure of one thing. If she has guessed it, she knows I'm no tramp. Couldn't you feel the difference this time?"

The plea in her voice stopped him at the door. She was right. And somehow he couldn't just walk out on her. He needed her too much. "I'll take you to dinner tomorrow night."

Melting at her relieved look, he strode back across the room to take her in his arms. She wondered how his big hard arms could be so full of warmth and tenderness.

"Please don't, Vic. You'll just make it worse."

"I have a problem, too, Isobel," he whispered. "You know what it is. That's why you told me so much. I'm in love with you."

"I know. Please go now, Vic, before I start blubbering."

He tried to give her a jovial smile as he closed the door.

Where would he go now? He recalled an article he had once read in a medical journal. "A morbid and uncontrollable sexual desire, which we identify as nymphomania . . ." He was in love with a nymphomaniac.

Vic went at once in search of Tom DeWitt. The administration building, the *Byrne*, the waterfront office, personnel office. No luck.

He walked around the Yard. The hospital? He recalled that Tom knew a good doctor there. What in hell was his name? At that very moment, he heard someone approaching him from the rear, and he turned to face none other than Tom's doctor friend.

"Vic Hadley! You made it again—was it bad?"

"Better than last time." He recalled the man's name now. Dr. John Elliott.

"Can we talk somewhere, doctor? I know you and Tom are good friends and I have a real problem. I don't want to talk to him about it yet, not until I talk to you."

Dr. Elliott frowned. "It *must* be serious, if you don't want to tell Tom."

"It is. There's no better man. Can we go to your office?"

In Elliott's office, the doctor's face grew serious. "All right. What's wrong with you?"

Vic took in a deep breath, then took the plunge. "It's my girl. She's the one who's sick. She's a nymphomaniac. And I'm in love with her."

The doctor's face went blank. "She poured it all out to you?"

"Yes, yes!" Vic jumped up and stalked about the

room. "Medically, this thing may not be within your province—but I thought maybe you'd know someone who could help her."

Elliott looked ruefully at his desk, pushing things around. "Boy, when you cut your throat, you do a job! Nymphos! Look, Vic, give me a little time. If I can find someone, it'll be quite a session. The three of us— me, your girl, and you, because you'll have to help talk her into seeing the specialist. Okay?"

"Can you help, doctor?"

Dr. Elliott was long in answering him. "I don't know. I don't know."

13

TOM AND GAIL saw a lot of Henry Carlson after their move to Woodbury, and many of their evenings together were spent discussing the war in the Pacific, the strategies of either side, the personalities of the leading figures in that arena of the war. Aside from Tom's desire to see action in the Pacific again—and, in a sense, to avenge Phil's death—he was as keen a student of history as was Henry Carlson. And because of Carlson's connections in high places in both the government and the military, their conversation sometimes went beyond what was known to the general public.

They talked late into the night, discussing each new development, watching in trepidation as Ad-

miral Yamamoto pushed southward to complete his
basic strategy. He was to take Tulagi and Port Moresby, New Guinea, and make the Coral Sea a Japanese
sea. Next was Midway Atoll and western Aleutians,
and finally he would bring out the U.S. Pacific fleet
for complete extermination. He was an imaginative
man who was moving with all speed. There were a
number of unknown quantities in the strategy, but
this only spurred him on. He knew that Admiral King
was shifting ships of every category into the Pacific,
and he decided not to wait until Japanese intelligence
could provide him with the disposition of these forces.
Of one thing he was certain. General MacArthur was
building air power as one of the preparations for his
return to the Philippines. MacArthur had already been
able to assemble some 400 B-17s and medium bombers. He was, however, a long way from having enough
ground troops for the effort.

Yamamoto did not need much in the way of striking
force and support force for the eleven transports,
which included both a naval landing force and regular
army troops. He had the *Shokaku* and *Zuikaku*, the
light carrier *Shoho*, four heavy cruisers, three light
cruisers, thirteen destroyers, a minelayer and a seaplane tender. They occupied Florida Island and Tulagi,
at the cost of the destroyer *Kikuzuki*, several landing
craft, five seaplanes damaged and a minelayer badly
damaged.

The *Yorktown* and *Lexington*, under Admiral Fletcher, moved to intercept the movement of Japanese
forces, which the U.S. rightly construed as a prelude
to occupation of Midway. With a destroyer screen, they

were accompanied by Admiral Kinkaid's support of *Minneapolis, New Orleans, Portland, Chester* and *Astoria,* all heavy cruisers, and seven destroyers and two fleet oilers.

Word reached Admiral Nimitz of Yamamoto's southward movement toward Port Moresby. In addition to the peril to Australia, he deduced that with the Solomons already in Japanese hands, Japanese possession of the New Hebrides, the Fijis and Midway would mean that a long line would separate Australia and the United States. He could not be certain that this thrust was a prelude to an occupation of Midway, but he proposed to stop anything that would interfere with MacArthur's build-up. What followed was the Battle of the Coral Sea.

The American forces attacked at flank speed. The Japanese light carrier *Shoho* was mistaken for the larger carriers which Admiral Fletcher wanted. *Shoho* took a severe beating from the *Yorktown* and *Lexington* dive bombers. And the torpedo-planes, under cover of the smoke, could hardly miss; they zoomed in and got at least ten torpedoes into the dying *Shoho.* She went down fast, with great loss of life. Three of the slow American torpedo-bombers were lost, and nine of *Shoho*'s fighters. The Japanese took their turn at mistaken identity. An American oiler and a destroyer were sunk when planes from the Jap carriers thought the big oiler was a carrier.

In the meantime, the large fleet of Japanese carriers and the *Lex* and the *York* were searching for each other. Contact was made, all carriers were damaged, and planes were lost on both sides. *York* scored first, making two 1,000-pound bomb hits on the *Shokaku* that wrecked her flight deck and started a booming gasoline fire that took this carrier out of the fracas. The *Zuikaku* was damaged largely by near misses which caused enough damage to put her out of action; *Zuikaku*, also as a result of near misses, had to retreat to Truk for repairs.

The price of this victory was the *Lex*. She bore the brunt of Japanese air and torpedo attack. For a while it seemed that Captain Sherman's skillful ship handling and the determined fighting of his crew would somehow manage to save the big carrier, even though the attacks were coming from all directions. The crew did succeed in putting out the fires, and the *Lex* began to retire from the scene. But accumulated gases from ruptured gas pipes filled several compartments and there was a sudden terrific explosion, followed by succeeding explosions through other compartments. Saving the ship was beyond the best efforts of the damage control parties. Finally, when fire main pressure died, Admiral Fitch ordered Captain Ted Sherman to abandon ship. It came hard to the carrier's crew to give her to the deep. They had fought the enemy and the damage to the ship to the point of exhaustion. Admiral Fitch and Captain Sherman were filled with pride for their personnel.

The cruisers and destroyers did a masterful job of rescue. Twenty-six officers and 190 men were lost of a stubborn crew of 3000. The *Yorktown* also suffered damage, but not fatal. She was able to make Pearl Harbor.

The Americans had not been let off easily in this

victory. Besides losing the *Lexington*, they lost the destroyer *Sims*, a fleet oiler and sixty-six planes, and the death toll was 543 officers and men.

But the Japanese, in addition to having their thrust toward Port Moresby scuttled, had lost the light carriere *Shoho*, the destroyer *Kikizuki* and four landing craft. The *Shokaku*, *Zuikaku* and *Okinashima* were crippled, eighty planes had been lost, and the death toll was 900 officers and men. Perhaps the most disheartening factors to Yamamoto were the diversion of two fleet carriers required to capture Wake atoll, and his failure to destroy what was left of the U.S. Pacific fleet. Add to this his ignorance of just how much that fleet had been reinforced from the Atlantic, and he was the picture of a sorely perplexed man.

However, from the inception of Yamamoto's and General Tojo's master plan, the destruction of the U.S. Pacific fleet remained the principal objective, and Yamamoto still had at hand a very powerful force to accomplish the job; including the striking force, main body and occupation force—there were ten battleships, four carriers, eighteen cruisers, fifty-seven destroyers, three seaplane tenders and fleet oilers. To meet and defend Midway, Nimitz had three carriers, eight cruisers, sixteen destroyers and two fleet oilers—a disparity of forces that would have driven Nimitz to despair had he not had one advantage. Nimitz knew that Yamamoto was coming and that his own forces, thin as they were, could be shifted to keep the Japanese guessing.

The battle for Midway was the turning of the tide.

Yamamoto lost the sea-and-air battle for a few simple reasons. Admiral Chester Nimitz had better intelligence reports, he was more flexible of mind, and Yamamoto failed to use the superior forces at his disposal at the proper time.

The report Yamamoto was taking to the emperor was more than alarming. The U.S. Pacific fleet, greatly outnumbered, had lost one carrier, one destroyer, 150 planes and 307 officers and men. But the Japanese had lost four carriers, a cruiser, 253 planes and 3500 officers and men, the best in the Imperial Navy.

If this was not good news for the emperor, it merited a full celebration for Tom, Gail and Henry Carlson. They broke out a bottle of champagne and celebrated into the wee hours, their mood reflecting the renewed hope all across America.

14

A FTER what he judged to be a reasonable interval for Dr. John Elliott to do some investigating, Vic Hadley sought out the doctor at the hospital. The nurse outside Elliott's office nodded, and he knocked and went in. Vic closed the door and leaned against it. His palms were moist as the two men stared at each other.

"Are you going to give me bad news, doctor?"

Elliott smiled and shook his head. "You're in luck. Someone's just been recommended to me. Name's Dr. Celia Jordan, at the Philadelphia Naval Hospital. I've never met her but I've read a great deal about her. She's something of a specialist—a pioneer, even—in this field."

At Vic's jubilant expression, the doctor held up his hands in warning. "Wait a minute. Finding Dr. Jordan isn't the same as finding a cure. This is a tough case. You must understand that most psychiatrists deal with patients who are in some sort of depression. Treatment consists of drugs plus getting to the underlying cause of their trouble, usually emotional, sense of guilt, whatever. Yet you say that your friend doesn't appear to be aware of any psychological reasons for her problem. That makes it harder, because either she's resisting the source of her problem or there's some other cause altogether, which may take a while to uncover. It could be a long haul, Vic."

"What's Jordan's batting average, doctor?"

"If my memory's good, and I think it is, of thirty-five girls who went to her for help with this particular problem, Dr. Jordan effected complete cures in twenty-one cases. Some of them resulted in good marriages."

Hope surged through Vic. "If Dr. Jordan will consent to interview and diagnose and treat Isobel, then you've pitched the hot potato right back in my hands."

"You mean getting the girl to see Dr. Jordan?"

"Yes. It'll take some persuasion. She's a sensitive person. Damn, I may have plenty of trouble." He went to the door, wiping the sweat from his brow. "It's been good to see you, doctor. Thanks a million."

John Elliott stared hard at Vic Hadley. "Vic—you really love this girl, don't you?"

"You're damned right I do," Vic said softly. "If you had me in the X-ray room, you'd see my guts all knotted up."

As he knocked on Isobel's apartment door, he decided that he would approach the subject slowly, carefully. She came to him swiftly, put her arms around his neck, pressed that soft kiss to his mouth, the kiss that had become so different in so short a time.

"Tonight it's your choice as to where we eat," he said. "But don't make it too expensive, my black-haired beauty. Remember, I'm starving on a j.g.'s pay."

She laughed, went to the closet, took out a leather jacket, slapped a knit cap on her head. "I know a place. We can walk, save gas. You remember that ice cream parlor on Chestnut Street? Well, next to it there's a small door, and a flight of steps. You'd think it was a hole in the wall, but downstairs it opens into a sizeable place, bigger than the Cathay House in Frisco."

As she talked animatedly over dinner, he silently reviewed his conversation with Dr. Elliott. Celia. Surely a lady physician would make things easier. He was certain of one thing. The solution here would be tougher than any combat. It was one thing to fight the enemy, quite another to fight something you couldn't see.

They took a leisurely walk after dinner, then returned to Isobel's apartment. As he hesitated at the door, she opened it and pulled him inside.

"My new roommate, Dorothy, won't be back tonight, Vic. Come in for a while."

They lay on the sofa, full and drowsy from the Chinese food. He figured he must have napped, for he was awakened by feeling her unbuttoning his shirt.

"Follow me, my little friend." She led him toward the bedroom. She already had on her new negligee, and she methodically undressed him, smiling all the while. Then she threw off her delicate gown, pulled him on her and coiled her warm soft body around him.

Until recently, when he took her, he had a wildcat in his arms; now it was different—a soft, writhing tigress, the new lovemaking that had convinced him their relation had changed. Isobel Strawn was no call girl, and if he could help it, she'd be no nympho, either. He cared to his very depth, and he was going to put up one helluva fight to save her. He was frightened at the urgency of this thing, knowing that at any time he might get orders to be underway, back to sea duty.

The next day, Vic vowed, was the worst in his naval career. There was some welding to be done on the starboard side of the ship on the forecastle, and he sent his shipfitter and two strikers to the wrong place. He could not get Isobel out of his mind; he still hadn't told her about Dr. Celia Jordan, hadn't even hinted at the subject. His men returned to him, saying there was nothing wrong where he had sent them. He shook his head, put his hand on his first class shipfitter, Lewandowski.

"Ski, I botched it up. Come with me." He showed the husky young man the job he had meant for them to do. "Get your strikers, finish the job, and report to Mister Bloch. I've got to shove off."

"Aye, sir, we'll get it done in jig time."

That evening Vic lost no time in getting to Isobel's apartment. Dorothy was there, and he practically pushed her out. "Please leave. Don't come back for half an hour. An hour would be better—and I apologize."

Isobel, in a form-fitting pale green dress, rose from the sofa, her wide eyes uncomprehending.

He went straight to the point, and the hell with slow and careful. "This is intimate, and also very important, for me as much as for you." Almost ruthlessly he told her what he had done, while her face grew colorless. Then she flew at him in a fury of flailing arms, tears flooding from her eyes. She slapped his face, sharp, stinging blows that quickly brought out big red blotches on his face. He stood and took the blows.

"Oh, you unfeeling bastard!" she cried. "To tell everything about me to strangers!"

"Not strangers, Isobel! People who want to help you. It's because I *do* care that I've done it! God, I love you—I want you more than anything in the world—but you know I can't have you as long as you're sick." He tried to cough the dryness from his throat. "You were married before, and you know that one man can't be enough for you. Tell me that you don't want to marry me, and you'll never see me again."

She stepped back, and for the first time saw the tears coursing down his cheeks.

"Isobel . . . do you think it was *easy* for me to tell Dr. Elliott, or to tell you?"

She staggered back and crumpled into a chair. "Vic . . . I can't do it . . . I can't go through with it." Then suddenly she flew into his arms. "I'm sorry I hit you . . ."

He held her head close against his shoulder. "You *can* do it, Isobel. My doctor and I will take you to this specialist's office . . . then you and Celia Jordan will beat this thing together."

"Celia?"

"A lady doctor, sweet girl, and she's cured twenty-one of thirty-five girls who went to her for help. Several of them had attempted suicide, because they weren't tramps and couldn't bear the way they were living. Dr. Jordan cured them permanently." He held her face in his hands. "I'll go now. Relax, sleep. Dr. Elliott is taking care of setting up an appointment for you with Dr. Jordan. I'll call him tomorrow to find out when and where."

"I can't face her, Vic!"

"It's been a shock, I know. But I'd like to see you in her hands before I leave. All of the alterations on our ship have been finished. It might be day after tomorrow or next week. You know how this war is."

"It's a dirty business," she agreed, wiping the tears from her eyes. "Somebody mentions the name of a ship, and a German put a torpedo into it. There must be spies everywhere in this yard."

"Everywhere in this country. And our spies are all over Europe. The trick is in knowing when and where the enemy moves. Courage is a relative thing, Isobel. I talked to a navy fighter pilot several days after he came back from the Pacific. He said nobody will ever get him to volunteer for submarine service, that he just didn't have the guts for it. And he had shot down twenty-two Jap planes in the Pacific. See?"

"What you're saying is there are different kinds of courage."

"Right. And I know a World War I vet, a grey-haired captain of infantry who got a citation for wiping out German machine gun nests in the Argonne. But he has to take a couple of stiff drinks before he can go into the dentist's office."

A smile finally broke through, though she kept clinging to him tightly. "Vic, don't make me laugh when I'm so miserable. I know you're right, and I love your friend, Dr. Elliott, for caring. But when you march me in to see that specialist, it isn't going to be easy."

"No, certainly not, but no victory ever is. Look at Midway. Piece by piece we're getting information about the battle. The jigsaw puzzle is almost complete now, and we have a major victory, fashioned by an admiral who had only a handful of ships and couldn't be outguessed or outmaneuvered by a vastly superior force."

She sighed deeply. "And when you boys with your small carriers, destroyers and cruisers escort a big convoy of cargo ships and transports, you have something to fight with. But how about us cowards? How do we fight something we can't see?"

He kissed her and put her away from him. "You *can* see *me*. Just have a little faith that I'm there to help you fight this battle. Now take it easy. Elliott says that Dr. Jordan is a modest person, that she'll tell you she can't guarantee a thing. But her record speaks for itself."

* * *

Vic met Tom DeWitt walking toward the main gate, threw up his hand and ran toward him.

"Hey, Tom, got to talk to you. I know you're off duty and going home to Gail, but this is important."

Tom stopped. "It must be. You seem bursting with something. Can we go to some quiet place to talk about it?"

Ever since Vic had started dating Isobel, Tom hadn't said another word about his suspicions. Tom's and Gail's demeanor and the occasional glances that passed between them when the two couples had been together had rightly led Vic to believe that they hoped things would go well between him and Isobel, that Isobel would somehow straighten out.

Now, with the future looking brighter, Vic had the courage to talk to Tom about it. He'd hated holding anything back from Tom, but for a long time it had been too touchy a subject for him to even admit to himself. Now, over drinks in a small bar, it all came pouring out.

Tom, aware of the long silence between them on this subject, was relieved it was in the open, and even more relieved to see the tension drained from his friend's face. He was apprehensive over the outcome of Isobel's treatment—but hell, Vic and Isobel were trying, weren't they? That, and the fact that they loved each other, might do wonders.

"Hey, look," Tom said as they got up to leave. "Let's all four of us do it up tonight. We'll get Gail and Isobel and take 'em both to Old Bookbinder's—wine and everything."

It was a good evening. They launched into a discussion of the war, gossiped about various characters they had seen in Point Affirm—and, most important, made up itineraries of cross-country sightseeing tours after the war ended and they could fill their tanks without the gas rationing tickets.

"Now, hear this," declared Tom. "I'm going to see my creaking old Plymouth repaired and drive all the way from Philly to California, just to see all the big redwood trees."

A good evening. Because Vic and Tom had determined to make it so.

The next morning Isobel met Celia Jordan, M.D., at the Philadelphia Naval Hospital. A spritely woman of perhaps forty-five rose from her desk and stepped briskly around to greet Isobel, Vic, and Dr. Elliott. Isobel felt the firm handshake of a woman with bronze hair and an abundance of red freckles over her nose and on both cheeks. There was warmth and friendliness in her open expression.

Dr. Jordan was smiling and pointing an authoritative hand at the door. "We'll get these males out of here and then get acquainted, Isobel."

As they started for the door, Dr. Elliott turned and asked, "When may Mr. Hadley see Miss Strawn again?"

"When I notify you."

"I may be at sea," Vic protested.

"All the better," said a smiling Dr. Jordan. "Isobel and I will have more time together before you return."

Left with this doctor who opened her desk, took out a clipboard and attached a sheaf of different forms to it, Isobel felt a coldness in her stomach and a sudden desire to run from the office. Without looking up from her desk, Celia Jordan said, "Scared?"

"Scared? My legs can't get me out of this chair."

Celia Jordan's gaze was direct now, and she smiled faintly. "Give me the straight pitch, Isobel. Do you really want this man, Vic Hadley?"

Isobel's mouth went dry. "More than anything on this earth."

"Then we'll try to lick this thing together. I can't promise a miracle. But as the boys at Franklin Field say, 'I'll sure give it the old college try.' So, step into this room and strip for your physical."

"My physical?"

"Sure. In here. You see, we have to begin at the beginning. Your Vic has to find out what he faces out there on that ocean before he can fight it. Right?"

Isobel nodded.

"Good. So we have to eliminate every physical possibility first." Dr. Jordan smiled reassuringly as she picked up the first of her instruments.

15

FOR A WHILE after the convoy crept into the sea
to continue the Battle of the Atlantic, Tom De-
Witt, Lieutenant (j.g.) USNR, could think of
nothing but his best friend and his seemingly insurmountable dilemma. But then his attention shifted
to the tankers and cargo ships all about him, the mass
of supply ships screened by destroyers, corvettes and
small flattops and constantly harassed by German
wolf packs who managed to get through and send to
the bottom ships so desperately needed by the Allies.
The destroyers and corvettes themselves were not immune to attack. Tide conditions and rough seas made
the sonarmen's work very difficult.

As he toiled with a strip-cypher, Tom suddenly heard from above:

"Torpedo wake to port!"

The torpedo struck the *Byrne* on the port side just forward of the torpedo tubes. Planes had been aloft, but Tom knew the sea was rough and periscopes and torpedo wakes were hard to see. It was too late when Tom thought of the navy admonition to hit the deck. A man can suffer broken legs from the tremendous jolt from below, and Tom felt a sickening wrench in his leg as he was catapulted from his feet to lay sprawled on the floor.

"All hands, abandon ship!" came the captain's voice. The *Byrne*'s list was to port and was increasing so fast that she was capsizing. As Tom limped outside, dozens of lines went over the side and sailors raced along the deck, cutting loose life rafts so that the men could slide into the sea beside the mortally stricken ship.

Down came the lines with sailors sliding on them. As Tom stepped forward to follow, he felt a stab of pain in his left ankle. "Hell, I've sure cracked something," he muttered. He had already tossed his leaded code books into the sea. Now he had to get a good start into the sea and swim like hell or be sucked under with the capsizing ship.

Another destroyer was after the sub, swinging in a circle, dropping ash cans packed with hundreds of pounds of TNT, but maneuvering carefully to prevent killing her own men in the water. Another explosion roared and flame and black smoke shot skyward—a cargo ship had been hit by the German sub. Tom swam faster, looking back briefly to see his remaining shipmates hitting the water and swimming like mad to get away from the ship. He heard the whoop-whoop-whoop of destroyers after other subs, with the last whoop rising higher in pitch, almost like a whistle.

Tom DeWitt was a strong swimmer and he struck out for the open sea, but the oil was closing in on him, clinging to his arms, getting thicker and thicker as he swung one arm, then the other, and tried to kick his legs. His arms were lead and he felt as if he was thrashing in a bowl of thick mush. Something was pulling his legs, and he was rolled over on his back. He was being pulled down and under. He couldn't see through the damned oil—damn it to hell, this wasn't the way to go. Something more heroic, with torpedoes launched from the main deck and the 5-inch .38s cracking and smashing and the chug-chug of the 40 millimeter guns.

"Over here, sailor!" he heard from behind him. Suddenly there were hands grasping the back of his blouse, jerking at his neck, those heaven-sent strong hands pulling him free from that damned oil!

His legs thrashed as he strove to kick off his shoes to help the bluejacket get him aboard a life raft. It seemed far in the distance that another cargo ship blew up. Other destroyers were skimming about, rolling off more ash cans.

"The *Radford* got one!" yelled one of the sailors on the life raft.

A tremendous geyser rose in the air; then there was debris, and later, a large oil slick appearing on the surface. Tom was beginning to form a sincere admiration for the British who had endured these nightmares while he had stood watches in a navy yard. His whole body felt like one huge chunk of solidified oil. Something terrible was in his mouth, then some of it got down his throat. He was sick and he heaved until he thought he would bring up his shoesoles. A dozen hands were wiping the mess from him. Then, mercifully, came oblivion. His last vision was of Gail's perky, round face.

"Good morning, Lieutenant."

Tom stirred at the sound. He knew, without knowing why, that he was accustomed to this crisp British female voice. As he opened his eyes and looked about, he began to remember. He had gone through the worst of it, the cleansing, the glaring lights, the needle, oblivion again, the awakening to a huge, noisy room filled with doctors and nurses scurrying about, here and there a man in American or British uniform, a French or Polish accent . . . and finally a small, quiet room occupied only by himself and another patient, a man he recalled saying, "God, I'm tired!" through the intermittent sedation. And there had been a male voice, saying, "You'll rest here a bit before we send you back, Yank." That was a doctor, he judged.

"How are you feeling today, Lieutenant?"

He tried to smile at the young British nurse, but his face felt stiff. "I can't move very well. Come around here and tell me who you are." She complied, and he saw a slim girl with sandy hair, hazel eyes and freckles beneath the small cap perched on her head. His head swam again, and he muttered, "Gail . . ."

"Your girl?"

"My wife . . . in Philadelphia." He rolled his eyes to his right, saw the tube in his arm.

"We're feeding you intravenously. Your stomach won't take food at the moment."

"You didn't mention your name."

"Louise Conti. You're pretty well sedated. Have a broken ankle, you know. And a bad lump up here," she said, pointing to his head.

"What about my friend over there? Is he going to be okay?"

"He is. Lieutenant Tip Hawkins, this is our American friend, Tom DeWitt. Tomorrow I'm going to take him for a walk, and if he does all right we'll send him back to America."

"Greetings, Tip." He tried to sit up in bed, then was distracted by movement at the door. There stood a girl of proud carriage, a brunette with wide black brows, green eyes and full, sensuous mouth. She wore a dark blue dress with a gold pendant. She stared a moment at the man she had obviously surprised.

"Roxane!" Hawkins cried out.

Her decorum broke, and she ran and dropped to her knees to embrace him. "You did—you did come back to me!" The green eyes filled as he held her tightly. "Oh, Tip, thank God! How awful it must be out there, not knowing—not knowing—"

He brought his thumbs up to wipe away the tears from her cheeks, then caught her face in his hands. "No," he said thickly, "I had you with me all the time. Never a moment did I lose the picture of you in my head—not once."

Tom turned his head away, feeling like an intruder. A spasm of pain hit him in the ankle, traveled all the way to his knee.

"I'll get you a shot for the pain," the nurse said. "You'll hurt a while, you know, even after you're dismissed—which should be soon."

"And on cold rainy days," he murmured.

The nurse returned with the needle, and the point went in deftly. "How does it feel now, Yank?"

"Ah—peace that passeth understanding," replied Tom as the easing flow blotted out the pain. "Tell you what—all of you—you don't call me Yank and I won't call you Limey. Okay?"

"Okay," they responded, laughing.

"When you begin to walk better, we'll take you on a tour," Hawkins said, "if you can see anything beyond the sandbags and rubble."

"Trafalger Square," responded a peaceful DeWitt. "'England expects every man to do his duty.'"

The raven-haired Roxane laughed. "That's the first thing you'd think of, you navy men, with all the things to see in London."

Tom didn't hear the last part of her sentence. In his pleasant glow he saw Gail again, striding along with those neat ankles, those legs that were so trim and strong. He heard her rapid throaty speech, remembered her unsinkable optimism and the sincere concern she felt for other people—and for him. God, how he missed her. . . .

He came out of his half-sleep and heard again the buzzing of conversation, the stamping of feet outside in the hall. Tom sharpened his ears to a loud British voice from the room next to his. "Do you know the big mistake old Hitler's made? He's running all over Europe, getting himself spread out so thin, he'll not be able to keep stoppers in all the holes he's made. And if Rommel can't hang on to Africa, he may find himself in a bad way for oil! Tanks and trucks can't run on air."

Tom prayed the man was right. If it was true, then the war on the European front might ease off some and perhaps it would be easier to get a transfer to the Pacific to help mop up things over there. And then, with the war over, he could go home, to Gail and the life they would share. He smiled at the thought and drifted off to sleep.

Tom DeWitt did not get in all the sightseeing he had intended. Like so many other wounded American servicemen, he was hustled into a van with no advance notice and driven down to the waterfront.

The ships, half a dozen of them, ploughed, pitched and rolled westward through thrashing seas and weather that could only be described as capricious. Packed below in three-tier sleeping quarters were men who, despite their various degrees of discomfort, were thinking of home and were oblivious to all but one thought—each hour brought them fourteen knots closer to those they loved.

The rolling of the ship did Tom's stomach little good, and between the pain his ankle caused him and the lingering dizziness from his light concussion, it was a period of semi-exhaustion. This had been Tom's first experience of war—the attack of the German wolf pack on the convoy, the exploding ships, the hammering and cracking of gunfire, the screams of men meeting their end in burning oil—and his own near escape from death. The scene kept replaying in his head, and not even his efforts to turn his thoughts to Gail could completely erase the memory. When the weather permitted, he limped outside on his crutches to escape the fevered mutterings of the other wounded soldiers.

Tom stared at the angry Atlantic, letting random thoughts drift through his mind. It seemed so incredible to him, this war which had changed the lives of even the most ordinary people, throwing them into the mainstream of history. He, too, had been lifted from what would have been a routine and perhaps mediocre life and thrown into the midst of this turmoil, and he was feeling more and more frustration at not having a say in how he would play out his role.

The Pacific. That's where Phil Armstrong had gone—and died—and that's where I will go, to see the finish of this thing. No frustration next time, like turning back and leaving those marines on Wake Island. A personal vendetta? Damned right—for the marines, but mostly for Phil. Phil, a big gentle bear of a man who would raise his fist only when his people were injured or threatened. The Pacific. That's where the navy will make its stand. A tremendous ocean, an unbelievable fight for control. . . .

Tom was able to walk without crutches, hurrying as best he could, by the time he walked down the main street of Woodbury, N.J. There was the red brick apartment, the big trees standing back in the yard, the small ones along the sidewalks. And there— She came out of the apartment, shading her eyes against the sun, that half-girl, half-woman. The sight of her made something jump in his stomach.

"Gail! Gail!" He broke into a lopsided run.

She turned toward him, a frozen figure for a moment. Then she started running toward him and several passers-by were witness to a head-on collision.

"Tommy, Tommy, Tommy!" He felt her surprising strength as she held to him, kissing him on both cheeks.

"I'd almost forgotten how it felt to hold you," he said.

"You're lying, and you know it," she laughed. "Come into our little sanctuary. I remember when one of us suggested that we have dinner first, just after you came in. Do you recall which of us it was?"

"I don't at all. But going out to dinner is *not* going to come first now."

As they lay in bed, quietly content in the aftermath of their lovemaking, Gail said, "He has been waiting to see you."

"Who has?"

"Henry Carlson, you nit! Jenkins too, for that matter. I promised them both I'd bring you right over when you got back. If you're up to it, why don't we get cleaned up and go see them?"

Jenkins opened the door. He stepped back, his thin face blank.

"Hello, gentleman's gentleman," Tom said, grinning at him.

Jenkins, British as beef, forgot his etiquette and grabbed Tom by both elbows. "Mister Tom, sir! How good to see you, sir!"

They found Henry Carlson standing by his cherished red leather chair, pipe in hand. "Well! Home is the sailor!"

Tom yielded to impulse and in an instant had both arms around Carlson. Then he held him at arm's length, returning Carlson's broad, warm smile.

"Tom, son, sit down, you and Gail, and I'll get the bourbon."

Tom looked around. So familiar were the shelves of books and curios from all over the world that he felt at home. Perhaps some of these things should have brought Irene to mind, but he felt nothing. Absolutely nothing, other than his affection for a man who had become like a father to him.

Jenkins was invited to join the group and sat primly in a chair, listening with obvious pleasure. Tom noticed a pile of newspapers and magazines on the coffee table.

"Not reading any classics these days?"

"Perusing the American press for a while." Carlson scowled at his glass. "It seems to me there are three categories of reporters: those who form their conclusions from hearsay; those who write to give the public sensational stuff—remember how they expanded on Pearl Harbor, had Japanese troops landing on the west coast? And there are those few who try to get the truth to the public, even going to the extent of being war correspondents, by actually being where the hell is really going on."

"From what I understand, the hell is about to be spread around even further. I stopped at the navy yard before coming up here, and there's plenty of scuttlebutt about our launching an attack across the Alantic, probably somewhere along the African coast. The general idea up to this point has been a build-up in Britain, then a massive second front across the English Channel. But this is something different—this direct attack farther south. Navy men, from apprentice seamen to admirals, have suddenly been hearing scuttlebutt for days. I've learned that where there's so much of it, there's generally some truth in it."

"Roosevelt and Churchill opening a second front," Carlson murmured. "We're producing unbelievable amounts of equipment and training plenty of good manpower."

"And a damned good thing," Tom declared, "especially with the war in the Pacific still raging." He leaned toward Carlson. "Say, those admiral friends of yours—"

Carlson's eyebrows went up. "Not again Tom! Not after what you've just been through!"

"I'm on restricted duty for now," Tom conceded, "but plenty of men are wounded and go back to combat duty. They're experienced."

"I don't mind trying again, Tom. But let's wait and see what the medics say—then await your orders." Carlson smiled and shook his head. "I'm almost sorry you found out I had some influence with those men."

Tom laughed and turned to Gail to explain. "Some of these guys played on the same football team with Henry at the Academy."

Jenkins took a sip and blinked, eager to hear more.

Carlson nodded. "True. But my military career was cut short. I was injured at sea—my back—and subsequently retired on disability. My family had some money, got me started, and I've done rather well. I thought I wanted to stay in the navy, but . . . I've managed to see a lot and learned a lot even without the navy. And I've been lucky in picking up a son and daughter."

Gail knew he could only be referring to Tom and to her, and she went to her knees by Carlson's chair and kissed him on both cheeks. He flushed with pleasure, then looked up. "Well, Jenkins, get us another drink!"

"Yes, sir!" Jenkins had been mesmerized, but leaped to obey.

Carlson rubbed his chin. He hated to admit to himself that the seed had been planted. He sipped his drink, and thought—after all, it wouldn't hurt to go to Washington and have a word with Al.

He sat turning his glass, watching the amber glint in the light for a long time after his guests had gone.

Tom DeWitt resumed his duties in the military department at the Yard. Each day, except those nights when he had the duty, Gail was waiting at the main gate to drive him over to Woodbury. Except for his anxiety over the change in his status and whether or not he'd go back to active duty, he enjoyed the perfect life with Gail.

Henry Carlson, in the meantime, had the advantage as far as progress in obtaining information on the new Atlantic venture. He renewed his long-standing friendship with Rear Admiral Allen Brubaker, USN, and they relived the old days. Carlson tread carefully. Not once did he mention any specific event. The war was discussed in generalities. Carlson was mildly surprised that despite the endless defeats the U.S. had suffered in the Pacific, Brubaker's confidence in ultimate victory was unshaken.

Periodically, Tom was called to the treatment room of his orthopedic surgeon, who moved his fingers around the ankle, took a couple of x-rays and studied them.

"Don't find anything bad, doctor," Tom pleaded. When the doctor didn't answer, he asked, "Will I have a limp? Look, doctor, I'm serious! I've got to get back into action!"

The doctor glared up at him. "Mister DeWitt, I know what's on your mind, and how you feel. But a limp? At the moment, I don't know."

"Are you finished with me for today?"

The doctor shook his head. "You're afraid I'll turn in a report that will remove you from sea duty. I can only report what I find. It *will* be an honest report—that much I can guarantee."

16

WHILE the battle of the Atlantic was one of logistics, and its outcome was still in doubt, Tom and Henry Carlson continued to follow the events of the navy in the Pacific.

The American public was astonished on 7 August 1942, to learn that 19,500 U.S. marines had landed on Guadalcanal and Tulagi, two of the Solomon islands in the south Pacific. Guadalcanal was to dominate the Pacific war news for the next six months, involving vicious battles on land, in the air and on the sea. After every engagement there were the usual exaggerations and months passed before the pieces could be put together to get the complete picture.

Tom learned that this operation had been conceived

by Admiral Ernest King, who had been toying with the idea since February.

"Why in the hell are we taking the offensive down in the south Pacific, when the talk about the Atlantic attack is getting stronger every day?" he asked Henry Carlson.

Carlson smiled. "Australia. These are guesses, mind you, but perhaps King wants to strengthen the American-Australian line. He takes Guadalcanal, goes from there up to Rabaul, and then MacArthur can return to the Philippines. We have the New Hebrides as a base, also the Fijis. But it's important to strengthen our position. Whether or not the Japanese have figured out how they were shellacked at Midway, despite having a hundred ships to our thirty, they know they still outnumber us. And they found out, as we did, how inferior our torpedo planes and torpedoes were."

"But that's changing fast; they don't know how fast. They haven't seen all those big battlewagons that can make thirty-five knots."

"Those are aces up our sleeve. Plus the U.S. marines. When the Japanese move in to dislodge those leathernecks, they're going to run into a buzzsaw."

With his fingers tracing lines on Pacific maps during every spare minute, Tom DeWitt began to develop a rather pessimistic view of the south Pacific venture. True, Guadalcanal might not be the spot the Japanese would have expected an American landing, but thus far they had shown themselves quick to react, although sometimes in the wrong direction. He did not believe Tojo had given up the idea of taking Port Moresby, for that was too close to where MacArthur was building up his forces. As far back as February, the principal area commanders were known. General Patch had the American division in the New Hebrides, the Free French had New Caledonia, and the southwest Pacific was under General MacArthur. Admiral Nimitz commanded the Pacific area, with Vice Admiral Robert Ghormley, commander of the south Pacific. The First Marine Division, commanded by Major General Alexander Vandegrift, USMC, went into the Solomons—and remained there despite vicious efforts of the Japanese to root them out.

Yamamoto felt that he held the greatest advantage, with his reinforcements in Rabaul and Truk much closer to the Solomons than were the American marines and army. Destruction of naval and army air power and ships and constant night bombing would eventually cause the resistance of the marines to collapse.

As the news, in bits and pieces, filtered back to the States, the Yard at Philadelphia showed more and more grim faces passing to and from the building ways, supply buildings, machine shops, power house, and waterfront facilities. Gloom, anger and shock hung over them all.

For the first real confirmation was the stunning news of the loss of the U.S. heavy cruisers *Vincennes*, *Astoria* and *Quincey*, with heavy damage done to the heavy cruiser *Chicago*, and the loss of the Australian heavy cruiser HMAS *Canberra*. Unbelievable! How could it have happened?

Details came later. All the public knew initially was that a clever Japanese admiral named Mikawa had led a fast-moving force of heavy and light cruisers and destroyers down from Rabaul, past Bougainville, between Choiseul and Santa Isabel. They had struck at tiny Savo Island, just off the northern tip of Guadalcanal, and sent to the bottom the major part of the transport covering force. Mikawa had moved with speed, using searchlights, torpedoes and gunfire, making a comedy of errors of the unexpected attack. Except that it was no comedy from the American point of view; it was, indeed, a wretched showing on the part of the U.S. task force. What was left of the U.S. transports and other ships had to withdraw, leaving the marines in the position of having to hang on until reinforcements could arrive. The path used by Mikawa—and later by other Japanese officers—became known as The Slot. The Japanese ships coming down with troops and supplies were labelled as the "Tokyo Express."

There were, to be true, spots of good news, and the American press gave them the largest spread possible, trying to report accurate figures. Henderson Field became a strategic spot. Whoever held it could control the narrow seas around it with air power. The Japanese ground troops therefore threw every effort into wrestling Henderson Field from Vandegrift's weary but stubborn leathernecks. In an area of the Tenaru River, a Japanese patrol of thirty-four men were ambushed and thirty-one men wiped out. In open hand-to-hand combat, seventy-five marines were wounded, thirty-five killed; but fighting with bayonets and gun butts, they killed close to 1000 Japanese. So much for Japan's highly touted jungle fighting ability.

Again, in an infantry engagement on Edson's Ridge

—later known as Bloody Ridge—forty marines died, and 103 were wounded. But the Japanese lost 1700 men, destroying the myth of the invincibility of the Japanese soldier. The American marines had proven themselves beyond a doubt.

Tom lay on the sofa, his head in Gail's lap. "You know," he mused, "if I don't get my orders soon, I'll be nuttier than a fruitcake."

Her round eyes looked down at him. "You've got one. The doctor released you, approving you for sea duty." She straightened. "Are you preferring a mermaid to me? After all, how could a mermaid—"

"No, no, no! But so much is happening, and I'm just sitting here in a navy yard sifting through rumors. The latest dope is that we've lost the carrier *Wasp* in the south Pacific. Who in the hell keeps maneuvering those carriers around in those restricted waters?"

"You've certainly asked an expert," she said dryly.

"Then we get good news—we've won the battle of Cape Esperance—but the figures are distorted. U.S.S. *Boise*, will be back here from that engagement any day now, and the factory whistles will be screaming and the crowds shouting, and the papers writing about the 'one-ship task force' and how she sent four cruisers and four destroyers to the bottom. The *Boise* men would not mention any other American ships involved, but I did pick up one leak. With the heavy cruiser *Salt Lake City* they actually sank only two destroyers and heavily damaged three cruisers. They won the battle, all right, but the figures given out by the press are all screwed up."

"So? The press is trying to keep up morale. You know we need it."

"True enough. But something crazy is going on. Even with some new ships in the Pacific there'll be only a handful of ships out there, and the marines are hanging on by the skin of their teeth. And yet there's all this talk about an attack across the Atlantic. And they're speaking in terms of hundreds of ships. Roosevelt, King, Marshall and Churchill must have given priority to the European theatre—which means that's probably where I'll be assigned."

Tom was unaware of it, but he had made a good guess, although it was circumstances rather than any unanimous agreement among the Allied leaders that had given Europe the military priority. His feelings were no different from those of anyone who wore the navy blue and gold. The European plan was still in the making, whereas the Pacific struggle had been going on since 7 December, 1941. Like any navy man, officer or enlisted, he still burned over the Pacific fleet's poor showing.

It seemed that good news and bad came in showers. Tom received two highly significant morsels of news in one day. One of his friends in the communication department showed him two dispatches, one of a general nature, the other pertaining to him personally.

Tom ran two blocks in the wrong direction to find his old Plymouth, and then drove through three red lights in his rush to get home. He raced into his apartment, grabbed a surprised Gail and swung her in a circle.

"Guess what? Guess what?"

"I can't imagine what—but I think you've split my dress."

"Number one, Ghormley's been relieved as Comsoupac, and has been replaced by Vice Admiral Bill Halsey! And number two, I've got orders, in the communication department of the *Cleveland*, a light cruiser, first of her class. She's right here in this yard. In the morning I'm going down to have a look at her."

"Sit down," said Gail, "and let me digest the meaning of all this. I've heard of Halsey. He conducted the raid on some Jap-held islands right after the attack on Pearl Harbor. What did he do at Midway?"

Tom grinned. "Sat at Pearl Harbor and scratched. Had some peculiar skin rash and missed the big show. Sure was mad. But the main thing is—he's a real leader. His men are important to him, they know it, and they'll follow him to hell. If Nimitz can get him some of those new ships, the Japs are going to have a bad time down in those Solomons."

They went out for dinner to celebrate, but Tom found his head filled with a hundred ideas about the Atlantic venture. Surely his ship would be involved. He knew that no one aboard the ships would know the details until the last couple of days, but how could his ship *not* be involved? The Allies were punching both ways at the same time out of necessity. The Japanese were hanging over Australia like a cloud and the German army had its boots on the edge of the English Channel. To top it off, Rommel had driven all too close to Algiers. This was it. His orders *had* to have something to do with the new Atlantic offensive.

Winston Churchill must have done some soul-searching when the Americans declared that their ships and troops were ready to hit the Atlantic side. What of the British? Could he spare what was needed? He must provide British ships to escort some 23,000 British troops to embark from Britain and capture Algiers. He would have the aid of 10,000 additional American troops. American troops, about 40,000 men, would embark in Britain and hit Oran. It was one of the greatest seaborne ventures ever, something like 800 ships all told. For the Americans to cross 4000 miles of ocean and land troops on foreign land was a stupendous task, especially when they were employing so many inexperienced men, new sailors who had never been to sea, and green troops who had never been under fire.

Tom's attention was now centered on his new assignment. After presenting his orders, he made a thorough inspection of this new light cruiser. It was a big ship; slightly more than 600 feet overall and 14,000 tons loaded for sea. Her complement was sixty-five officers and 1200 enlisted men. Plenty of fire-power, with estimated speed of thirty-three knots, but Tom had read enough figures on ships to know that her real speed was in excess of this.

He knew Vic was still somewhere in the Atlantic. The *Augusta* had not been in his convoy, nor had she come into the Yard at Philadelphia, so he had not seen Vic. He'd have to talk to Gail to see if she'd heard anything about Isobel and that Dr. Celia Jordan, he reminded himself. In the meantime that odd little

instinct that the *Cleveland* was going to rendezvous
with other ships persisted to the point where he was
now reasonably certain that all this scuttlebutt had a
solid foundation. The only questions were—where,
and with whom? He had not long to wait. October's
falling leaves were decorating the city when the
cruiser's P.A. system gave the word:

"Prepare to get underway! Go to your stations, all
the special sea details!"

From the quarterdeck came the quartermaster's
voice: "The officer of the deck is shifting his watch
to the bridge. All departments will make their reports
for readiness for getting underway to the officer of
the deck on the bridge."

Just before taking the bridge, the officer of the deck,
one Lieutenant j.g. Barry Terence, instructed the boatswain mate of the watch; "See that all boats are
aboard, and see our stern clear."

The routine progressed smoothly. Terence stalked
about the bridge, enjoying the babble of voices as
each man carried out his function.

"Test whistle and siren! Test bridge instruments!"

The quartermaster was moving down his check-off
list. "Fourth Division ready for getting underway."

"Engineering officer requests permission to turn
over main engines."

"Get the mush out of your mouth in radar plot—
can't hear a damned thing over these headphones!"

Terence glowed inside. Action. Action. Things were
going on. Two of the destroyers were already standing out in the stream. Busy feet were running around
one of the escort carriers. Soon they would be inhaling

good fresh air. The Delaware River was not the most aromatic water he had ever sniffed.

Then, with all reports in, the executive officer, Commander McCall, came up the ladder.

"The ship is in all respects ready for sea, Commander," Barry reported.

"Very well. I have the deck."

So a portion of the big movement was underway: three escort carriers, the U.S.S. *Ranger*, her antiaircraft cover, the *Cleveland* and nine destroyers. In the wardroom, consensus of opinion was that this was only a part of a much larger force going into action, though no one knew for certain yet. The executive officer, at the head of the table, remarked, "This force must be coming from different places, because if it is as big an operation as scuttlebutt has it, so many ships leaving one port at the same time would be a dead giveaway. We'll rendezvous at a predetermined place and then descend like a horde of locusts upon the enemy."

"Didn't know you were so lucid and poetic," commented Kibble, the engineering officer. "You sound like Pearl Buck's *Good Earth*. Tell me; no one appears to know our ultimate destination. If you knew, would you confide in one or two cherished friends—like me?"

The exec slanted a smile at him. "No. You wouldn't have anything to think about."

They broke into the open sea and the ships began to rise and fall in that graceful motion so satisfying to the seafarer. Tom DeWitt stood on the forecastle with

Barry Terence, watching the big *Ranger* ploughing her majestic way through the endless blue.

"Dakar," said Tom.

"I don't think so. I agree that it's going to be Africa, after we stop and pick up more ships. The Azores?"

"Too close. These guys must have it figured so that we won't be seen until two or three days before we hit the beach."

From the P.A. system came the booming voice of the boatswain mate of the watch:

"On deck, section three, condition three—*relieve the watch!*"

"That's me," muttered Terence, moving forward. He was one of those who stood bridge watch underway. "I wonder who in the hell started that tradition of relieving the man on watch fifteen minutes early?"

Tom stared at the sea. Any day now other groups of ships would show and the anticipation would sharpen.

Five hundred miles east of North Carolina, they found the first part of the answer. Bermuda. An isolated speck of land, twenty-one square miles, a British Crown Colony since 1684. The navy vessels began to drop their anchors in Great Sound, well beyond the harbor of Hamilton, the capitol. The view was one of green hills, red-roofed houses and brilliant flowers. Because of the shallow approaches of the piers, navy men going on liberty had to go in sixty-foot motor launches, winding through rippling beautiful turquoise water, so clear the jagged white coral could be seen below.

Tom DeWitt remained aboard the ship, his watch

on duty. Barry Terence, however, was at liberty and had the time to look, to absorb, to wander at his leisure, once he reached the pier that paralleled Front Street. He looked from left to right, his whole being relaxed. Hamilton. It was like a painting. Hadn't he heard someone aboard say it was only one hundred and fifty acres? Once you stood on Front Street, it didn't seem that small. To Barry it seemed this delightful little town had stopped changing somewhere between the nineteenth and twentieth centuries and seemed quite content to remain as it was. There were dozens of people on bicycles and a near absence of automobiles, and the atmosphere seemed to be one of leisure and contentment.

Once he had his feet on shore, he began his slow stroll, delighting in the old-fashioned shops and stores, feeling reborn in the crisp October air fanning his cheeks. He had left Front Street and begun walking north on Queen Street, keeping an eye out for likely looking restaurants.

"Good morning, Yank." It was a British voice, cheery and bright. Barry had met many British on the convoys, but there was something distinctive about this one; perhaps a reflection of the way he himself felt on this sparkling day. He turned to see the speaker. He was a scarecrow of a man, burned leather-brown by the sun, wearing the kind of smile that evoked a smile in return. The man flapped a wrinkled hand at a stand of bicycles. "You can see more in less time for a fair fee."

Terence shook his head. "Glad to see your pretty little island, sir. But I prefer to see as much of it as I can walking. This war has made me hurry enough. I'd rather take my time." He gave the man the courtesy of a traditional U.S. Navy salute. "I may use one of your bikes later."

"Well, damn my fading eyes," said the other. He glanced sharply at the ships in Great Sound. "First Yank I've ever seen who wasn't in a hurry."

"Good day to you, sir."

Barry continued casually up the street, turned right on Church Street—and there, before the city hall, met the girl.

"Morning, Lieutenant."

He liked everything he saw; the smile, the red-bronze hair, the shapely tanned figure in white shorts, the smooth calves. She was on a bicycle, leaning against the curb. He watched her eyes scan him from head to foot. He snapped his salute.

"My name's Barry Terence. I'll be here a few days. Shall we make a deal?"

She laughed. "My name's Jennifer Townes. You approach things in a headlong dive. What do you mean by a deal?"

"This delightful place is completely new to me. Take me around to see things—everything in the limited time I'm here."

She gazed thoughtfully out where the ships' silhouettes stood sharp and clear against the blue sky. Then she fell quickly into the first of many American phrases she was to learn. "It's a deal."

The road climbed up among the little houses with the flower gardens all around them. Their mode of transportation was a highly polished black carriage drawn by a white horse with red trappings. Their driver, a dignified Bermudan black wearing a high silk hat, waving his whip now and then at some point of interest.

"Do you think he's ever been anywhere outside of Bermuda?" asked Terence.

"Probably not. He'll live out his life here."

Jennifer pointed out the sights and explained the history behind them, but Barry was silently paying more attention to her, to the way she looked and the sound of her voice, than to her guided tour. At last he said, "Look, I was supposed to have dinner at some good restaurant tonight with two officers from my ship. Would you like to make a foursome? I'm sure they'd enjoy it, and I'd like to have you along."

"A jolly good idea. Where shall we meet?"

They both laughed at her forthrightness. "Let's see," he said. "Wherever you work—about six o'clock. You do work?"

"Yes. You see that old fashioned building down beyond that church? That's the Cathedral of the Most Holy Trinity. And the store is Talbot's. That's where I work. I'll be there, awaiting with keen anticipation the opportunity to meet your friends."

"Great! I'll let them pick up the check."

She laughed. "Take us back," she instructed the driver. "I'll have to look around for something to wear."

It was his turn to laugh. "English or American, always looking for something to wear."

Jennifer looked radiant when they all met at Talbot's. "Three men, all to myself," she said as they walked toward the restaurant. The Ace of Clubs was a low building of stucco, half-hidden by clusters of what seemed to be palm ferns. They went inside, Terence, Jennifer, a young ensign named George Becker, and a chief warrant boatswain named Matone.

The restaurant's proprietor approached them from across the room of rattan furniture. He was a big man who could have passed for the distinguished actor, Charles Laughton. He gave his guests a short bow and smiled.

"My lady—gentlemen—I must begin with an apology. Our menu is limited, due to lack of personnel to work the gardens, and shipping to import foodstuffs. We can provide potatoes, long green beans and brandied soup. And we do promise a most palatable charcoal-broiled steak. If you will have a seat, I will place your order. And may I recommend our Jamaica Rum Collins? My attendants here are most competent bartenders. Satisfactory?"

The drinks were served and they talked. Terence felt the drink slap his stomach and descend to the bottoms of his feet. It tasted of different kinds of fruit juices, but somewhere in there lurked rum that was like a jolting punch. Terence saw the moisture come into Jennifer's eyes after her third sip.

"This stuff reminds me of a concoction in Singapore," Matone said, turning his glass around in his thick fingers. "It went down as innocent as lemonade, but when you tried to get out of your chair or away from the bar, you couldn't move."

In due time they were summoned into the dining room and the men vied to seat Jennifer at the table.

Red blossoms and palm fern were in abundance and shapely waitresses in pink dresses scurried about. They were black with dainty features and their British accent sounded odd to the men. The soup warmed the diners still further after their potent drinks, and the steaks were superlative. They departed from the Ace of Clubs completely satisfied.

"Good evening," said their host, "and do come back."

"You can be sure of it," replied Terence, wondering if he would get back to the boat docks upright or horizontal.

He did make it to the liberty pier. A launch picked up navy personnel and put them off at the various ships out in Great Sound. Terence got up the gangway, saluted the quarterdeck, then the officer of the deck.

"Permission to come aboard, sir."

"Permission granted—provided you can make it." It was Tom DeWitt, grinning from ear to ear.

For the men of the American task force, that trite old expression "time passed all too quickly" was quite appropriate for their stay in the clusters of islands that made up Bermuda. As they wandered among the flowered elegance, gazed at the old fort and the stately Princess Hotel, rode bicycles along narrow roads and loafed in lazy luxury, a few of these seagoing men tried to make mental maps of the place—no drawn maps could be sent home, anyway.

When Barry Terence took Jennifer to another restaurant, the Twenty-One Club, then to a small Chinese restaurant, Tom DeWitt remarked, "I'm not sure whether she's taken you over, or vice versa. What's she like? I know you introduced us, but you can't learn much in a few minutes."

"Like myself, middle class. Unlike myself, very nice. She enjoys a good laugh, she's well-informed and reads everything she can get her hands on, like all of these isolated people, and she has a great curiosity about the world outside. I've noticed a funny expression come over her face every time she sees another ship drop anchor in Great Sound. 'In from the world to touch here briefly, then gone, never to return,' her face seems to say."

"You make them seem like prisoners," said Tom.

"In a way, they are. Maybe a man can choke to death on tranquility."

After dinner that night, a little ferry took Barry and Jennifer across a small river and to her place in St. George's Parish. It was a small cottage hidden behind lush foliage, quiet, with only the light tinkling of a hidden stream to be heard.

They went inside. The room was dark, with only two lamps in the far corners. The night was cool as they stood by the sofa. She backed to him, put his hands upon her breasts, and he could feel her tremble as his hands cupped them and gently moved them up and down.

"The world spins in odd ways," he said. "Men are everywhere killing each other, men who might well be friends otherwise . . ."

"For what? An idea?"

"For us—survival. We had no choice. Other than wars, a woman will die only for a child."

"What other things does a man die for? A change in his way of living? A sense of duty?"

"Yes, I suppose."

She put her arm around his waist and they walked into the bedroom. She kissed him, and he returned it, full and moist.

He held her hands and said, "I can think of an example of what a man will die for." He pulled her close to him, and she did not resist. "Once there was a man who stole a loaf of bread. He had tried to find work but could not. He was sentenced to pull an oar in a galley. It was hard work, and poor food. But he was a hard man, and vowed to survive and make something of himself." They were lying on the bed, and she felt a slight movement of her blouse.

"He escaped and was befriended by a priest whose kindness he never forgot," his voice continued more softly. "He was a capable man and developed a huge business. He showed every consideration to his employees, so that they would have worked themselves to exhaustion if occasion demanded."

"Yes—?"

"There was a police officer who knew of his theft and escape, and doggedly searched for him, inquired about him. In the eyes of the law he still owed part of his sentence. In this sense, the officer was a dedicated man. At the same time, he learned of the good this man was doing everywhere, of how he had helped to save many from starvation. So tenacious was this officer, he finally had his quarry in a position where he could arrest him and send him back to the galley. What a hell this officer must have suffered! Ultimately, he threw himself into the river, rather than commit an injustice. For his life was to render justice—which meant more than payment for a loaf of bread."

"Yes. Mr. Terence—you have me naked!"

"Why, yes, I believe I have," he said gently, letting his hands caress the length of her body.

"And you are, too!" She reached forth, clinging to him eagerly, and he was upon her.

Later, as he started walking down the path in front of her house, she stood in a white dressing gown at the doorway and hissed at him softly, "Barry, you sneak-thief—that story was from *Les Miserables*!"

"Why, yes, I believe it was." He touched his cap. "I will see you again—soon, Jennifer."

17

B EFORE THE SHIPS had departed Great Sound, their
personnel had left various impressions, not all
of them necessarily fair and impartial. Some of
the local people had received the Americans with stiff
indifference. They resented the swarms of sailors who
drank too much and indulged in fisticuffs that brought
the civilian police and the shore patrol on the run,
forgetting that their own British tars were doing the
same thing in Charleston and Boston and Philadelphia.
Tom DeWitt was *Cleveland's* shore patrol officer one
day, and he was sympathetic to the shore patrol officer
housed in an office for the duration in Bermuda. The
bulky lieutenant-commander growled as half a dozen

Cleveland men were poured into an omnibus that would return them to their ship.

"I'm not including all of you fellows, mister, but I'll be damned glad when that CL five-five weighs anchor. Maybe they'll save some of that energy for the Krauts."

"They will, sir, they will," Tom said, thinking of some of the gunnery exercises the light cruiser had displayed in Chesapeake Bay when she had outdone two British cruisers.

Of course Tom had met many amiable citizens here, men who had travelled over much of the world and decided to live out their days in this spot. He had met the man who had tried to rent a bicycle to Barry Terence that first day, a fellow named Wellington Travers. In Tom's words Travers was "as British as you can get" and he told stories of Singapore, Burma, India and the Portuguese colony of Macao, boasted of being one of the few westerners who had entered the forbidden city of Peking, and on and on.

Tom didn't care whether even half the tales he told were true. He was a superb storyteller, and when the day came that Tom stood at the boat dock and everyone knew the following morning would find Great Sound empty of the American warships, he wrung Travers's hand hard.

"Take care of your little island, Travers. It's worth more than gold to any man who sets foot on it."

"Bless you for your kind words, DeWitt." As Tom stepped into the boat, he lifted a gnarled hand and shouted, "Good luck, Yank!"

"Eastward we go, even as Columbus stuck to his

westerly course," said Barry Terence, who stood at Tom's side taking a last look at the port.

"Aye," grinned Tom. "And one of these bright days, we'll come topside and see more damned ships than we've ever seen in one place."

Tom spoke more truly than he knew. These were ships that were part of the Western Task Force, the force that was due before many days to slam the enemy with gunfire, planes and troops. It was an experience that would be new to most of them, but there was not a man unwilling to seize the tasks that lay ahead.

The name of this operation was TORCH, and it had been relatively hastily assembled. Many units had never worked together and the largest battleship, the U.S.S. *Massachusetts*, was one of the newest, having just completed her shakedown cruise. Commanding the Western Naval Task Force was Vice Admiral Henry Hewitt, USN, whose task it was to land 35,000 troops and 250 tanks at Fedhala, Mehedia and Safi on the coast of Morocco, starting at 0400 8 November 1942. General George S. Patton, Jr., was in overall command of the army forces, and he was quoted as saying: "The enemy may know Admiral Hewitt and I are coming, they may know how inexperienced our seamen, flyers and soldiers are—but they don't know where or when we'll hit."

Because of Rommel's constant annoyance to the Allies in the African desert and the threat he posed to Algiers, Churchill now had to throw his Sunday punch. He threw one from the Atlantic. Under Commodore Thomas Troubridge, Royal Navy, about 39,000 troops embarked in the United Kingdom to take Oran. Another force under Rear Admiral Sir H.M. Burrough, Royal Navy, and made up of 23,000 British and 10,000 American troops, set sail from the United Kingdom to capture Algiers.

Fedhala, 8 November 1942. Admiral Hewitt's Task Force 34 had arrived. Standing off the coast were twelve transports and three cargo vessels, carrying 19,870 officers and men, with the naval personnel of this group numbering about 17,000 men.

The army troops, well-trained and equipped with the best arms available, were well aware of their inexperience, but except for whatever hints they might have picked up aboard the ships they were probably unaware that the navy personnel were just as green as they were.

The troops started loading into the landing boats, also known as Higgins boats, but the first landing went badly. The boats were easily wrecked in the rough surf and soldiers were tossed into water waist high, slowing their progress toward their objectives and giving the defenders more time to pick off the desperately scrambling men as they fought their way up the beaches.

The enemy artillery to be overcome was the Batterie du Port, three 100 millimeter coast defense guns, two fixed 75 millimeter guns and four formidable 138.6 millimeter coast defense guns in sunken emplacements. These armaments made landings even more difficult, and two ships with excellent gunners were sent to neutralize them. The light cruiser *Brooklyn* was joined by the husky *Augusta*. In silencing the shore batteries and clearing the way for the soaked infantry, *Brooklyn* shot up about sixty percent of her ammunition, and the *Cleveland* was ordered to replace her. Up to this point, the *Cleveland* had been the watchdog for the carrier *Ranger* against air attack, and had taken her share of risks from submarines.

Aboard the *Cleveland*, Tom DeWitt heard a bluejacket with headphones sing out in a dry voice, "Torpedo wake to port!" Every man on the bridge saw the white streak coming through the water at the *Cleveland*. The captain was on the bridge, too, refusing to take his battle station in the conning tower, which offered six inches of solid steel protection but very poor visibility through the narrow slots.

"Flank speed!" he ordered.

The ship fairly jumped ahead. Had she maintained her position on her original course, the torpedo would have struck her on the port side, central station, below the waterline. "Left full rudder!" was the next order.

The helmsman, his eyes wide at the onrushing torpedo wake, fairly stood on the wheel, spinning it to port.

Tom DeWitt could feel the beads of sweat pop out on his forehead as he heard the call, "Hit the deck!"

Every man in that compartment was flat on his belly, sweating it out, feeling the ship respond, ever so slowly. But the *Cleveland* was a fast ship; she swung until the torpedo was running parallel to her and ran itself out and disappeared. It struck no ship, because no ship was astern of her. It hit no rock or part of the coast. It simply disappeared. And twelve hundred men could breathe easily again.

"Resume your stations," said the assistant damage control officer at central station. Central station was practically a duplicate of the bridge, complete with all instruments in the event the bridge was demolished by a hit. The same thought was running through the mind of every man down there. The captain and the officer of the deck had done some excellent maneuvering, but no man in central station could understand how that torpedo had missed. For days the same thought was in the mind of each. Where did it go?

Now came the destroyers, the *Corry* and the *Hobson*, rolling off their depth charges astern of the fast-moving cruiser to hit the submarine. And they scored. A tremendous geyser rose in the air, then there was the debris and finally the oil slick and wreckage.

The operations at Fedhala were proceeding well. Later in the war, the Western Task Force's performance would have brought smiles to the faces of the more experienced men in the enormous fleets in the Pacific; but this initial effort was doing a creditable job and learning by its mistakes. Like the army and the naval personnel, the navy pilots had been trained in the States and had known no combat, but what they lacked in experience they made up in enthusiasm.

"Look at 'em go!" said Tom to one of his compatriots in communications. "They're tearing in there like a bunch of Red Barons!"

"Agreed," said the other. "But I'm still wondering

about that damned torpedo. If and when we get back to the States and go into drydock, I hope we don't see a German torpedo hanging underneath the port side of our hull."

By 1700 hours resistance in this area had ceased; 7,750 officers and men were ashore and three cargo vessels had been unloaded. Admiral Hewitt had hoped to have had more men on the beach by this time, but he knew inexperience was the key word and the youngsters who had rendezvoused in mid-Atlantic were men now. He wasn't concerned about Patton to the south. Casablanca, some fifteen miles from Fedhala, was the chief obstacle; any sorties from the French warships would bring his own firepower into play.

The next and principal point of attack was Casablanca, for this was where the French were most strongly fortified—and here they would fight. With France being governed by Vichy, one could be certain that it was national pride rather than loyalty to the Germans that spurred the French to their repeated efforts to hold Casablanca. Rear Admiral R. C. "Ike" Giffen had the responsibility of holding the French ships at bay while the transports disgorged their troops in the Casablanca area. If the French sortied, as Admiral Giffen expected they would, it was the responsibility of *Massachusetts* to obliterate "El Hank," a casemate whose gunners had displayed great tenacity, as well as the battleship *Jean Bart* and the destroyers. This was the only way that the landing American troops could be provided air-sea protection.

The French ships came out and when they sortied

a genuine slugfest ensued. They were destroyer leaders *Frondeur* and *Albatross* and destroyers *Milan*, *Frougeuex*, *Brestois* and *Boulonnais*. They were intercepted by *Augusta* and *Brooklyn*. The French depended on speed and torpedoes to take care of the heavier ships, but they were hit by bombs from the *Ranger* and suffered hits from the U.S. destroyers *Wilkes*, *Swanson*, *Bristol* and *Boyle*. The *Milan* was driven onto the beach, *Boulonnais* disabled and sunk. The *Frougeuex* was also sunk. The *Massachusetts* and *Jean Bart* exchanged fire and after *Jean Bart* suffered five hits she was through.

The French had tried valiantly to defend Casablanca harbor but the results were very one-sided. If Admiral Hewitt appeared to display a bit of strut in his gait, he could be pardoned. He had taken his Western Task Force across the Atlantic without the loss of a single ship; indeed, so proficient had been the work of the destroyer screen that not a single one of the German wolf pack tailing the convoy had been able to get in position for a shot without putting itself in a suicidal situation. And during the Battle of the Atlantic, no German submarine commander ever showed himself to be an idiot.

The southernmost objective to be taken was Safi. It was taken quickly, due chiefly to the best army-navy cooperation shown in the entire operation. By 1300 hours on November 8, three coastal batteries at Safi were out of action. And at daybreak of November 11, it was determined that with the collapse of resistance at Casablanca, every objective of Operation TORCH had been achieved. The capture of Oran and Algiers by the combined American-British forces had secured the Mediterranean. Now, President Roosevelt, Winston Churchill and Joseph Stalin were making preparations for a meeting at Casablanca.

Once again Tom DeWitt heard the all-too familiar order over the P.A. system:

"On deck, section three, condition three, *relieve the watch!*"

His watch again. As he ascended to his station from the *Cleveland*'s main deck, he noticed about him the ships steaming west, back to the States. To their starboard, about 2000 yards, were the reliable heavy cruiser *Wichita*, two of the escort carriers and six destroyers. And, of course, the *Cleveland* was also going home. They had accomplished their mission; Morocco was secured, and Algiers and Oran were a British responsibility. More words came over the P.A. system.

"Our destroyer screen is very thin. Every man will exercise the utmost vigilance. You are to be congratulated on a job well done."

And now, after all those days of tension and moments of heart-stopping anxiety, he could relax and think of Gail. With his guts tied up inside, waiting for the clap-clap of 14-inch and 16-inch guns and the nasty crack of those fast little 5-inch guns, he had almost forgotten what she looked like. Now it was over, they had made their contribution and he could stand at the rail and watch the pitching and rolling in a still-rough Atlantic, gulp in the cold fresh air and think of other things, other places, other people. Gail. Henry Carlson. Tree-lined Woodbury. . . .

The *Cleveland* made good speed on the return trip to the States, but it wouldn't be fast enough for Tom now that the job was done. It was an eternity docking the ship. Then he was down the gangway and looking among the searching faces of hundreds of civilians. He saw her compact running figure before he could recognize the face.

"Tommy! Tommy!"

He was caught in a maelstrom of hugs and kisses, and her tears were running down the sides of his face. There was a lump in his throat, and all he could do was to crush her in his arms and keep whispering her name.

"Let's go home," she finally said. "But first we're going to Henry's." They began to walk along the pier.

"Can you tell me more?" she asked. "The papers were full of it, but there wasn't much detail."

"Not much. We didn't know where we were going until we were three days from the landing spots. But what's the news from the Pacific?"

"You know better than to ask *me* that. I'll tell what little I know, but you'd do better to ask Henry."

The drinks were mellow and warming. The company was even better. Henry Carlson was there. And, surprisingly, Isobel Strawn. With a soft gasp, Gail ran to embrace her.

"*Where* have you been?"

Isobel looked radiant. "Dr. Jordan has had me in isolation until now. Gail, she's wonderful! Can't wait to see Vic when he comes back from the Atlantic. How long do they keep ships in one area?"

"Oh, they don't handle it that way," put in Carlson. "The *Augusta* may stay there for some time, but they rotate men in small groups. Some kind of point system, you know; they're back to the States for a stretch, then back to sea again. You may see Vic before you know it."

Tom leaped to his feet, raced across the room. "Jenkins!" Carlson's manservant had just come into the room, and Tom almost floored him with a resounding whack across the shoulders. "You have one of the prettiest faces I've seen since getting back to Philly!"

"I *beg* your pardon, sir." Jenkins lowered his head. "I came to see if you'd like something more to drink."

"Sure, we'd be glad to have another round, all of us. Tell me—how are all your women?"

Jenkins stepped around, collecting the glasses, placing them on the tray, red from his stiff white collar to the edge of his receding hairline. "*Mister* DeWitt, sir—"

"Pay no attention to him, Jenkins," laughed Carlson. "He may have a few skeletons in his own closet."

Tom DeWitt was summoned to face a battery of physicians the following day—the usual routine following a return from combat duty in foreign territory. He declared to them that he felt fine, but there was a great to-do over his ankle.

"That didn't happen on this assignment," he growled. "Can't you see that?"

"Of course. You healed well. X-ray shows that. But

the trouble is, no matter how well it mends you'll have a bit of pain there from now on. The weather, of course, will be a factor. But if it's any consolation, your collection of pretty ribbons and medals will go with your dress uniform. There's a ribbon for that Atlantic convoy duty, another for the invasion of Africa with a battle star on it, and of course the Purple Heart. And probably more to come."

"I can't wait," Tom muttered.

Henry Carlson took Tom, Gail and Isobel to dinner that night at a most pretentious restaurant with a French name Tom wouldn't even try to pronounce. The wine made his head spin, and the entree was so embellished he had no idea what he was eating. But it was delicious.

After dinner, Carlson said to Isobel, "I'll drive you home, dear. I daresay that Gail and Tom have some unfinished business—or at least some catching up to do."

"Henry Carlson, you're positively vulgar!" Gail snapped.

Back on the road to Woodbury, Gail asked, "Tommy, how do you feel, really feel, about this war?"

"Ask the Japs and Germans. They started it. I don't hate anybody—except when my sleep is interrupted. When that damned beep-beep-beep starts going at three o'clock in the morning, that's when I begin to hate 'em. And when I have to be at my battle station before daybreak is another time."

"Before daybreak? Every morning?"

"That's right. That's when the submarine commanders figure two-thirds of a ship is asleep, but we're ready for 'em."

"Do you get a sub now and then?"

"Our destroyers do."

"Must be terrible, being sunk in a submarine—not a chance in the world of escaping."

"Yeah. But don't forget the guys on our ships, in the forward engine room below the waterline when that torpedo comes through. The pieces of men floating around afterward don't look like anything human. Of course the submarine man is only doing what he's told to do, just as we are."

"Tommy, it just doesn't make any sense!"

"Who said it made any sense?"

They put the car in the garage and went into their apartment. "Give me a big old bear hug," he said.

She threw off her coat and he could feel the trembling strength of her as he crushed her in his arms. In three minutes she was in the bed naked and he was right there beside her, devouring her with kisses.

"Darling, I've felt you in me a hundred times while all that was going on over there," she murmured. "I've missed you, I've missed this . . ."

"Remember, you started it."

She laughed and held him closer. "How?"

"The September day those legs of yours led me into the Bellevue-Stratford. From that moment, I knew you had to be mine."

"Just for my legs?"

"No. For all of you." He came up on one elbow. "You know, I'm so contented with you, I feel guilty about Isobel and Vic. He should be back soon. I just hope Dr. Jordan has something good to tell him. I wish we knew what was going on, but I don't suppose either one of us can really ask Isobel anything that personal."

"Poor Isobel—I believe she'd commit suicide if that doctor fails. . . . Tell me, Tommy. Did those Casablanca girls have better sugar than mine?"

He looked aggrieved. "I'm the faithful type. Besides, we didn't even get into the city. After we got the troops ashore, we set our course for home. It looked romantic, all right, beautiful minarets and tall palms— but you've changed the subject in a hurry. Come here. I haven't finished with you."

"No, you haven't."

She came to him and he found her insatiable. She went at her lovemaking eagerly, arousing him past anything he remembered, anything he had dreamed of.

18

THE JAPANESE had not yet given up getting a hold in New Guinea, so in March, 1943, a convoy of eight Japanese transports escorted by eight destroyers left Rabaul and headed south. This operation ended in massacre. The convoy was spotted by a heavy American bomber, a B-24, and so lost the element of surprise.

General Kenney, MacArthur's air commander in the area, had evidently learned one point from the Battle of Midway. There the army bombers had tried to hit carriers at 20,000 feet; it was the navy's dive bombers, going in close, that had sunk the entire Japanese carrier task force. Now Kenney sent in B-25s and A-20s to skip-bomb the ships, dropping bombs that exploded five seconds later, having the same effect as mines. P-38s, P-40s and 13 R.A.A.F. Beaufighters came in to strafe Admiral Masatomi Kimura's convoy. The bombing was horribly accurate. Out of thirty-seven 500-pound bombs dropped, twenty-eight scored. As the transports and destroyers heeled over from the bomb hits, the B-25s and A-20s came in close, strafing the ships from stem to stern. One ship after another went down. Kenney had evidently instructed a clean sweep of this Japanese operation; survivors clinging to wreckage and rafts were mercilessly strafed.

At length the Japanese Admiral Kimura had had enough. His remaining destroyers, with 2,734 survivors, headed north at flank speed. They were all that remained of the venture. All eight transports and four destroyers were on the bottom, with a loss of more than 3000 men, thirty planes. The Americans lost two bombers and three fighters out of 335 planes engaged.

There were glum faces at Imperial Headquarters. Those who were present recalled that some of them had been reluctant to bring the United States into the Pacific. Yamamoto, for one, had advised that it was a mistake unless a Japanese victory could be accomplished quickly, perhaps in ten months. And Admiral Nagumo, despite his success at Pearl Harbor, had always had misgivings. Midway, too, had been a disaster.

Tom DeWitt, seated in Henry Carlson's study during one of their discussions of the war, leaned toward his host, his expression intent. "Explain to me how on earth a force of one hundred Japanese ships could be defeated by thirty American ships." By this time the entire story of Midway had been pieced together and was known all over the nation.

"Yamamoto split his forces, for one thing," said Carlson. "He sent ships and troops up into the Aleutians but Nimitz wouldn't take the bait. He never seemed aware of Nimitz's carriers at the northeast of Midway and hung around the west side of the island with powerful battleships when we didn't have a single battleship that wasn't sitting in the mud at Pearl Harbor." Carlson let out a puff from his pipe and gazed at the ceiling. "Whatever his reasons were, we'll never know." He levelled his gaze at DeWitt as if enjoying the bolt he was about to deliver. "He's dead."

Gail came up straight upon the sofa as if stung. "How? When?"

"I think the reason he was killed is more interesting," Carlson said thoughtfully. "He was aware for a long time of the magnetism of Bill Halsey's leadership. To be sure, Halsey lost ships and men and planes, but he kept on the offensive from the time he arrived in the south Pacific. The men down there would have followed him into the pit of hell. Actually, I think Admiral Raymond Spruance is just as good as a tactician—and Kinkaid is no slouch either. But Halsey has that quality that inspires men."

"And now old Mac is building up a tremendous force in Australia, that convoy is destroyed in the Bismarck Sea, and Yamamoto is dead," said Tom. "How?"

"Yamamoto decided to inspect bases in the upper Solomons. He was emulating Halsey, mingling with the men and building up morale. U.S. intelligence found out about it. About the middle of April, Yamamoto and his staff boarded two Betty bombers at Rabaul, escorted by six Zeke fighter planes. The Japanese planes never had a chance. Major John Mitchell was flying low along the west coast of New Georgia, leading eighteen P-38s. Just as the bombers were about to land and the Zekes left, the P-38s shot in under the Zekes. The bomber carrying Yamamoto was shot down and fell in the jungle. The other, carrying Vice Admiral Ugaki, his chief of staff, fell into the sea. A neat bushwhacking job."

"They surprise us now and then," Tom mused, "but lately it seems that most of the time we know their intentions before they act. Have we developed a system of breaking their codes?"

Henry Carlson got up and paced around. "No doubt of it. The navy broke the Japanese code before the summer of 1941 was out, and though the Japanese repeatedly changed it, the navy broke it again—too many times for it to be coincidence. What burns me—and all of us, I suppose—is that several messages were sent to Washington just prior to the attack on Pearl Harbor, and Washington took no action. Admiral Kimmel and General Short are just scapegoats." He broke off abruptly. "We've all heard enough of that."

"But this Bismarck Sea slaughter and our P-38s knowing exactly where Yamamoto was—was it coincidence or decoding?"

"It's plain by this time that the navy's decipherers are very adept at their work. Talk to Mr. Roberts, the communications officer of the *Cincinnati*. He'll be helpful."

Tom smiled, "If you mean my ship, it's the *Cleveland*, which is out to sea now. And it's Commander Roberts now; he's just been promoted." He yawned. "Gail, time to heave short and bring in the anchor cable. We'll let the army take care of Europe. In the meantime, we'll keep an eye on the Pacific."

One can well imagine what thoughts were behind the lined visage of General Tojo as the reports came in. American ships were coming into the Pacific in a flood; there was a new *Lexington*, a new *Hornet*, battleships such as the *New Jersey* and *Iowa*, task forces that made those of the Midway days look like a small collection of outboard motor boats. The American torpedoes had improved, Japan's merchant marine was disappearing, new Japanese pilots were too hastily trained and were making a poor showing against American pilots. The quality of the Japanese planes had not deteriorated, but the accelerating pace of production in the U.S. was forging far ahead of Japan. Admiral Yamamoto was not here now to remind Tojo and the other military strategists of his prediction of the historic conference before the Pearl Harbor attack. Cries of "banzai!" still echoed as the Japanese continued to battle in the air, at sea and entrenched on land, but they were now on the defensive throughout the Pacific—on the defensive, but still fighting with the same valor as when the war had first begun.

General Tojo was aloof, distant, and just when he

accepted the realization that Japan was losing is not known. But it was as obvious to him as to the rest of the world that the U.S. Navy, through bitter experience, had adjusted to night fighting and was improving with every contest. The flow of new ships, planes and troops grew every week; and Nimitz, with that inexplicable instinct for out-guessing the Japanese, now had more hardware with which to follow through.

"They did it! They did it!" cried Tom as he rushed into Henry Carlson's den one evening. "Have you heard about the Battle of Empress Augusta Bay?"

"No," smiled Carlson. "Enlighten me. I'll bet you the *Cleveland* had something to do with it."

On the return from North Africa, the *Cleveland*, heavy cruiser *Wichita*, escort carriers and their destroyer screen had passed through the canal and were now in the Pacific.

"Here's the way it was." Tom poured himself a drink, half-swallowed it and went into spasms of coughing.

"Sit down now, and see if you can give me a coherent account."

"I don't have all the details—oh, a few, and a summation. There were four destroyers in the van, then the main body; Admiral Merrell with *Montpelier*, *Cleveland*, *Columbia*, *Denver* and four rear destroyers under Commander Austin. Our boys tangled with the Japanese force—four CLs and six destroyers. As I say, details will have to wait, but old Merrell had his ships skimming the seas like a pack of sharks, flares in the air, pouring out 6-inch shells. Two Nip cruisers were sunk, and three destroyers put out of action.

Denver suffered three hits. Admiral Merrell scored a neat victory, if you ask me."

The steady march across the western Pacific continued. The new ships took the time to lob a few heavy shells into Jap-occupied Wake Island, and U.S. subs with their improved torpedoes kept sinking supply ships. The Japanese on Wake were a miserable and hungry lot; to them it began to seem a very long time since they had taken over and marine Major Devereux and his handful of survivors had been marched away as prisoners.

In the south Pacific, the American task force admirals did not expend their ever-increasing numbers of ships and troops by attempting landings on all the Japanese-held islands. After shelling and bombing islands which would have been hard to take, they simply went on, leaving behind islands that were now isolated and no further menace to the U.S. Pacific fleet.

Tarawa, 19-23 November, 1943. As Tom continued his duties at the Yard and details of the determined American advance could be released, he and Henry Carlson pored over maps of the Pacific, discussed what had taken place, and speculated on future moves. The Japanese had launched their last offensive thrust, and were now on the defensive everywhere.

The U.S. Pacific fleet's next move was an enigma. In some places, they shelled and bombed the islands, in others they attacked and took them, believing them to be a possible threat. Halsey and MacArthur were in accord on some occasions, differed on others. The wisdom of their individual moves was discussed in cocktail lounges and truck stops throughout the United States, but it has never been established whether the assault on Tarawa was justified.

The navy and marines went to the attack under Rear Admiral Harry Hill, who had his flag in *Maryland,* indicating that the renovated ships sunk at Pearl Harbor were returning to action. His forces attacked the southern part of Tarawa. The veteran *Tennessee* was also present for bombarding before the LST's and LCI's disgorged their marines and tanks. Tarawa was only one of the tough nuts to crack in the Gilberts and Marshalls chain. And the Japanese had thrown up rugged defensive barricades and had elite troops to defend them. Along the entire beach at Tarawa were logs, sand and corrugated iron. These barricades were three to five feet high and were armed with 5.5-inch to 8-inch guns.

The Japanese garrison numbered about 4500 hand-picked men, physically much larger than the average Japanese soldier. Rear Admiral Keiji Shibasaki, the Japanese commander of this atoll, had proudly declared after inspecting his defenses that the U.S. could not take Tarawa with a million men in a hundred years. He was killed on 21 November at his command post, just two days before the Japanese flag was lowered.

The landing force, however, had somehow been so indoctrinated that they did not believe an island existed that could repel the U.S. Marines. The attacking party was the Second Marine Division, made up of components that had mopped up the Solomons. For about seven minutes the carriers *Essex, Bunker Hill* and *Independence* bombed the Japanese installations; then the battleships and heavy cruisers unloaded their hardware. The transports had loaded their boats, and at 0830 the first wave of marines moved in, wearing green, brown and yellow battle regalia—too hot for this climate and cloth-covered helmets, camouflaged in jungle colors. One would have expected the covering bombardment and work of the dive bombers would have the defenses in poor condition. But the first incoming waves of marines were wiped out by vicious cross fire that hit the landing craft. Marines looked at each other in disbelief at seeing their comrades falling in the shallow water, with small pools of blood beginning to move under the inert forms. Naval gunfire could not resume at this point because the thick smoke impaired their accuracy and endangered their own men.

The marines kept coming in, and reached the beach with bullet-riddled men still falling. The survivors gave no thought of retreating, but their rifle fire and hand grenades, while killing some of their antagonists, were not making much headway.

By noon the situation appeared to be a stand-off. Some progress was made by a hand-picked group of thirty-five men, who killed at least ten times their own number of Japanese. But at about 1300, General Holland M. Smith (generally known as "Howling Mad" Smith) received a message from Admiral Turner in *Pennsylvania*, saying that the "issue was in doubt"—a chilling reminder to all of Wake Island's famous message.

However, this ship-to-shore movement was not about

to be stopped anywhere short of annihilation. Regardless of casualties, regardless of the fanatical resistance of Tarawa's defenders, boats kept moving into the lagoon all day. By the end of the November 19, the marines had 5000 men ashore, with casualties of 1500. The destroyers *Ringgold, Dashiell, Frazier* and *Anderson* kept up a cracking of 5-inch guns and a steady thum-thum of their twin 40-millimeter guns. The marines continued to make their bloody progress, carrying the 75-millimeter pack howitzers. Ammo, blood plasma, bandages, morphine and reinforcements came in all during the night. The invaders spent the night on the beaches, watch-and-watch. Half the men slept like drunks in a flop house, and those on watch fought drowsiness. A counterattack of any strength could have swept them from the beaches into the water. But it was impossible for Admiral Shibasaki. Naval gunfire and carrier bombs had killed too many of his men. And those marines who came close enough to use their rifles picked off Japanese like so many clay pigeons.

21 November: the day opened with more marines pouring ashore, many men still falling, but the survivors, grim-faced and sweating, still hitting the beach. At one time the stolid-faced Japanese drove a landing party back into the water. One marine officer, bleeding from two wounds, led a hundred men in to take out a troublesome machine gun; by the time he reached the spot and obliterated the Japanese with hand grenades, he had only two men with him.

The end came on 23 November 1943. Marine tanks rumbled over the hard ground as the Stars and

Stripes went up over Tarawa. Admiral Shibasaki lay dead in the pulverized mass of logs and concrete that had been his command post. The marines had paid a price for this victory, but the Japanese death toll left only one officer and sixteen enlisted men to be captured.

If Japan had been considered an immovable object, it had finally been dislodged by an irresistible force—the United States Marines.

19

Tom DeWitt found it hard to suppress a grin whenever he came away from the communications office and found the press outside, waiting for the release of details of specific operations from the heavy book labelled Top Secret. The reporters would rush the public relations men, like the surge of the offensive line when the ball is snapped, as they came from the building. Now, with Tarawa demolished, the navy and other armed forces risked nothing in releasing more details of the continuing battle of the Pacific, and the military decided the public was entitled to know more about the navy's unstoppable surge.

Tom, Gail and Isobel were talking to Carlson in his sanctuary, discussing the giant Task Force 58.

"Well, the Gilberts were taken, then Tarawa," said Tom. "God, what a bloody mess! And now Kwajalein, the core of the Marshalls."

"Yes," Carlson agreed. "I hear a thing or two. I don't think I'm betraying a confidence when I tell you it appears that the striking forces and supporting forces are basically the same that took the Gilberts."

"No." Tom was seeing the names of ships and their functions, and the only difference he could see was that Admirals Spruance and Turner had made sure that Kwajalein was in for more pulverizing than Tarawa had taken before the marines and soldiers started moving in from the transports. This had been no bloodbath for the invader. Compared to Tarawa, the marines and soldiers virtually walked ashore. From the Japanese point of view, the casualties were horrible. Spruance had intended to flood Kwajalein from every angle with naval gunfire and each beach with troops. This he had accomplished. Of 42,000 men attacking, 400 had been killed and 1500 wounded. Of the small Japanese garrison of 8,675 men, 7,870 had been killed and 805 were taken prisoners.

"The *Maryland*, the *Pennsylvania*, the *Tennessee*, Henry," Tom suddenly blurted out. "They're out there now. Intelligence would wring my neck for telling you, but Admiral Hill had his flag in *Maryland* at Tarawa!"

Carlson's eyes widened. "So the old boys have come from the mud to fight again. God bless 'em, I hope the rest of them are out there too. Do you know? Might as well tell me—you've told me this much."

Tom shook his head. "Maybe. I'm sure of only those three." He stared at Henry's jade Buddha as if mesmerized. "There's one other ship, Henry. If she's out there, then that's where I want to be."

Carlson poured himself a drink, while the girls stared at him. "I know, I know. Now, look here, Tom. There are only three major obstacles standing between the U.S. Pacific fleet and Japan. That fool Halsey's got enough ships and carriers to clean up the rest of the world's navies. We're getting near the end, and I know how much you want to get in on the last big wallops. But—"

Gail reached over and clasped Tom's face in her small strong hands. "Is it the *West Virginia*, darling?"

Tom nodded glumly.

"And Tommy wants his admiral friends to get him a berth on the *West Virginia*," said Isobel. "I wouldn't be surprised if most of the men on those ships were also at Pearl Harbor."

"Eight battlewagons were sunk there," said Tom, "two lost forever. But ten to one, the other six are out there now. Henry—"

Carlson levelled a finger at Tom. "Admiral Murphy, who pulled the strings for you before, has been transferred to the Atlantic. I don't know the other admiral quite as well, Tom."

"He wouldn't mind doing you a favor?" Tom was almost pleading.

"It'll be difficult. There's so much more personnel to handle than before, and he's so dedicated to wrapping this thing up."

"Henry," Gail interrupted, "you said only three major obstacles were left for us before Hirohito is through?"

"Actually, there are a number of them—and then Japan has to be conquered. Remember, the main body of Japanese troops are still in their islands. The three objectives I had in mind are the Philippines, Iwo Jima and Okinawa. They'll be tougher than the ones already conquered. Then comes Japan." His face was grave. "We have more carriers, battleships, cruisers, destroyers and auxiliary ships than the rest of the world combined. Even our own drydocks and repair ships. In the end, the tank, armored car and foot soldier will decide the issue. We'll take them. But I turn cold at the cost in blood."

"Tougher and tougher," said Tom, his voice no more than a whisper.

Just as Carlson was beginning to anticipate a renewed request for help with a transfer, there was a pounding on the door. Carlson, glad for a brief reprieve, quickly got up and opened the door.

There stood Vic Hadley, tanned, muscular, grinning. Isobel came running and threw herself upon him, kissing his cheeks, tears flowing from her bright eyes.

"Jenkins!" Carlson called.

Jenkins promptly appeared—and was practically crushed breathless by Vic.

"Jenkins, you stately old bastard, it's good to see you."

Jenkins shook hands, his face pink with pleasure.

"Mister Hadley, sir, it's good to see you, sir. And it warms me to see no harm has come to you."

There was a moment of embarrassment, while Gail kissed Vic and Carlson wrung Hadley's hand. Then Carlson broke the awkward moment:

"Vic, if you'd like you can take Isobel for a walk. It's pleasantly cool outside, and also a trillion stars to look down on you—and perhaps hear what you have to say. Then come back and let us talk to you."

Vic gave him a mock bow. "As usual, you're the soul of tact and diplomacy—and we will be back. Now, let's go, you delectable creature."

Isobel took his arm and they walked into the night. "God, you've been on my mind every hour, Isobel. I wasn't as afraid of the bombs and torpedoes as of what was going on between you and Dr. Jordan."

She laughed happily. "She did it, Vic. She did! I was dismissed three weeks ago. I was put through every medical and psychological test ever invented and for a while it looked as if we'd never find out what was wrong. But Dr. Jordan finally discovered that the underlying cause was a glandular disturbance which has been corrected with medication. I was so afraid, Vic, but now it looks as if everything is okay."

"Better than okay," Vic said, his eyes moist with relief and happiness as he took her in his arms.

They talked for a time and then went back inside, to sit with the group of smiling faces. All except Henry Carlson. He wore the expression of a man who faces a distasteful decision.

"Tom has something on his mind," Gail said as they entered the room.

"Gail, hold off on that for a minute," said Carlson, "and give Tom and Vic your presents for them."

In a wink, the two young men were dazzled by the sight of two sets of silver bars, to be worn on naval officers' collars when they wore khaki.

"Full lieutenants, you are," said Gail. "I went with Isobel when Tom came home with his new commission in his pocket. I hadn't seen Vic, but I knew he had his commission; they went on active duty at the same time, and both have enough sea duty—combat stars, too. Isn't it great, Henry?"

"It is." Carlson shook hands with them.

"I feel sort of selfish about this," said Tom, "but, what do you say, Henry? Will you give it a try?"

"Damn it, I don't know how I'm going to do it yet," Carlson grumbled. "I've got one friend who's terribly busy and of whom I want to ask a favor, and another young friend who's like my son who has a request I may have to reject."

Vic studied Tom's unhappy face. "I think I know what it's all about. All of you knew when I came in here. Tom's got some information from communications, right?"

"Everybody will know soon," said Tom. "The *Maryland*, the *Tennessee*, the reborn battlewagons, are in the Pacific. Yeah, and the *Pennsylvania* too, all looking like new and blasting the Japs."

"Joyous retribution," said Vic. "What about the *West Virginia*?"

"No word yet. But she was the newest, best-built battlewagon of the fleet. The boys at Bremerton must have sent her back in excellent shape."

"And Tom wants me to persuade Arthur Franklin to have him transferred to the west coast, and from there to the *West Virginia*," Carlson muttered.

"Taken unawares and smashed," said Tom, "the hero returns to skin the villain. Don't you find a bit of romance and heroics in that, Henry?"

"I'm not sure whether all present would go along with that," Carlson replied.

Gail, who was sitting on the floor by Tom's chair, came up on her knees, her face inches from Tom's. "Tommy, I've grieved for Phil Armstrong, too! And for all the others who died on the *West Virginia*. Now you've had enough sea duty and combat for a stretch of shore duty and the navy is willing to give it to you—but you want to go back, and it's awful out there!"

When she buried her head deep into Tom's shoulder, he put his hand on the bronze head, heard her sniffle and smiled faintly. For the moment she seemed childlike. And Henry Carlson, ever hungry for a daughter, was struck with compassion and put a hand on her shoulder and squeezed it hard.

"There have been a lot of momentous events today," he said. "Disclosure about the war, Vic's arrival, promotions . . . So why don't you all go home and discuss the things young men and their girls discuss. In the meantime, I'll have some thinking to do and perhaps a word with Jenkins."

Jenkins, obviously flattered, nodded with some authority. "All of us, indeed, have borne some strain. I think your suggestion is eminently sensible, sir."

They stood at the door and Isobel looked at the

fatherly man who seemed so happy for her. She threw her arms around Carlson's neck. "There's no man like you—God, I love you!"

In their apartment Tom slowly undressed while Gail sat curled on the sofa, her lips puckered, a deep frown across her brow. "Tommy, this is really important to you, isn't it? I mean getting Admiral Franklin to get you aboard the *West Virginia*."

"I'm not at all sure the admiral will even have time to listen to Henry now. This is a big drive, Gail. Our admirals and generals are burning the midnight oil, trying to figure which islands to take and fortify, which to bypass and let wither on the vine. For example, we sure as hell couldn't take the Gilberts, garrison them, then bypass the Marshalls, Kwajalein and go on to tackle Saipan. Some of the decisions are tough. If we reach the Philippine Sea—well, if we take it, Japan will be desperate, because we'll be too close to the Philippines."

"Oh, the hell with the Philippines!" she cried. "You haven't answered my question! You're given me a resume of the war, and I don't understand half of what you're talking about. I want to know just how much this means to you. How much does our relationship mean to you?"

"Everything. That's why we have to win. It *could* mean preserving our way of life for us." He sat with her, grabbed her fiercely. "I don't say one lieutenant in an American battleship can preserve our way of life; but I do know the tide of war is running fast against the Japs in the Pacific. We have to be sure it continues that way so they'll no longer be a threat. I'm making a poor explanation, sweetheart, but it's just something I have to do. We have to keep rolling westward toward the Philippines. And if we get close, MacArthur will be waiting to make his return. The Japs will see more soldiers, ships and planes than they knew existed. Historically, the American military man is at his best on the offensive. And he's moving now. For me, I have to admit that I'm also considering Phil, of course, and all the other men who died before they had a chance to fight . . . Can't you understand me?"

"I understand that you could be killed. Oh, Tommy, Tommy, why?"

Her face held a sullen look, but he knew she understood every word he had said. She went to bed, sobbing softly, and he held her until she went to sleep.

The next morning Tom was summoned to the personnel office and handed his orders, pay accounts and health records to the U.S.S. *West Virginia.*

"You must have some pull with that Carlson," Lieutenant Carnes said, "if he can convince Admiral Franklin that you should have a special request approved for the Pacific. Well, here it is. You know the procedure. Happy days!"

Tom left the office, muttering, "I'm not particularly happy at the moment. How the hell do I make her understand, anyway? She's got a guy on a shore station, with an occasional escort voyage with a convoy, he's nuts about her—and the damned fool wants to leave her and transfer to the Pacific! How much is she supposed to take, anyway?"

He had his things ready quickly. He and Gail walked about Woodbury and went by Carlson's so Tom could thank him, but the conversation lagged stiffly, and they didn't stay long. The day passed swiftly, both ill at ease.

Tom suddenly said, "Gail, shall we eat out tonight—good old Arthur's Steak House?"

"Sure, sure." Her normally full face had seemed thin recently, and her enthusiasm seemed forced.

"Say, put on that grey knit dress and the red shoes. Please?"

For the first time that day he saw her smile. "If that's what you want, Tommy. And can I have one of those filets? About as thick as both your hands, the kind the knife just slides through?"

"My pleasure, fair lady."

At Arthur's, they made an effort to regain the high spirits of previous visits to the restaurant. The food was good as always, but somehow their talk faltered, and they left early.

Bedtime came and they lay unclothed together. He took her in his arms and never had she felt so rigid.

"Gail," he said softly, "I once worked for a man who had the happiest marriage I'd ever seen. He told me once, 'We never go to bed angry with each other, my wife and I, or out of sorts in any way. You'd be surprised at how good I always feel the next morning.'"

As he talked, hoping to break this barrier so strange to them both, he could feel her gradually relax. Then she reached up for his face and her kiss brought a tightness in his throat. Later, she awoke and saw him asleep, on his back with his right arm up and in back of his head.

"Bless you, darling," she whispered. "I know how you feel and I do understand."

20

A S JUNE PROGRESSED, the Fifth Fleet, with Admiral
Raymond Spruance steaming with his flag in the
heavy cruiser *Indianapolis*, swept north, then
northwest. This fleet was known as Task Force 58,
and it seemed a navy in itself to the desperately fighting Japanese. The heart of it was split into four task
groups: 58.1—fleet carriers *Lexington*, *Yorktown*, light
carriers *Belleau Wood* and *Bataan*; 58.2—fleet carriers
Bunker Hill and *Wasp*, light carriers *Monterey* and
Cabot; 58.3—fleet carriers *Enterprise*, *Hornet*, light
carriers *San Jacinto* and *Princeton*; 58.4—fleet carrier
Essex and light carriers *Langley* and *Cowpens*. Fleet
carrier *Hornet* was sometimes in Task Group 58:1.

The carriers had sufficient air power to carry them

through Kwajalein, Saipan and the Philippine Sea. Some of the carriers were shifted from time to time from Spruance's Fifth Fleet to Halsey's Third Fleet. Indeed, both in the United States and in Japan it was some time before it was known the two fleets were one and the same.

Task Force 58's fast carrier striking forces hit Saipan on 15 June 1944. The assault teams came in fast, the Japanese met them furiously, but there were 8,000 marines ashore in the first twenty minutes. The marines kept up the pressure; all day and all night landing craft kept up a steady flow from the transports to the beaches.

On 15–17 June the beachhead was secured, but not the island itself. Twenty thousand marines had landed at the cost of 2000 men. The Japanese made several furious charges to drive the marines into the sea, but destroyers from offshore and tanks and rifle fire broke their efforts. Night illumination and naval gunfire helped to weaken Japanese resistance. Here was a different picture from that of 1942. The skies were filled with planes bearing the big star, and the ships that casually moved in to bombard flew the Stars and Stripes. Men spoke in terms of ten to fifteen carriers, where before it had been three or four.

Perhaps the factor that most hurt the defenders was the difference between the skill and combat proficiency of the fighters from Spruance's fleet carriers and the relatively inexperienced Japanese pilots. The Japanese threw raids from Guam and the Marianas, but planes from U.S. carriers met them and fighters with the prominent "meat ball" went streaking through the air like miniature comets into the sea. Coral Sea and Midway had taken the elite and now these green flyers went into the sea in hissing flames. Navy fighters and marines released streams of metal that blew Zekes into splinters in the air.

On the ground, a battalion of Japanese, after emptying their rifles, charged the marines with fixed bayonets. The marines methodically chopped them down, leaving windrows of bodies. The Japanese infantry came on, stumbling over the bodies of their comrades, and then it was hand-to-hand conflict, the marines emptying their rifles, then using bayonets and gun butts.

The slightly curving chain of islands including Saipan, Guam and Tinian made up the Marianas. Having virtually wiped out all of the Japanese air power in this area, Task Force 58 turned due west to take the Philippine Sea. The U.S. fleet was in for a fight, for with General MacArthur readying himself for his return, the loss of the Philippine Sea left only Iwo Jima and Okinawa before the fleet stood fairly on Japan's doorstep.

The carrier strength at Spruance's disposal was an ominous portent for the Japanese defenders, as was the fact that many of his men were veterans, men who had served on the ships that were blasted in 1942 and who now manned those ships' namesakes. Over Guam and the Marianas, the Japanese combat pilots were no match for the Americans who had known the dark days. Twenty-nine American carrier

planes were lost, while the Japanese lost 315. It was
known as "the Marianas turkey shoot," unquestionably
the greatest air battle of the war.

Guam was mercilessly pounded. According to the
sailors, it was "Geiger by land, and Conolly by sea,"
referring to the two most popular officers in these
operations. Rear Admiral Richard L. Conolly, USN,
was dubbed "close-in Conolly." He would bring his
Pennsylvania within about 600 yards to bombard and
to make the marine landings easier by getting them
on the beaches more quickly. General Geiger took
position on *Pennsylvania*'s bridge, assisting Admiral
Conolly in directing fire where it would be most ef-
fective; then his troops ashore kept up relentless pressure until the Japanese capitulated.

Saipan was finally secured on 9 July, 1944. There
were still ample forces to garrison the islands, because
Task Force 58 had anticipated determined resistance.

The Japanese fleet, worn thin by their losses, managed to escape the coup de grace only through Admiral Spruance's lack of reaction after the Marianas
turkey shoot. Three of Vice Admiral Ozawa's nine
carriers had been ambushed by American submarines,
his fleet had lost its air cover, and fourteen of the
fleet submarines had been sunk by the swarms of
U.S. destroyers operating through the area of the
Marianas and Philippine Sea. Ozawa had no alter-
native except to run northwest—which he was doing
at flank speed. Spruance ordered carriers after the
Japanese, but he had hesitated too long. Spruance
had won a victory, but he met with severe criticism

from the press for permitting that Japanese fleet to get away.

Other things were happening. With the fall of Saipan, Tojo and his entire cabinet resigned and Admiral Yonai became the new foreign minister. And on July 6, Admiral Nagumo shot himself with his pistol—an obscure finale for the man who had achieved perfection in his attack on Pearl Harbor. Those who found and viewed his body must have thought it eons since the barracks of Hickam Field had flown into the air like splinters and the waters around the sunken battle line had covered over with oil.

The Philippines were wide open. MacArthur looked at his subordinates and said he had been advised to launch his attack on Leyte as Operation King Two. With the approval of Roosevelt, Churchill and Nimitz, the man with the beautifully braided hat said simply:

"Gentlemen, we are ready. We have the air power, the ground troops; send a dispatch to Admiral Halsey for speedy ships."

Halsey complied. He sent nine fast fleet carriers and eight light carriers, five fast battleships, fourteen cruisers and fifty-eight destroyers. Mindanao had been considered the landing point, but since Leyte Gulf had been selected, MacArthur had organized his attacking forces in what he termed his K, K, and K: General Krueger's Sixth Army, Kenney's air force and Kinkaid's fleet. The Japanese organization to meet this invasion was Plan Sho-Go: nine battleships, twenty-three cruisers, sixty-three destroyers and four carriers. The Japanese commander-in-chief was Admiral Soemu Toyoda.

When Rear Admiral Barbey began the landings of General Sibert's X Corps on the Philippines, no one could measure the depth of feelings within MacArthur's tall proud figure, standing somewhat stiffly on the bridge of his flagship, the U.S.S. *Nashville*, to watch the smoothly efficient movements of transports and landing craft. These men were expending their pent-up energy by their very motion, going down the lines and hitting the beach running. But the tall silent man? How many sweating hours had he spent prior to this moment, going over details, sometimes with his aides, sometimes pondering alone? Had he picked the right places for the right movements of men, ships and planes? Had he put the most capable men in the places where their particular talents were best suited for sweeping this group of islands end to end? For that was what he was here to do.

He had been standing straight with his hands on his hips. Now he spun, slapping his hands together, calling out for all to hear:

"Man, look at those boys go! Nobody's going to stop them, nobody! They've been trained too well for that! And Admiral Barbey has done a superlative job!"

This was 20 October 1944, and waves of khaki-clad troops were swarming ashore. General Douglas MacArthur, now the Supreme Commander of Allied forces in the southwest Pacific, had returned to the Philippines.

Fighters and dive bombers from the escort carriers were covering the landings, the movements of the Liberty ships and the maneuvering of the LST's. The U.S.S. *Mississippi, West Virginia* and *Maryland* were there, lobbing their murderous 14-and 16-inch projectiles ahead of the advancing troops. Then they retired and Rear Admiral Berkey's destroyers came in to relieve them.

Ashore, MacArthur discussed the forthcoming battle in Surigao Strait. Admiral Kinkaid indicated that the *Nashville* was needed elsewhere and that MacArthur should establish headquarters ashore. The general kept his thoughts to himself but he recognized Kincaid's reluctance to take the Supreme Commander into a battle in confined areas; the man most valuable in retaking the Philippines might be killed. MacArthur genuinely wanted a part of this action, but appeared cooperative and accepted the suggestion.

By 25 October the Northern Attack Force had 80,000 men ashore with all necessary supplies and equipment. The Southern Attack Force had completed landing 51,000 men and General Krueger, one of MacArthur's K's, had set up his command post. "Close-in" Conolly had provided the fire support.

Thus far, MacArthur was content. He had plenty of men in reserve. Intelligence was a bit vague on the strength of Japanese forces and could only estimate about 100,000 men. This figure was placidly accepted by MacArthur and Kenney. They would now see what Admiral Kinkaid would do in Surigao Strait.

The American bluejacket saw Surigao Strait as another "torpedo junction" similar to those in the Solomons. Due to the confined waters, ships on both sides got out of position and blips on the radar screen showed objects where they should not be. The result was that a general melee developed in the strait. Vice Admiral Shima of the Fifth Fleet and Vice Admiral Nishimura of the Southern Force believed they had enough ships to control Surigao Strait, perhaps because they supposed that MacArthur had allocated so much of his available seapower to other operations that they had no cause to worry. It was a costly miscalculation.

Kincaid had sent Admiral Weyler to Surigao Strait with *West Virginia, California, Mississippi, Maryland, Pennsylvania* and *Tennessee,* battleships that had been rehabilitated and that bore crewmen who had thought of little other than the treacherous attack on Pearl Harbor. They fairly simmered now with the desire to square accounts with the sons of Nippon. Accompanying the main battle line were Rear Admiral Oldendorf's heavy cruisers *Louisville, Portland* and *Minneapolis,* Rear Admiral Berkey's light cruisers *Phoenix* and *Boise* and heavy cruiser H.M.A.S. *Shropshire,* Rear Admiral Hayler's light cruisers *Denver* and *Columbia,* and nineteen destroyers. The American force was certainly enough to raise some Oriental eyebrows; they had expected meeting nothing like this.

Captain Coward's four destroyers went into action at about 0200, launching torpedoes at Admiral Nishimura's battle formation. Coward's DD's missed the Japanese destroyers, but U.S.S. *McDermott* got a torpedo into the battleship *Fuso*, and Melvin hit *Yamagumo*, which exploded. During these first exchanges, the Japanese ships seemed to be firing almost without effect.

The firing from the main battle line began about 0350. *West Virginia* was the first to fire, later being accused by the other ships of getting off her first salvo just before the order to commence firing. The night was black, with icy bits of stars looking down at the bright flashes of gunfire and explosions. *West Virginia*, *Tennessee* and *California* were getting off the most salvos. Outside, the flash of searchlights, spurts of fire; and inside the turrets, sweating yelling men. *This* was the way it should have been on December 7, 1941, so very long ago.

"Retribution!" yelled one sailor.

"Revenge!"

"Retaliation! Shoot the butts off the bastards!"

Tom DeWitt had been elated over his assignment to the communications department of the *West Virginia*. There was plenty of personnel in the department, more than he had ever seen; a three-striper as communications officer, a lieutenant as his assistant, half a dozen officers available to stand watch, a signal officer, a radio officer, radar officer, radio electricians, signalmen, including a chief signalman—plenty of everything in this reborn slugger.

The *Wee Vee* was now delivering her 16-inch projectiles of murderous A.P. and making hits. In the coding room, he sat with headphones, listening in on the JZ circuit and trying to hear some of the TBS going on at the same time—hard to do, with the thunder of the *Wee Vee*'s main battery blotting out nearly everything else. No, not everything; nothing could blot out his grim satisfaction on this marvelous night. He heard some voice calling out that the *Fuso* had been hit. One of the Japanese battleships! He knew what a 16-inch shell could do, piercing steel and exploding inside—God, what a mess.

"They're paying in blood, Phil," he found himself murmuring, and wondered how he could feel so vindictive, so full of hate, so unfeeling for the men dying in the battered and sinking ships of the Japanese Imperial Navy. It wasn't good to feel this way. It should make a man sick.

Holy mackerel, those guys in the turrets were really pouring it on! The *Wee Vee* was shuddering from stem to stern. How many of those murderous projectiles had she thrown? Then he felt the ship's engines slow a bit. Two-thirds speed? Could be. They were turning; it came through on the TBS. The whole battle line was turning. They were leaving the strait. The *West Virginia, Tennessee, California, Mississippi, Maryland,* and *Pennsylvania*—the avengers had delivered a paralyzing blow.

The new Japanese cabinet was shocked at the final tally of the Battle of Surigao Strait. They had lost two battleships and three destroyers, and two light cruisers and one heavy cruiser had been crippled. The Americans had lost none of their ships, and the only damage suffered was to one destroyer.

21

A HARD FIST knocked on the door of Tom's room on board the *West Virginia*. Then a grinning, sandy-haired j.g. came in.

"I'm the bearer of great good tidings, do you know that? You may now put on your shoes and get to the personnel office. You're being transferred to the States!" He started out, then turned. "Can't figure how a man operating from the Fourth Naval District got aboard the *West Virginia*, anyhow."

Tom smiled for the first time in many days. "That'll be my secret. Thanks, Carson, for the good news. Hope you get something pretty, say like the Silver Star, before this thing's over. And it *will* be very damn soon."

He brushed his hair, then had to take out his handkerchief to wipe the tears from his cheeks. Gail. Henry. And you, too, Jenkins, you old bastard. He hurried down the passageway, stepping over the bottoms of the watertight doors. He'd have to find Vic and Isobel, too.

Tom was shipped first to Mare Island, a scant thirty-five miles from San Francisco. As he stood looking in at the officers' club, he had the sense that he was stepping into another world. The bar, the music and dancing, the lights out over San Pablo Bay, the relaxed conversation and laughter . . . he had forgotten that such things existed. It seemed like only last night that Kinkaid's ships had swept the Japanese from Surigao Strait, only last night that the deck of the *Wee Vee* had been cleansed of the blood of Phil Armstrong and his dead comrades.

There was the usual routine of paperwork before Tom could leave for Philadelphia. Eager to be home, he went through it all by rote. He was no sooner done than he was approached by a pretty Wave with a handful of papers.

"You'll have to have a physical before you can go home. It's routine for everybody back from the Pacific—checking for fever that might be hiding in you, and all those fungi, diarrhea, and bugs that doctors here have never even heard of."

There was a cough behind him, and Tom turned to see a solemn-faced man in uniform. He held a paper in his hand and as he lifted his arm Tom saw the insignia above the gold stripes.

"Good morning, padre," Tom said.

The chaplain handed the dispatch to Tom, saying, "My name's Jernigan, Mister DeWitt. As you know, delivery of mail is difficult to ships in action areas, sometimes even in foreign bases. Sorry we couldn't reach you earlier. Radio was used when possible in relaying word to next of kin, but—"

"Next of kin?" Tom snatched the paper. The words were so formal . . . "The Navy Department deeply regrets to inform you—"

The next words blurred his vision and he ran from the building. "Mister DeWitt! Mister DeWitt!" The words trailed after him. He did not hear them. He ran past one building, then another, the paper crushed in his hand.

"Gail! Oh, God, it's a mistake—it can't be Gail!" He stopped, flung himself against a brick building, began to pound both clenched fists against the wall. The pain flashed through his hands, but he kept flailing his arms. His knees buckled and he began to slide down the side of the building. There was no feeling in his hands now. It was blotted out by a far deeper pain. "Gail, sweetheart . . . oh, God, why? Why . . . ?"

Officers, bluejackets, the chaplain and a shore patrolman came running.

"Get hold of him!" cried the officer. "Go like hell for some corpsmen!" He threw Tom to the ground, tried to control the thrashing figure. "My God, look at his hands—he's beaten them to a pulp!"

Three bluejackets were already running toward the hospital, their shiny shoes kicking up the dust. The chaplain held the wild-eyed Tom down, and the officer managed to get the bloody paper from his right hand. He squinted and shook his head. "Can hardly read it."

The chaplain took the paper and said softly, "Either his sweetheart or his wife. He must be among those rotated from the Pacific. An automobile wreck. The signature at the bottom looks like Isobel."

For the next week, Tom was aware of only a hodgepodge of images, sounds and sensations. The ponderous turrets of the *Massachusetts* swinging around to belch black thunder . . . the terrible stabbing pains in his hands . . . the swift prick of a needle and numbing peace . . . and a girl walking in front of him, a quick swinging figure in blue, and patent leather shoes. Gail . . . Gail . . . Figures in white working over him . . . crackling thunder and bright flashes through the night . . . a Japanese destroyer exploding in a huge ball of red and yellow . . . the *West Virginia* gun crews still shooting after the cease fire order. . . .

The hallucinations shattered like thin glass and Tom drifted through to settle in the solid present. He was lying in a hospital bed. Through the open door he could see swiftly moving figures; corpsmen, nurses, doctors, men being brought in and then the sound of laughter.

There was one other officer in the room with him, sitting on the edge of the bed, wiping his face. He smiled and said, "Been out for a walk. Still a bit weak."

He was in uniform, and Tom looked at his ribbons. There was the plain gold ribbon with fleet clasp, indicating he had been in the Neutrality Patrol back in the thirties when the U.S. was trying to keep out of the war. And there was the blue American Theatre with a star, the Purple Heart, the African and Middle Eastern green ribbon with a star. So the guy had been in some of the same places, thought Tom. Same rank, too.

Introductions followed. The man's name was Albert Kearney. Tom didn't much feel like talking, but the friendly Kearney soon had him acting more sociable than he felt.

"Kearney's a famous military name," Tom commented. "Indian-fighter. Descendant?"

Kearney laughed. "Hell, I don't know. Wouldn't bother to find out. I didn't want to fight anybody."

Tom tried to smile, but his face felt stiff. His whole body had been rigid for God knows how long. "Sometimes you don't have a choice," he replied. Funny how the two men seemed reluctant to wave the flag. He and Kearney had both volunteered.

There was no more talk for some time. Tom lay in bed with his hands bandaged up like two small pillows. The pain was bad in the afternoon, and he was given a shot, then another that night, along with a sleeping pill.

A nurse came in, smiled at Tom, then said to Kearney, "Come with me to the lab."

Kearney grunted. "Not another test? When are they going to run out of things to do to a man? I thought our enemies were the Krauts and Japs."

"This is the last one, you good-looking bear," she said. "Then back to duty, if it's negative."

The room seemed so still after they left. Tom began to feel drowsy and finally fell so deeply asleep that he did not feel the prick of another needle. He was deep in sweet exhaustion, free at last of the tension, the thundering hell of night battles, the eye-strain, the tautness of every muscle.

When he awoke the next morning he saw Lieutenant Kearney across the room, sitting on the edge of his bed.

"I've been wondering, DeWitt," he asked, "how in hell did you get shot in both hands? Damn, but some weird things happen in this war."

"I've heard a thousand weird questions asked since I've been back in the States—and it's nobody's business," Tom snapped—and was immediately ashamed of himself.

Kearney's face turned pink. He opened his mouth to make some rebuttal, then snapped his lips shut. At this point the nurse came in and levelled a finger at Tom.

"We're going to take a hike, a long one this time. Too much sack time will make you weak."

Tom went to the door with her. He turned and looked at Kearney. "Hey, Kearney, I'm sorry. I mean it. Okay?"

"Okay, sport. It really isn't any of my business."

Outside, Tom and the nurse strolled, and he knew she was right. His legs did feel weak. His orthopedic surgeon joined them and spoke to Tom. "We did the best we could, Mister DeWitt. I never saw such a mess. We're going to get those boxing gloves off your hands and do one last job. You'll leave here with bandages that will at least give you a little flexibility. Your orders have been written for the Philadelphia Naval Hospital. You'll report there, and they'll have another look at your hands. Dressing, shaving and such will be clumsy, but the pain will gradually go away. Just how much flexibility you'll have is something we can't tell."

Tom walked on in silence. The doctor squeezed his shoulder, muttered something about things to look after, and left. Tom and the nurse continued their walk.

"Is Philadelphia your home?" the nurse asked.

"My ship's home port was Philly. I live in Woodbury, New Jersey."

"You don't talk like an easterner."

"That's because I'm not an easterner. I'm from the south. Come on, we've walked enough and I'm tired. I'd like a big steak tonight. Okay?"

The sun was faintly warm on the sidewalk of Woodbury, with now and then a light breeze caressing his cheeks. There were not many people on the streets and he walked slowly. Flags hung over the doors of shops and restaurants.

Emotions do strange things to a man. He had been released from the tension of the war, from his total immersion in its outcome. But as for the other—he was still taut, with his stomach coming up tight every time he tried to take a deep breath. And as walked nearer the rustic one-story house, it grew worse. At least his hands didn't hurt anymore, but there was little flexibility in them.

"Tom! Tom, old boy!" It was big Vic Hadley, out in front of the other three figures he saw running toward him. He knew they had been looking for him, and now they came: Vic, Isobel, Henry Carlson and Jenkins. People on the sidewalks recognized that here was one of the men they had prayed for, one who had returned, and they yelled, "Welcome home, son! Welcome home!"

He didn't know them but he threw up his hand in acknowledgment. A wry twist of his lips was as close as he could come to a smile as he heard a small boy call out to his parents, "Look there, mother, dad! One of our heroes has come back!"

Then there was the collision with Vic, whose embrace was like a bear's. The others crowded around, Isobel kissing him on both cheeks, Henry Carlson grabbing him, Jenkins seizing one of his hands with both of his, then quickly withdrawing them as he saw Tom wince.

"Mister DeWitt, sir! Oh, heavens, how good it is to see you, sir! Look, Mister Carlson, he has two full stripes on his sleeves."

Carlson got them into his study, begging them not to make such a scene. Tom had been keeping a tight rein on his emotions during this reunion, but he suddenly felt overwhelmed. He fell against Carlson, his shoulders shook and the tears ran down his cheeks. At long last the flood broke over the wall of restraint that had frozen him since he had seen the message on

Mare Island. Carlson held him tightly, murmuring, "Let it go, son, let it go."

Then with the tension gone, all of them sat down, half-laughing and half-crying. When Tom saw Jenkins primly wiping his cheeks and replacing his handkerchief, he grinned and said, "Jenkins, you old bastard, you're beautiful! That's how good you look to me." Jenkins was radiant and stood back like a Whitehall guard at attention.

Tom was aware that they were consciously avoiding looking at his bandaged hands, that they didn't know whether or not to bring up the subject of Gail. It was Carlson, as usual, who broke the stillness.

"Tom, son, we know there's not a great deal you can tell us about the Pacific. But can you give us a general idea as to the validity of all we hear on the radio and read in the press?"

Tom smiled, appreciating the man's efforts to divert him from more painful thoughts. "You mean are the reports exaggerated? In the main, Henry, they're right. When they use the phrase 'one smashing victory after another,' it's true. The war correspondents are giving you the truth, subject to the restrictions of armed forces censorship. It's only the editorial writers and stay-at-home reporters who magnify the losses we've inflicted on the enemy."

"I'm not asking for figures and dispositions, Tom. But we hear so much about the size of the U.S. Navy. You know, with so much smoke, there has to be some fire."

"Right. It's the biggest fleet in the history of naval warfare. That's general knowledge, probably released to frighten the Japanese people. I've been in a part of the amphibious technique used. Beautiful to see. Good friends of mine have been in others."

"And the Japanese?"

"Good fighting men. Time and again they fight to the last man, but they can't stop the steamroller they started."

His throat felt dry. "Henry, are you still hoarding some of that good pre-war bourbon? Surely you've got a few drops for my homecoming."

Grinning, Carlson got up. "Jenkins, give me a hand —unless you've guzzled it all up."

It seemed to Tom that the warmth of the alcohol slowly trailed down his legs as he sprawled in a chair and looked at the faces around him. God, they'd never know what it meant, just to see them. They didn't have to formulate any words of comfort. At this time, there were no words. And what made these people so special was that they knew that and did not attempt to verbally share his loss.

When the reunion broke up Henry Carlson went with him into the street. There were just the two of them.

Carlson's voice was gentle. "Tom, time is the answer. You've taken the first step today. Check with your doctors as they direct. I believe they can get a waiver on your hands from the Bureau of Naval Personnel. There's a helluva lot you can do in the Fourth Naval District Communications—or Operations, for that matter. You've got the experience to pass on to so many young men who are ready to listen. As to your loss, no one back there attempted any words—"

"I love them for that, Henry."

"Take your time, son. Think. And when you're ready, this door is open, any time."

Tom looked straight down the street, avoiding the eyes of the man he had admired since first meeting him. He couldn't turn to say good-bye; his eyes were filled. He forced a laugh. "You know I'm not the sloppy kind. I'll take your advice. And I'll see you soon— Pop."

Henry Carlson watched until Tom was out of sight, then turned toward his house. He put a hand to his head, tried to rub away the sudden ache there. Isobel had said nothing about her pregnancy, and he was glad. It was going to be a happy occasion, but this was not the time to tell Tommy. Isobel and Vic had instinctively withheld the announcement, and Carlson was grateful to them for this.

Time, he had told Tommy . . . He had felt like the perfect heel, even as he had said it. Time would take away some of the pain, enough time might ease all of it. But one could not forget. No man who knew Gail could ever forget her.

Epilogue

T<small>OM</small> D<small>E</small>W<small>ITT</small> walked the street, drawing near Point Affirm at the Bellevue-Stratford. His status had been changed to lieutenant (S) USNR, restricting him from sea or combat duty, but he was quite eligible for his specialties ashore. The deep void that Gail's death had left was still there, as was his anger over the senselessness of her death. He would never know if the accident had been caused by sheer bad luck or by the problem with her eyes. Maybe he should have pushed her harder to have them checked out. . . .

The worst of the grief had passed, though, and he had done his best to blot out his thoughts of Gail with plenty of hard work. He liked the looks of the keen-eyed young ensigns he was training. And there was Henry Carlson and Jenkins, and Vic and Isobel now had a beautiful baby girl they'd named after Gail.

As he looked ahead on the street he suddenly felt his flesh crawl and tiny beads of sweat broke out under the shining visor of his cap. There was a pert, swinging girl in front of him, and above the sweet curves of her legs, a navy nurse's uniform. My God, he thought, I'm going crazy. She's the same trim size . . . I've got to know, even if she yells for the shore patrol.

He quickened his pace, came alongside her, and she gave him a quick look from blue-gray eyes. A brunette, with smooth round cheeks, she smiled and said, "Are you going to flirt with me? I see your ribbons and battle stars, you're home from the wars." She broke off and started laughing. "I'm just ribbing you. Had a good day and feel good."

He laughed. What a grand, light feeling filled him! His day, too, had been good. Then she nearly shrieked. "It's Tommy! Tommy DeWitt!"

"Come over here." He pulled her to one side and let the crowd of pedestrians swirl by. This was the last girl he'd ever expected to see. "Pam! Pam Waldren! Oh, hell, you look cute in uniform. Forgive me for standing here looking like a gaping fool, but I haven't seen you since school days. Say, can you spare a few minutes with a guy who likes you very much? Let's have a cup of coffee."

She smiled and nodded, and they stepped into a nearby coffee shop. As they sat and looked at each other, he decided to get one thing out of the way.

"Pam, what do you see? The truth, now."

The blue-gray eyes stared at him over the cup. Then she said, "I see a good-looking young guy. But there are shadows under his eyes and some lines in his cheeks that shouldn't be there." She glanced at his hands. They were covered now with some light silky material. One could almost see the redness through it. "War wounds? Somehow I don't think so. You've been deeply hurt, a heavy loss that has at times been almost unbearable. You can tell me whenever you want to—or you don't have to."

"I have several good friends who are beginning to fill that black emptiness better than they know." The words came out in a hurry now, words that he'd never spoken to anyone. " I came through the Golden Gate, jubilant over an important victory—couldn't wait to get back here to tell her. She had been killed in an automobile wreck. I went crazy." Odd, that he could speak of her now.

"What a horrible jolt! Your girl?"

"Yes. My wife." He would have said more to this girl. She suddenly seemed like a friend of long standing, despite all the years that had passed. But she understood that he wasn't quite ready.

"We'll say no more. Take a pull on that coffee and I'll tell you about the really funny things—the women giving victory parties because they know it's coming, the people putting in orders for new cars from the automobile dealers and being told they'll have to wait at least ten months for delivery. And there are rumors about gas rationing being lifted . . ."

They separated shortly after that. Pam had to go on duty. They waved their good-byes and she went swinging down the street. He listened to the clicking of her heels until he could hear them no more. Bless you, Pam, for showing up when you did. You finished a perfect day.

When he reached the yard, he saw a spanking new cruiser of the *Baltimore* class. She had just backed into the stream and would soon be on her shakedown. He heard the voice coming through the P.A. system:

"On deck, section three, condition three. . . . *relieve the watch!*"

Her colors had gone up. He faced the river, snapped out his salute. How beautiful she looked! It was indeed a perfect day.

THE FIFTEENTH AND FINAL BIG NOVEL
IN THE DRAMATIC SERIES
FREEDOM FIGHTERS!

Junglefire

by Jonathan Scofield

Phu Bien Air Base, Vietnam, 1969: An infamous conflict tears the world apart, throwing together heroes, killers and fools. Captain Jack Hunter, ace helicopter pilot, is dubbed the "reluctant hero", as he dares to question American involvement in Vietnam, yet leads a bold corps of aviators to victory in and above the seething jungles of the war-torn country.

Meantime, Hunter's superior—and rival in love—schemes at his destruction, and the beautiful but deadly "Dragon Lady" seeks to seduce and betray him. As the battle rages to a bloody peak, Captain Jack Hunter finds himself caught up not only in a brutal struggle against the VietCong—but in a fight to free himself from the treacherous manipulations of "friends" and "allies."

DON'T MISS THE EXCITING
CONCLUSION OF
THE *FREEDOM FIGHTERS* SERIES!
JUNGLEFIRE
COMING IN MAY FROM DELL/BRYANS